Acknowledgements

The following stories were previously published in anthologies and magazines. Several stories have been revised and re-written for this collection.

A Visit to Lizzie's—*New Stories 5*: An Arts Council Anthology edited by Susan Hill and Isabel Quigly, Hutchinson, 1980; Pieces of Eight edited by Robert Nisbet, Gomer Press, 1982.
The Gift—*The Anglo-Welsh Review* No. 79, 1985.
Mirrors—*The New Welsh Review*
The Round—BBC Radio Wales March 1979; *Cambrensis*, 1979.
The Way Back—*Anglo-Welsh Review* No 67, 1981; *Pieces of Eight* edited by Robert Nisbet, Gomer Press, 1982; *Story Two* edited by Dai Smith, Parthian Books, 2013.
Working with Cyril—BBC Radio Four Morning Story 7th of Dec, 1982
Throwing the Punch— *Confrontation, Long Island University Literary Journal,* No 24, Summer, 1982; BBC Radio Four Morning Story, 1984; *The Anglo-Welsh Review*, No 76, 1984; *Stories from the Radio,* National Language Unit resource pack for schools.
Film Night—*Dismays and Rainbows,* edited by Robert Nisbet, Gomer Press, 1979; *The Western Mail, Words Magazine* No 8, 1980; BBC Radio Four Morning Story 9th April 1985.
Umbrella—BBC Radio Four Morning Story 15th of February 1985.
Into August—*Bananas Magazine*, edited by Emma Tennant, 1978.
Canada Dry—*The Anglo-Welsh Review* No 72, Autumn, 1982.
The Robinsons' Court—*The Mississippi Valley Review* Vol XIV No 2, 1985; also published in German in *Erkundungen* 28 walisische Erzahler, edited and translated by Hans Petersen, Verlag Volk und Welt, Berlin, GDR, 1988.
H.M.S. Cassandra—Considering Cassandra—Poems and a Story by Tony Curtis, Gwasg Carreg Gwalch Corgi Series, 2003.
A Night with Nina—*Paris Lit Up*, No. 3, 2015
Some Kind of Immortality—*The New Welsh Review*, Summer, 2017.

Contents

A Visit to Lizzie's   9
Shakin' All Over   22
Mirrors   36
The Gift   50
Umbrella   68
Some Kind of Immortality   74
The Round   80
The Eighth   88
The Way Back   95
Working with Cyril   108
Hedging your Bets   114
Throwing the Punch   120
Film Night   127
Bill Rowse   135
Into August   144
Canada Dry   148
The Robinsons' Court   167
Terminates at Newport   182
A Night with Nina   192
A Cuckoo in the Nest   202
H.M.S. Cassandra   212
Memory Sticks   228

This book owes so much to so many people: friends and colleagues who worked with me at the University of Glamorgan, as well as Masters candidates who shared their work over twenty years of writing workshops; we learned the art and craft together.

I am grateful for friends who read the new stories and to editors and producers who chose to publish and broadcast many of these stories. Cinnamon Press are to be thanked for their support.

As ever, my wife Margaret has been the constant first reader and the dependable proof-reader and fellow editor.

Some Kind of Immortality

A Visit to Lizzie's

The side window was full of sky with dark clouds, purple ink spilling into the blue. Trees blurring, pylons stuck into green fields so that if he blinked his eyes with the rhythm of the trees and telephone lines the pylons became rocket ships from *Dan Dare*, and the rolling fields a strange planet's terrain.

'Over the border. Now the skies will clear. Never rains in Pembrokeshire,' Richard didn't need to sit up and take his bearings. His father always made a crack about the weather as they passed the county sign, around the broad curve before the straight half mile at Llanteg. Most weekends for the last couple of years they'd leave Carmarthen and drive west.

Sometimes it was to his uncle's big, crumbling house on the edge of the Haven. He liked these visits for it was a mysterious, old eighteenth-century rectory with cellars and numerous rooms. His father would check and maintain the wartime generator that they used for electricity, and Richard had his three cousins to play with. They'd sleep together on Saturday nights in one of the big bedrooms. Robert was thirteen and drove their old Ford tractor like a man. He had an air rifle and was even allowed to use the twelve-bore in the fields on occasion. Michael was eleven and the same age as Richard: they fished together. Whilst Sam, at seven years old, was a nuisance who got in the way of everything they did.

Richard ran his finger along the groove where the arm rest fitted into the back of the seat. A train: pulling the rest down by its leather strap made a bridge. He wished they were going to the Rectory. But this time it was to Lizzie. If that had been the county line then another twenty minutes would see them at Kilgetty. He hated their visits to Aunt Lizzie. She wasn't a real aunt anyway; his grandmother's sister, did that make her a close relative? His face screwed into a Mekon face at the day's prospect. When had she ever given him a Christmas present, or remembered his December birthday? Did she really know his name? Always it was 'that bittie boy' or 'the child'.

Ashburnam was a house with a smell of its own. He could tell where he was without opening his eyes. There was chicken meal and stale cooking, wood smoke and dog smells and damp smells. Walking in through the door made him feel sick.

'Now take your toy box in and don't get under Auntie's feet.'

She'd come to the side door; no one used the front door except strangers, and there couldn't have been many of them. The privet hedge from the railings, edging the few yards of path to the front door, was never cut. It was as if Lizzie was proclaiming an unwelcome. Once in the holidays Richard had seen a new postman approach the front. Scamp, Lizzie's mangy collie, had padded round the corner like a wolf, with the old woman close after. The poor man left the parcel on the side wall and was quickly back to his van. The front door itself was quite sheltered from the westerly weather, but had been the same muddy brown colour since the previous occupants.

Lizzie had moved to Ashburnam fifteen years before. Her husband died the following year. Richard had heard his parents talking about the man, but he couldn't imagine anyone actually living with her. Certainly, she'd never mentioned him and there was no photograph to be seen.

On the mantelpiece over the stove that served as both heating and cooker was a snap of Lizzie herself that his father had taken the previous summer with his squeeze-box Kodak. She was standing square on to the camera, dressed as always in a shabby, voluminous pullover and skirt, a sack tied around her waist and thick, frayed woollen stockings going down to her wooden clogs. Her face was screwed up against the sun, her left hand clutched the collar around Scamp's neck.

Richard liked photographs. He longed to be allowed to use the Kodak, turning the dials and flicking the shutter.

His father had a leather case for it that reminded him of Rommel and binoculars and desert war films.

The photograph was real. He'd seen his father take the film. Somehow that photograph was how he'd like Lizzie to be. Here in the flesh she made him squirm.

'You watch them things on the floor!' and she clattered over his Dinky cars and lorries with her great battleship clogs, bending the axle of his new jeep.

'The tyre's got twisted on my jeep, Dad,' he complained.

'I've told you not to get in your aunt's way,' his father said, examining the damage. 'Why don't you take them outside and play around the flower garden?'

Richard gathered his cars and soldiers from the Lino of the back room and, stepping over the collie who was sprawled across the back door, went out into the afternoon air. It was October and the weather promised the beginnings of winter. Still, the wind was fresh, carrying the sea in on it, and he lifted his head to take in a big breath.

Across from the house was a flower patch bordered by a green and mildewed rustic fence. He could pitch a battle around the spiked roses and the jungle of drooping chrysanthemums. Richard was soon in a world of his own. His mother was at her knitting and his father was working to patch up the wire of the chicken run further up the garden.

The old woman always had a huddle of chickens, keeping herself in eggs and selling or exchanging the others with neighbours. The box of eggs with which they usually drove home to Carmarthen was the nearest thing to generosity that Lizzie ever showed. Meals, when they stayed, were particularly rough and ready.

'Good wholesome food in Pembrokeshire," his father said, adding, 'when your Gran and Aunt Lizzie and her sisters lived down here on the family farm they'd have everything fresh. Nothing posh, but you didn't see people having bad stomachs and the illnesses you see now. That's the country, boy.'

Richard didn't care, though there was something special about the small, sweet new potatoes they'd eat after the first early picking at his uncle's rectory fields. In any case, according to his father, nothing ever went wrong in Pembrokeshire. After their previous visit to Lizzie's a few weeks back he'd been half dozing in the back of the big Vauxhall when they'd begun to talk about Lizzie and Ashburnam and that someday perhaps they'd be living in Pembrokeshire. His mother said something about her being as tough as old boots and probably outliving them all.

'It's only what we're entitled to. After all the work I've put into keeping that place going for her: the rewiring, and that damp under the stairs. Look at that plumbing in the kitchen. Where would she have been on her own with that?"

'But shouldn't Florence get the place?'

'Florrie's too violent. Certified. You go up to see her in that ward and it's like she's walking in her sleep. If you ask me she'll never leave the place.'

'Fancy saying that,' objected his mother. But it was a stock response, for Lizzie's daughter had been up at St Teilo's asylum since her early twenties, before the war. At home she frequently disappeared; just wandering off to be found picking hedgerow plants down some aimless lane. That, and her violent, incoherent outbursts, had surely hastened her father's stroke. 'Anyway, I'm not so sure I'd want to move down here and live,' said his mother, dampening the discussion.

As the first few drops of rain came down through the shrubs and flowers onto his soldiers, Richard thought back to that conversation and shivered. He felt tired and cold. He was sure that he didn't want to leave the town and his friends and the park and the school to live down here, where there was no corner shop or football in the street, and where sweets meant taking a bus ride. What did people do down here ? There were the visitors and day trippers in the summer season, but everyone was busy making money out of them. Every week or two the faces changed. More and more houses were growing B & B signs in the front garden. The Williamses in the smallholding next door had started with visitors that summer, and Lizzie reckoned that they had pots of money. One thing was certain, the old woman herself would never take visitors. Who would want to step inside the place even? Except relatives.

'Where's that trap then?' his father shouted down the path as Richard emerged from the flower patch holding his toys close with both hand against his chest to keep the rain from them.

'It were under here last night, I saw it sure,' said Lizzie, as she fussed in the cubby-hole under the stairs.

'What's the matter, Dad?'

'The feed box. Looks like a rat's been at it. There's teeth marks,' his father replied, kicking mud off his wellingtons against the rough facing of the side wall.

'Do rats eat chickens, Dad?'

'They're likely taking eggs. There's broken shells which could be that. Though chickens get stupid sometimes and go for the eggs themselves.'

''Why don't we shoot it, Dad?'

'That's a fine suggestion. You'd enjoy sitting up all night with a torch taking pot shots everytime the trees moved,' and he picked up a soldier that Richard had dropped near the door, making a machine-gun noise. 'Now don't get under your Auntie's feet, you hear!'

'Can't find nothing,' said Lizzie, emerging from under the stairs, 'but that Williams next door will have one likely, from them rats they had in the shippen that time. You go ask them, Jim.'

Richard went back inside and moving his mother's knitting from the worn armchair settled himself by the stove. It was a strain to read his comic as Lizzie never put the light on early enough, unless she had her pools to do or some post to decipher from the morning. It was one of a handful of old Eagle comics he'd swapped a scout badge for in school on the Friday. He realised that he'd read it before anyway. Still, his father was returning from the Williamses with the rat trap and that was far more interesting.

They'd first done something about the Great Plague and the Fire in top Juniors. He remembered a drawing of a rat in that page in his encyclopaedia too and he always flicked on past it to the Battle of Trafalgar and the bright red uniforms with their tall hats and muskets. The thought of dirty, diseased rats made him shiver. Your face broke out in sores; no matter what they did for you, you died, horribly.

Robert had chased one from the stocks of seed potatoes in the Rectory's outhouse once. Richard had stayed back by the door but his cousin had thrown a garden fork at it and showed him where there was blood on one of the prongs. Richard had a broken sleep that night dreaming of a huge rat dragging itself up the long stairs of the Rectory and coming for them. Always he imagined the archetypal rat, like the animal on the front of horror stories, teeth bared, claws drawn.

When his father had finished and they all sat down for a meal Richard could not face the fat strips of bacon that Lizzie served up. Having to watch the old woman putting the greasy pieces into her mouth was bad enough.

'He's too finnicky, that ba,' she said as she sponged the plate with her bread. 'Towns and television, all furren stuff,' she added, mysteriously. His father had come home with a television just a few days before the Coronation. That was quite something down their street.

'Only the fifth in the town, the bloke said,' he'd boasted. It was more pleasing for Richard that they were fifth than having to sit through the hazy, grey images of distant regal glory in Westminster Abbey: it might as well have been on Mars, a strange ritual discovered by Dan Dare.

They never went short, with a car ever since he could remember, but his father often worked into the early hours, cooped up in his tiny shed on 'fiddles', repairing dynamos and starters for farmers who were customers at the garage where he worked. He did electrical jobs on cars and could turn his hand to fixing inside the backs of radios and things. Richard could see the skill, the fitting back together again of all the small details, but the way his father hunched over the parts, pulling himself into a closed and private world, smoke hazing around his head from the constant cigarette, worried him: was that what his life would be too?

He'd got an old repaired radio for Lizzie a few years back and they listened to the music programme after the tea things had been cleared. His mother survived these weekends by knitting steadily. Sometimes she would fix up a cotton reel for Richard to knot wool chains that you could make hats out of: looping the bits of spare wool over and around the nails and slowly pulling a coloured snake from the bottom of the reel. But when they'd settled, his father announced, 'A surprise for Richard,' and produced an Airfix model plane. It was a Faery Swordfish, with two wings, one over the other, and a great bulbous propeller, with a torpedo slung under its fuselage. The illustration on the box cover showed an attack on a German battleship with the torpedoes slipping into the waves, heading towards the iron bulk of the warship.

Glueing and putting on the transfers with the markings took them all evening. Richard did the bigger pieces like the wings and the stand to mount the model on. But his father did the smaller details and controlled the tube of glue. He'd once completed a Lancaster bomber in full camouflage green and brown paint long after Richard had exhausted his interest.

His mother knitted until her hands stopped moving and she fell asleep. Lizzie leaned her elbows on the table and squinted down at her Old Moore's Almanac until she'd turned a couple of pages. Every year his father had to make sure that she got a copy. An unshaven man in his fifties in an old mackintosh sold them in Carmarthen market; he just stood there and held them out, blank faced as if the dire events and joyous promises that the flimsy pages foretold, were of no concern to him. Every December he appeared, like slush.

Richard didn't know what the Almanac was about, but lying in bed that night he wondered about the way she pored over the thing. All those symbols, crescent moons, stars and signs of the zodiac. He remembered the stories his-father told about the old woman when she lived in Gorse Bank, the stone cottage on the edge of the moor; how she'd learned the ways of the gypsies, could cure warts with a cut onion, hedge herbs and mumbled words. 'Charmers,' his father had said they were called, 'Your Auntie's one of the Pembrokeshire Charmers. She's special.'

The next morning he woke to the sound of a church bell. The rain had stopped in the night and he could see out of the box room window that the main road just beyond the gate was drying rapidly. Beyond that the common stretched darkly green to Begelly Hill and the church. The silver and cream gypsy caravans dotted around with rough shelters of corrugated iron and sacking gave out breakfast fire smoke that rose reluctantly in wisps. You could believe in magic seeing them living as they did among the gorse bushes and rough moor grass, trapping rabbits and even hedgehogs, baked in mud to draw the spikes out, his father had said. And they collected plants to make up potions for illnesses despite the fact that a couple of the younger men now drove lorries and bought modern clothes. These were rusting, misshapen vehicles grinding round the winding Pembrokeshire lanes collecting scrap. His father had done repairs on some of the lorries that summer. They paid him immediately in grubby pound notes. 'Faster than any of those so-called gentlemen farmers,' he'd said. From three generations of gypsies Lizzie had learned the oldest country skills.

He could hear her in the back bedroom: the squeak of the old metal bedstead. The predictable sequence of moving noises, then she would groan to bend to the chamber pot. A cough on the stairs as she made her way down; the slop of pee into the lavatory pan; the clang of the chain as she pulled at the rubber ball handle. He hated this, each morning the clumsy ritual, but had to listen to it. He couldn't understand the mixture of disgust and fascination he felt. Lizzie was an relative, part of their extended family, but almost completely alien. It was that fact of not knowing what he was really feeling that unnerved him.

He waited until his parents had gone down before getting dressed. His father had left the completed Swordfish on its stand on the side table by the bed and Richard imagined the plane's low runs in for the kill, slowly clipping the spray until the torpedo just couldn't miss the tall side of the ship. The enamel washbowl was time and again sunk as it rode the eiderdown on his bed.

His mother had boiled eggs for their breakfast and they ate them out of wooden cups with Lizzie's tarnished apostle spoons. The old witch was mashing something up in a bowl for the dog, but didn't appear to need anything for herself.

'Let's see what's happening in the world,' said his mother. And his father responded by trying to coax the tired radio onto station. The way the tuning light built up to intensity always excited Richard. He had a quiet pride in the way his father seemed to be able to bring machines to life. It was really mysterious the way that those tubes and wires and bits of solder gave out sound.

A few years before they'd been driving back to Wales from his great uncle's in Berkshire. It was the first car they'd had with a radio fitted and the whole journey had been made to the accompaniment of the BBC Home Service washing in and out of range as they wound their way through the hills. On the news that night the Prime Minister had declared a state of war—Egypt and the Canal. Richard remembered feeling frightened. Wars were for comics and games. In the big war, the Faery Swordfish war, his father had spent a few years on a searchlight at Milford Haven, good times, rabbits and taking vegetables ('borrowing' he called it, smilingly). There'd never be another one, everyone said.

'No problem there,' his father had said, 'Egypt's not like a proper war, is it?'And Richard had lost himself in sleep as the car slowly climbed up the Air Balloon in Gloucestershire..

Now the posh man's voice was droning on about some farmers and Parliament meetings and the boy went into the chilly front room, still stuffy after his father's pipe the previous evening, to look at his Swordfish model. The plane was complete but for the RAF wing bull's-eye and badges. The rear gunner hunched over his weapon, squinting through the sights; the slung torpedo was a silver metal shark. A sky full of Swordfish could settle Germany, Egypt and all the rest.

But Richard's war was interrupted by a sudden raising of voices in the back room. Lizzie was shouting, excited about something, and the dog was whining, bouncing on its four paws and scraping its claws in the worn Lino.

'I knew it were, I could smell the bugger!' she screamed, her right-hand in a fingerless glove flapping in the air. 'Rats is dimp for any food.'

'Well, that trap and the eggs was bound to do the trick,' said his father. 'Where is it?'

'Here it is!' and she jerked her left hand up, the cage swinging from its short length of chain and the rat, looking enormous to Richard, flopping over, clawing to grip the wire mesh. Its squeaks went through his ears like a saw. He gave out a groan. As Lizzie turned to him something dropped from the rat.

'It's gone to the lav!'"he shouted. 'Take it away!' The he rushed out of the door, into the hall, catching the wing of the Swordfish with his sleeve as he turned. The top wing sheared off, splitting the struts to the lower wing as it went.

He was at the front room window, his hands touching the shattered left side of the model when his father came in.

'All right, Richard lad? Don't worry about your Aunt Lizzie. She's an old country bird and things aren't the same for her as for you and me. We've cleaned up the mess and the rat's outside now. Look—just to show there's no harm, come and help me fix up the hose to fill that old rain barrel. We'll see him off, eh?'

Richard followed the progress of a solitary car up the pencil straight road cutting through the moor. It gathered speed after the bend to take a run' at the hill past Ashburnam. He turned to face his father who was holding out a handful of broken plastic.

'I picked these up. And there's plenty of glue left,' he said to Richard.

The barrel took ages to fill. Richard couldn't see why they needed that much water anyway. Water was dangerous:

his mother always kept him from fishing in the Towy. The rich and wide provider; the reason for the town of Carmarthen. All those fat, glistening sewin and salmon his father brought home as tips from work and as payment for fiddles: salmon for a dynamo, sewin or dabs for a set of plugs. The coracle men's nets bulged with fish, and even Harry Evans from number 46, who couldn't read, had come home with something on a line. But always it was, 'People have drowned in inches. It's been in the papers.'

The hose spewed out water until the barrel was as full as it could be. Leaves and dead insects dislodged from the wood floated to the surface and Lizzie scooped at them to clear the water. Richard couldn't understand that either. The old woman cleaned nothing as far as he could see. The house was held up by dirt. Then she fetched a hammer and nail, and whilst his father held the cage between two sticks she nailed the end of the chain to the rim of the rain barrel. Then, taking hold of the two sticks, she flipped the caged rat over the side into the water.

'Swim yer bugger, swim!' she cackled as the trapped creature clawed for a hold on the water. It threshed for what seemed like minutes before coming up to the surface like an old rag to be squeezed out.

Richard didn't wait to see how she disposed of the rat. He went back in, through to the front room and sat with the broken pieces of his model.

An image came up in his mind. Years before, when Lizzie lived in Gorse Bank, his father and mother had wound their way down the meagre lane from the main Tenby road to be confronted out of the final bend by the sight of Lizzie pegging up what looked like a leather belt on the washing line. It was the first thing she had said to them as they got out of the car

'A mighty big angletwitch. Kill't it myself last night.'

It was an adder she'd come across near the water pump. She'd battered it with a broom and was drying the skin. His father told the story to people as a joke, a bit of Pembrokeshire colour. But it always made Richard shiver, and he was glad he'd not been there then. Did people eat

snakes and rats and things? Like the gypsies and their baked
hedgehogs ?

He didn't touch his lunch, but excused himself and went
outside. 'Are you all right, Richard?' his mother called
through the back door.

'Not hungry, Mum. Going for a walk in the garden,'he
said.

In the run the hens were clucking and pecking about like
clock work toys. His father had made a good job of the
broken wire fence and Richard knew that he could never
make it look as if that had given way. Instead he simply
pulled the peg that held the door frame of the run.

For minutes the hens seemed unaware of the opening.
'Stupid birds don't want to get out,'he muttered.

But at last the solitary White Sussex spotted some spilled
grain on the path and jerked and pecked its way out. Soon
the whole lot of them were bobbing and strutting over the
garden, giving the ground speculative stabs with their beaks.

He grinned and shooed them wider, hissing under his
breath. It would take ages for that old witch to chase them
all back in. He could see her now, scrawny red arms flailing
the air, tripping over the rough vegetable patch in her heavy
clogs. He had difficulty in hiding a smirk as he walked back
into the kitchen where they were drinking cups of Lizzie's
thick, dark tea.

A few minutes later, at the sound of the tyres
screeching, his mother's cup fell down into the saucer,
slopping tea over her knees. 'That's a crash !' and his father
was up and running to the door with the others following
close after.

A big black Austin had come to rest with its nearside
wing buckled up against one of Lizzie's front gate pillars.
The metal was dented and glass from the headlight had
fallen onto the tyre and twisted mudguard.

'Christ in Hell!' his father shouted and, though he didn't
normally swear, no one seemed to notice.

A plump, red-faced man in a thick tweedy jacket and a
farmer's cap was standing by the driver's door, his hands
covered in blood and white feathers.

'Chickens everywhere," he said, his face an expression of puzzlement and wonder.

Richard, leaning against the side wall of Ashburnam, turned away. He instantly felt hot and sweaty, his feet no longer feeling the ground. Turning his head to the wall, he vomited back his breakfast.

Shakin' All Over

Mervyn was playing carpet snooker when Jimmy called. The carpet was the one in front of the fire-place; it had something of an oriental pattern, with dark curves at its four corners. By putting his mum and dad's slippers at each corner, Mervyn made four pockets. The carpet was the most worn in the whole house and that meant that the balls ran straight. He had devised the game months back in the winter when the games he'd had for Christmas had broken, or become boring. He had worked out priorities for the marbles he used as balls, though they would have seemed just a jumble of random stripes and colours to anyone else. It was a secret, pleasurable arrangement. For a cue he used the brass toasting fork which hung from a hook at the side of the fire-place. At first his mother had told him off, but his grandmother had decided that there was no harm, and that was that.'You bought it for me as a present, and I'm sure the boy will take care of it, won't you Mervyn? It'll still toast well enough.'

The three-pronged head came off easily with unscrewing, and the Gloucester Cathedral shape fitted his hand well as a handle. He loved kneeling in front of the fire, his game lit as much by the flame as the daylight which filtered in through the curtains of the tiny front windows.

He had potted an orange into one of the corners and was lining up a black and green striped marble when his Gran called through, 'Mervyn, it's one of your friends.'

Although he didn't want any of the other boys to know about his game on the carpet, he had time to take his next shot, for there was no fear of his grandmother letting anyone in, other than a doctor or a man of the church, certainly not one of his friends. She was large and firm and would stand no nonsense, her grey hair tight in a bun and her farm girl's arms still full of work, but kind and enveloping when needed.

'Mervyn, it's that Jimmy for you, come on,' she said, popping her head round the door, and sounding disapproving.

Jimmy was a popular member of the boys' gang. He was almost a year older and the others took notice of him. He enjoyed an audience; though grown-ups always seemed suspicious of him. His manners were impeccable in front of them and he could put on a smile, a sort of assurance that was beyond his years. This cut no ice with Gran, though.

'It's Jimmy this, and Jimmy that,' she said, 'Boys sharp as a knife cut themselves. You mind.'

The striped ball skimmed the corner, past the slipper and clattered off across the Lino. Mervyn collected the balls, screwed on the prongs and hung the fork back on its hook before going to the front door.

'O.K. Masher?'

'Alright, Jimmy,' he replied, wincing inwardly at Jimmy's nickname for him.

'Fancy coming up the house this afternoon, for some records ? The old man's bought Johnny Kidd and the Pirates.'

'I'll have to ask my Gran.'

'Oh, come on, there's no-one up the park today, I been. And they're not home until late tonight, my parents.'

Jimmy was lucky that way; he was always being left to have the house to himself. That's when he had girls.

'I've shagged in all our bedrooms,' he boasted to the others.

At fourteen, Jimmy Hughes was definitely something special. He had the gang all wide-eyed and sticky-thighed with the stories of his exploits. The chance of an afternoon at Jimmy's place was not to be turned down. As far as Mervyn knew, none of the others in the Park gang had been inside the place. They all met usually at the corner of the Workhouse Hill, or at the bandstand in the park. Houses were a different world, grown-ups' places where you were told what to do, places you escaped from to school and the park.

Though both of Mervyn's parents worked, Gran was his more or less constant overseer at No 50. It was her house and they'd moved in after his grandfather had died: to 'look after her', though Gran was hardly in need of any looking after; everyone did as they were told. Mervyn rarely had the freedom of the house—there were places he longed to explore. There must be, he knew, mysteries, secrets, drawers he'd never opened, the dark corners of wardrobes.

They set off up the street with Jimmy leading, scuffling at loose chippings in the kerb and pulling leaves from the low, regular privet hedge. At the end of the road they stopped to pick handfuls of bells from Mr Ives's fuchsia hedge and slowly walked on, meticulously pulling the white stalk from the centre of each flower and drawing it sweetly across their tongues. They moved up the sloping street, past the old fire-station that now sold tyres. They watched a mechanic working at a wheel, straining his weight down on to the metal lever that puckered the rubber from the wheel-rim. The afternoon sun was out and it was too hot to watch such an effort. They walked on to the corner of Workhouse Hill, where Jimmy flopped down on the bench and pretended to strum a guitar.

'What you been doing ?' Mervyn asked him.

'Nothing much. Boring. You done anything since Friday?'

'Nah. Thought I'd go up the park and kick around before tea, until you called.'

'There's no-one up the Park. I told you. None of the girls. No-one. Catch me sweating today, anyway. See that tyre bloke?' Jimmy pulled a face. At school he always managed to be second or third from last. Too lazy to be picked for anything, but fast enough not to get shouted at too often. That was the way he got through most obstacles. Bright enough for the Gram., but always looking to cut corners.

'You seen Meryl ? Are you seeing her much?'

'Naw. Cow. But I've seen a lot of her before—get it. Hey,—see these railings here, Merv,' Jimmy reached over the back of the bench to strike the iron rods of the railings.

'There was this kid who kicked a ball over, and when he tried to get it back his trousers caught on one of the bloody spikes. He was standing, balancing on the top with his feet between the points, see. And his bloody trousers got caught, and when he jumped off he turned over and landed on the bloody spike. It went through his bloody balls. Right through his fucking balls! Skewered him. Gor!' Jimmy held his crotch like a cricket cup and jumped up and down.

'What would that bloody mean, then? You know, being injured like that.'

'Eh? Ruin your fucking chances, wouldn't it ?'said Jimmy.

Mervin wanted to ask, Chances of what, exactly ? but he held back from the question. It was probably obvious, and he didn't want to appear stupid. So much of what Jimmy said was nervously laughed at by the others. He had proper American jeans and slicked back his hair like a pop singer

'That happened years ago,' said Jimmy.

The clouds were high and rolling eastwards, leaving wide stretches of blue sky and room for real sun, so that Mervyn had to shield his eyes to follow a tiny tractor moving on one of the sloping fields on the hill the other side of the river. All the town sloped up or down, to or from the river. A bustling market town in the middle of good farmland. Mervyn liked to take bike rides along the main roads and then off any one of the lanes that wormed out into the country. These were rough, unmetalled tracks with pot-holes or narrow tarmacked ways that were streaked with dried, tyre-gouged mud. There were milk-stands with churns you could drum on with sticks and surprising corners that revealed loud barking, but daft and soft farmers' collies, suspicious and then friendly. The farmers' sons came to the Gram. They were slow talkers with the Welsh on them, big-boned and red-faced lads who kept to their own kind and left in old, scruffy buses promptly at the end of the day. They didn't sneak over to the Tuck where the townies bought single cigarettes and paid a penny to have the record player on.

'I might go to the country a bit in the summer,' said Mervyn, to himself, 'Might go exploring.' He had cycled out

25

on the Swansea road at the end of the last summer holiday. On his own. He'd got as far as Nantycaws hill and had gone exploring into the wood there. It had been close and mossy under the trees, quiet away from the noise of cars and lorries groaning up steep Nantycaws. In town they had the Park, but that was like school, noisy game-playing, only with girls as well, in the woods there was something old and clean, quiet and mossy.

'Catch me pedalling out there,' said Jimmy,' See the green,' he said, pulling down the corner of his right eye with his index finger.

Mervyn wasn't sure what this meant, though Jimmy had started doing it a few weeks before and now they all did it. Even Walrus Evans Chemistry had done the eye thing when their mate Williams had tried to bluff his way out of a missed homework. It hadn't worked, and the green eye was followed by a swift dap on the arse for Williams. Walrus had gone through his usual performance with the chalk first, though. He called the dap, a black worn and bending shoe, size nine at least, by the name of 'Bonzo'. Before administering the punishment Walrus would chalk 'Bonzo' in reverse capital letters across the sole. The name was then printed across the boy's behind for the rest of the day, though he didn't dap them hard and the word became a sort of badge of honour

'Walrus,' said Mervyn, to himself.

'Eh?' said Jimmy, 'more like a snail,' he said, pointing to the far distant tractor. 'Hey' he said, 'look here—one of them old buggers from the Workhouse. Let's trip him up.' He winked and clutched at his head as if concussed.

But they didn't. The old man shuffled past them like a large, sick bear. Mervyn had never seen eyes so grey and sunk deep in folds of skin. His Gran was old, but she never stopped moving with an energy that seemed endless. This man was ponderous, his height hunched over his walking-stick, his feet moving without appearing to leave the ground. The toe of one shoe was torn open and he wore a dirty-brown overcoat, despite the growing warmth of the afternoon. As they set off, following the railings and wall of the institution around the corner and up Brynmawr Road, Jimmy pointed up at the large Victorian building. He said, 'Old bastard. Fancy being stuck up bloody there. Like a prison '

'What is it then, the Workhouse?' asked Mervyn, 'Do you have to be poor, or what?'

'Used to be. It's not a proper one now, I suppose. My Auntie Bron works up there cleaning. It's just for old people, when you're useless and dirty like him. You should hear the things she says. Shit and old food all over the floor, everything in a state. Shoot 'em, she would. Catch me getting like that.'

They walked on down Picton's Parade, past the big, private houses with long lawns and flower-beds, houses with names—Cartref, Teifi, Malta, The Willows, big, black Wolsey cars and bottle-green Austins; a Triumph with a soft roof and a globe of the world on its nose which Mervyn touched for luck. On they went, across the top of the town to the Wellfield estate, with its lines of council houses; newer houses than Mervyn's Gran's, with different coloured doors and concrete and wire fences.

'You can see right up the valley, for miles, up here,' said Jimmy, pointing up over the roof of his house.

'All this here used to be just fields, my old man says,' replied Mervyn, who stayed at the top of the steps, waiting for Jimmy to unlock the front door. Mervyn envied him. He'd never unlocked their front door at number fifty, never been trusted with any key, except occasionally the back-door one with its clumsy string and cotton-reel dangling. Jimmy clipped the Yale key and its plastic disc back onto his belt and waved Mervyn on in.

There was a stale smell of cooking which he hadn't been prepared for. Did all houses have different smells? Of course, they would, wouldn't they? Houses were what you made them, and what you did in them. He wondered what his own house would smell like to someone else. Perhaps that was why no-one was ever allowed in. And the furniture: Jimmy's front room had a bright red settee with shiny legs, a radio-gram and an electric fire in the fire-place. It struck him immediately as being new and modern.

'Go on in, then,' said Jimmy, and pushed him across to the settee. 'What will we do?'

'That's a great radio-gram, Jimmy. Can I look at your records?'

'Help yourself, Masher,' said Jimmy, going through to what seemed to be the kitchen. 'We've got coffee. Do you like powder coffee?'

'Yes,' said Mervyn, who thought the stuff at Fecci's cafe in town was o.k. when they'd mitched out of school dinner times. They'd just had a juke-box installed with three records for a shilling. A shilling's music, chips or coffee and they had just enough time to leg it back to the school gates in time for the bell. His Gran made coffee with black treacly stuff from a bottle with a Scottish soldier on the label. He wore a kilt and was being served a steaming cup on a tray served by an Indian servant. That was the British Empire, where coffee came from and rubber and oil and everything that made the country work. 'We usually have tea,' he added, though Jimmy was clattering the kettle and cups and didn't hear him.

'What?' he said.

'You've got some long-playing ones—Lonnie Donegan, Buddy Holly—where d'you get the money?'

'It's the old man,' explained Jimmy proudly, 'He's great on records—buys all the ones I like. Spends quids and quids on 'em. And the old woman. I see them dancing right here in the front room some nights.'

'Are they young, then?' asked Mervyn, 'Mine only got a record--player at Christmas, and it's Winifred Atwell and Petula Clark and Teddy Johnson—nothing younger, nothing much good.'

Jimmy came in with two cups of coffee. 'You want to get them to listen to Radio Luxemburg, the Top Twenty Programme. I got the Everlys and Elvis.'

'We listen in the car when we come back on Sundays after going down to my Uncle's in Pwllcrochan.'

'Pull what?'

'It's down in Pembrokshire. They've got a big old house, like a ghost house. My dad does his electricity and things. They've got potato fields. But he's a teacher, really.'

'I wish Walrus Chem had been a flipping farmer, and Ben the Head. Bastard. Wait till I leave.'

'Can we put on Johnny Kidd?' asked Mervyn.

'And the Pirates—Shakin' all o-o-over... dingalingding ding ding ding ding,' Jimmy did the guitar bit with his hands. 'You go and put 'em on—it's in the end bit of the rack there.'

Jimmy went back into the kitchen, but Mervyn didn't put the record on, he wasn't sure how to work the thing, and the radio-gram. looked so polished and precious. He sat on the settee and read the label until Jimmy came back with some biscuits and snatched it off him.

'Here, let's have it. Want a biscuit? We got custard creams.'

Mervyn felt stupid. Jimmy put on the record and sang along, knowing every word of it and all the guitar bits. Mervyn's coffee was hot and sweet. The custard cream crumbled and sank without trace when he tried to dip it.

'What's the B side? '

'It's rubbish—'Yes, Sir, that's my baby' -it's old. Hey, listen to this.'

'Ok. You bring Meryl up here ?' he asked, as Jimmy was putting on the Elvis long-player. He was longing to know about Meryl,. She was chapel-Welsh from up on Town Hill, and her father ran a big baker's shop in the main street— Humphries Bread. He'd see the Humphries all parading past on their way to the Congregational on a Sunday, twice, three times sometimes. On rainy days they took the car, a big, black Jaguar with horns like trumpets. But Dan Humphries was happier leading his family to chapel in full view of the town. When he'd taken up with the rest of the park lot the previous summer, Mervyn had been surprised to find Meryl hanging about. She had long, dark hair, broad hips and large breasts already. If at first she was stand offish, it had more to do with who a boy was in the town, his family, rather than any religious misgivings about sin.

She was a flirt, and brushed against your arm or back with her breasts knowingly, and then she'd put on her Sunday-best look of innocence. The word was that Dan Humphries was strict chapel, but soft as cream with his only daughter. Meryl could get her own way just by pouting. A show of tears was enough to get her a new frock.

'Yeh, see that settee you're sitting on?' Jimmy pursed his lips and pulled down the corner of his right eye, 'Hound Dog. They said you was high class... ' she's been there. With me.'

Mervyn squirmed, and the cushion seemed to sag under him like marshmallow. Meryl on this settee—those breasts. Were her nipples like cherries? Did they taste like sweets? Was her hair pulled up in that bun, wisps left curling at the nape of her neck ? Did Jimmy and her lie down here ? Could you do things like that on a settee? It had to be Jimmy with her, didn't it; he was big enough and knowing enough.

Mervyn sat back and closed his eyes. Brenda Lee sang, 'Let's jump the broomstick.' Some weeks back he'd started to sneak upstairs to the airing cupboard. When his grandmother was at the washing-line or weeding, or crossing tongues over the fence with Mrs Hughes, he would chance it. He'd creak open the door, his hands going into the softness around the water-tank feeling for flimsies, lace edges, the clasps of underwear. His hands moulded around the stiff cups of brassieres and he imagined Diana Dors, the Vernons Girls, Meryl Humphries. The first couple of times he'd sort of pumped and leaked without even touching himself. This was a secret treat—better than the newspapers, better than the Kays catalogue, more real than the unsubstantiated workings of his mind. But now, as the radio-gram's changer clicked and slotted another record down, someone sang about a dark-eyed beauty. He felt his face flush with shame. No-one must know about that; he couldn't even tell Jimmy.

Jimmy had done it. With Meryl, and perhaps other girls, he was sure. He had done it and knew about the taste of nipples and the smell of things. Jimmy was like a man, could have had a moustache if he wanted; he used his father's razor. He had a pair of suede shoes and quiffed his hair. Mervyn's dad said that suede shoes were a sure sign of a nancy boy. Buddy Holly and the Crickets finished 'Rave On'. Mervyn walked over to the mirror hanging over the low side-board. He twisted his front hair round his finger, pulling it into a quiff until the pain began to water his eyes. Not Elvis, not the Everlys, just straight hair that lay flat and refused to be interesting.

'My Mum let me use her curling whatsits once,' said Jimmy, and without waiting for an answer, his hands planted in his pockets, he slouched into the hall. Mervyn heard him go up the stairs and then across the landing. A door opened and closed. He sat down again on the settee, stretched his arms above his head and leaned back. The electric-light shade had orange and green flowers. On the sideboard were two prize cups: he went over to look at them. The smaller was plain and as light as tin; there was nothing to say what it was for. The other, had large handles and was sitting on a wooden plinth. It was inscribed ' The Buffs Snooker Cup— presented by T.H. Jones. ' A row of tiny shields went round the base of the plinth. 'Johnny Hughes, 1960' the last one read. That must be Jimmy's father, Mervyn thought.

There was a television in the corner the other side of the fire-place, and a framed picture on the wall behind the settee—it showed a couple posed outside a caravan. It was sunny. The man in a check shirt and jeans had his arm around the woman and a cigarette in his other hand. She wore a summer dress and had a pony-tail. Mervyn wondered if this could be Jimmy's mum and dad.

Jimmy was still upstairs, though the sound of footsteps had stopped. Mervin walked through to look at the kitchen. There were shiny tiles on the walls, so much smarter than the rough brickwork painted green in his own home. The cooker was splattered with grease, though, and the sink was a jumble of unwashed plates and pans. His Gran and his Mum would have had sharp tongues about that. Two half-full milk bottles stood on the window-sill in the sun and one of them was turning thick and smelling. He felt a shiver in his stomach that was partly the smell and partly the guilt of prying into someone else's house; though Jimmy had left him on his own. He walked back to the front-room to look at the television. The clock said nearly half-past three. It was over an hour to go before the programmes started up again. It was Robin Hood tonight, but he should be home by then.

There was a hard, dull thump through the ceiling and Jimmy's muffled voice came through, 'Come on up, Masher.'

As Mervyn began to climb the stairs, he heard a door close. And at the top, 'Come and get me,' in one of Jimmy's funny voices, came from behind the closed door to the left of the landing. Jimmy opened the door and walked into a large bedroom. The heavy green curtains were drawn shut so that the room was as half-lit as a hollow under thick trees. The room appeared to be empty, so Mervyn jumped when Jimmy said, 'Here I am,' and slid out from the gap between the wardrobe and the wall.

'Jesus, Iesu Grist! What are you bloody up to?' Mervyn said, as Jimmy flung off the dressing-gown he was wearing. He had on a black, lacy brassiere and red-fringed panties. 'What are you doing with those?' he said, as Jimmy minced around the bedroom like a girl, but still with his socks on.

'I'm Meryl,' he simpered, pushing his chest out and placing a hand on his left thigh.

'Are those her things? Like, did she leave them here?'

'No, don't be twp. They're new underwear, from the catalogue. My old man bought 'em for the old girl, to make her sexy. They was an extra present for her birthday. To be unwrapped later, he said, so I guessed what would be inside. That was last month. There's lipstick and stuff here too.'

'What's it for, though? ' said Mervyn, staying by the bedroom door.

'Don't be stupid.'

'I mean, what are you doing with it like this?'

'Bit of fun, isn't it? I try anything once. Anyway, they won't know, will they?'

Mervyn knew that there was something wrong, but he couldn't think of the exact words for it.

Jimmy lifted up the cups of the brassiere in a parody of a bathing beauty. 'Touch them,' he said, 'they're like real tits —*Health and Efficiency*.'

'Neh. Get off, Jimmy.'

'Go on.' He stepped towards Mervyn, who was back at the bedroom door. Mervyn reached out and brushed his fingers against the left cup.

'There, see,' laughed Jimmy, who unclipped the strap and swung around, wrapping the bra and its two handkerchiefs of stuffing over Mervyn's face.

'Geroff—bloody stupid!' he shouted, disentangling himself. He went hot in the face and flung the brassiere across to the dressing-table. Sitting down on the edge of the bed, he realised that he had the beginnings of an erection.

'Let's talk,' said Jimmy, lying down beside him, 'Let's talk dirty'. He pulled off his socks, but was still in the panties. He began to stroke the front of the lace decoration beneath which his own hardness swelled. 'How many times you done it, eh? Last term, after the Christmas holidays, when I was in bed with the tonsils, I did it sixteen times in a day. What's your record ? You ever done it for someone else?'

'I don't know. I don't remember.'

'Like this,' said Jimmy, and he put his hand on Mervyn's trousers. Mervyn wanted to stop him, wanted to lash out and punch him in the face, but he didn't. His ache wouldn't let him. Instead he closed his eyes and his fists unclenched as if a spring had unwound inside him. Jimmy had flicked his buttons undone and was working the skin of his prick up and down. At the same time he did the same to himself inside the panties. Mervyn came in a rush, much wetter than he'd ever been before.

'You finish me off, then,' he heard Jimmy say. And he did—holding Jimmy's thing, there in the bedroom where Jimmy and Meryl had been. And then Jimmy said, 'Have you ever wondered what it's like, you know? Do it to me, if you like,' he offered. And he pulled down the panties to his ankles.

'No, I've got to go. Get some fresh air. I don't feel alright,' said Mervyn, his throat tight, and feeling as if he had swallowed a ball of fur.

He closed his trousers and, fumbling with the buttons, rose awkwardly from the bed. 'Got to go,' he said, and ran out on to the landing and down the stairs, tripping on the mat at the bottom. He banged his arm on a small table as he stumbled, and shouted out, 'Shit!' And then, 'I'm going. You're a dirty, bloody bugger!'

He had slammed the front door behind him before he'd realised that his trousers were still open. He turned back to the door and buttoned up in the shelter of the porch. He spat on his shirt-cuff and rubbed it over the stain he'd made. 'Soon dry,' he said to himself, and climbed the steps up into the street, now full of sunshine.

He ran down the slope to the corner, not once looking back, though he had a picture in his mind of the bedroom window, with Jimmy's hand holding the edge of one of the closed curtains and his eyes following him down the street. It seemed as if he were empty and was filling up with air and sun at every stride. He started to side-step lampposts like Bleddyn Williams did in his imagination when the matches were on the radio. Then he hop-scotched a whole street obeying the symmetry of the pavement's stones. By the time he reached the Workhouse Hill corner his mind had filled itself with rugby and he needed to sit down on the bench. The distant glint of the ploughing tractor from across the valley caught his eye as it stitched the bottom of the brown field. From the bench he could watch the last furrows drawn into place. But he turned the corner to find the old Workhouse man spread across the seat, legs wide in front of him, his heavy, stained overcoat undone and shoes loose-laced with string. He was humming the Tipperary song.

'Nice afternoon,' Mervyn said, surprised at the sound of his own voice. 'Might go for a ride tomorrow—see that tractor over the other side of town—might go for a bike ride. I've watched it from here—I could go exploring over Nantycaws way.'

The old man's eyes opened, peering out of the brown folds of his face. He said nothing, but continued humming. Pushing on his stick, he slowly rose, stood for a moment and then broke wind lengthily. Mervyn watched him hobble around the corner. Then the boy turned for home, his legs stretching into a run.

Mirrors

Julie picked at her tea while trying to read a book. It was cold lamb with fry-up. Sunday's dinner making do for Monday. She could have willingly left the meal; she didn't feel hungry because they'd got down to the cafe from school at lunchtime. Besides, fry-up was one of the things to avoid for your skin. The white lamb fat was tasteless, crumbly and sickly. It was bad for you.

Her mother nagged her from the kitchen, 'You'd do better to leave that book and finish your tea before your dad comes home.' She came into the living room with a plate and a tea-towel in her hands and shouted up at the ceiling, 'Our Richard! Come on—yours is ready.'

Julie had just started the book. It was The Dubliners, which she'd picked up from the library on the way back from school. They had done one of those stories, 'Eveline', in class that morning with Mr Wilson. He had read it to them, taking up the whole lesson. She thought it was strange, like moving towards something, but stopping short of it too. He had left the class hanging out over the edge of the story's epiphany, peering over the side dangerously. She was getting bogged down with 'The Dead', though, so she swallowed enough of her dinner to avoid her mother's tongue and decided to wash and change. Besides, Jean had stayed at school for second form netball trials, so the bathroom would be free. And Richard was coming down the stairs and he would turn on the television straight away. The boy never read and would obviously never come to anything at school. Ever since they'd got a television it seemed that meals were always accompanied by the thing. He had started at the comprehensive at the beginning of that term, in the D stream. The fourth Coles child at the school, and the first to be dull: three bright girls and then Richard. Just like his father: the son he'd always wanted.

She brushed past him on the bottom stair and climbed up to her room to change. She flipped the book on to her bed and pulled her bottle-green jumper over her head. It caught a spot on her neck and she swore 'Damn, bugger, hell!'

Why did she get spots? She picked up the hairbrush and scraped it in anger over the top of the dressing-table. Where did spots come from? Was it just greasy food? People on television and films never got spots. Even in books, books about real things, no-one got spots. Or was it that writers didn't bother to mention them? She held a tissue to the place. She had agreed to babysit for the Wilsons and had to catch the seven o'clock bus, so she hurried to take her jeans, check shirt and patterned pullover from the wardrobe. Her wardrobe. Her sister Sandra had left for college six weeks before, in October, but the bedroom was still littered with her things; two of her posters were still on the wall—Steve McQueen and the R.S.C. Hamlet. There was a drawer of half-used and discarded make-up in the dresser, so Julie helped herself to some face cream. The spot on her neck disappeared, the red bulb of her nose dimmed. She tried first the left, then the right profile of herself in the mirror. No Racquel Welch, was she? But then, who wanted to carry those lumps around, and be constantly stared at, the way men looked at women like that?

As she dressed, she heard the sound of her father's motor-bike in the yard, and the slam of the back door. He'd be barging into the kitchen now, bulky and clumsy, pulling off the helmet and goggles, the great gloves like paws. Julie smiled at the scene she imagined below, the routine. He was like an actor taking off the Toad costume after Wind in the Willows. 'But it's not funny, is it?' she admonished herself, 'You can only laugh at him when he's not here, can't you?'

The previous weekend had been a bad one at her house. It had rained all week and her mother was unable to cope with the weight of washing and drying in their cramped kitchen. The waste-pipe on the twin-tub had worn and slimy water had finally gushed out over the kitchen floor;

father's tea had not been ready when he'd arrived from work on the Friday evening. He'd come in dripping like a water rat, tearing his streaked goggles off and swearing about the bloody works traffic and how some mad bugger had almost had him under a lorry. Seeing Jean and her mother mopping up he said, 'What the bloody hell is this then?' Her mother said it was a rehearsal for the Titanic and why didn't he man the bloody lifeboats, or else do something useful? He'd stormed out, stepping on one of Richard's model cars and walking through to the bathroom to clean up. He had gone straight into one of the sodden nightdresses hanging like bats on the dolly to dry. He flung it off and tore the lace of the bodice. Then he'd marched out of the house with a face glaring like coals.

They'd all been in bed when he'd returned, barging through the house and stumbling up the stairs. Julie had heard him stop at the door of Jean and Richard's room and belch, then he'd pulled off first one shoe, then the other, dropping them there on the landing.

When Sandra went away Julie had moved her own bed further towards the outside wall of their room. She hated hearing her parents through the dividing wall; the arguments. But worst was the whining of her father when he was drunk, and then the rasping of the bed's worn springs. She would try to think it out. Sandra and she had rarely referred directly to sex, but they exchanged hard, knowing looks after a night when the noises were obvious. Time after time Julie had buried her head in the pillow and run songs over in her head, hymns, the Beatles, anything to shut out the sounds coming out of the wallpaper's roses as if they were loudspeakers. Sandra would turn up her nose, 'He's an animal,' or 'It's a miracle they've stayed together— we could all be orphans.'

They had no words for the thing. 'Lovemaking' seemed wrong. Sandra said that men only wanted one thing—the sex thing—and that she expected the boys at college to be no better. Julie envied her, though. She was stuck in school for another two years, trapped in the sixth form. One more hurdle. And the boys in the Sixth were hardly attractive:

38

those in the Science Sixth were distant; they played with their slide-rules and talked formulae and football. The Arts Sixth were even less promising: there were Martin Dobbs and Keith Johnson who were obsessed with historical battles and cricket scores; Dobbs, too, had the awful habit of picking his nose, blatantly. There were the Williams twins whose almost perfect, strange alikeness was their only interesting feature. The rest formed a smutty suggestive group, always leering at fourth and fifth form girls. Mr Wilson called them 'the laughing cavaliers'. He kept on top of the double entendres in the Shakespeare classes, but at times seemed to share a sort of camaraderie with them.

English classes were casual, but with a sense of direction. John Wilson had the knack of directing energy into positive channels. You found yourself talking about feelings which the books had made you discover in yourself. Quite often the class time passed too quickly and it was unnerving after the bell to be thrown out into the corridor's noisy tide of bodies again. Like returning to the world from another planet. It was tiring, Julie thought, to have to keep changing into different people: speaking up for herself in class; saying nothing of note at home except when the tensions in the cramped council house would snap into a row. It was then that she was most likely to lose control. Sandra had survived by bending to their father's stupid demands and then ridiculing him behind his back. She said, 'There's nothing to be gained by arguing with him, or trying to talk sense to him. He doesn't listen to half of what you say, and he doesn't understand half of what he does hear. We've moved too far away from him, you know. And Mum, for that matter.'

Julie pushed the brush once more through her hair and winced. Was it really that bad? Was there any sort of family living in this house? Were they, the Coles girls, some sort of gifted creatures, royal children being succoured by simple folk until they escaped to claim their heritage?

She put the brush down. Her hair clung to the plastic bristles. Hair, nails, a face in the mirror; not a lot to leave behind. She went down the stairs and collected her raincoat from the loaded hooks at the bottom. She pulled it on and leaned against the front room door, bracing herself by holding on to the front door handle. It seemed quiet, just the television chatting in the corner; no raised voices from the front room or the kitchen. She opened the door and poked her head around into the room. 'I'm off then, Mum. Mr Wilson's house to do some baby-sitting. Won't be late.'

The bus was on time and had few passengers. Julie sat upstairs, for although the smoke annoyed her, she could put up with it for the view. Looking down from the top deck was like snatching unobserved glimpses of other people's lives. The back gardens of the estate had homemade sheds, pigeon lofts, dog runs, dismantled cars, neat vegetable patches. As the bus climbed into the Brynmawr area the semis and bigger houses sat snug with their squares and curves of lawns; there was the glint of greenhouses, garage doors ajar with garden tools stacked or hung from the wall, the sleeping snakes of garden hoses above the chrome smiles of cars. It soon grew dark with the beginnings of rain on the misty bus windows. The street lamps threw down pools of starched light that dissolved into grey at the edges. At the corner of Conway Road the Wilson's house presented its side and rear to the main road. Julie waited until the bus slowed, then rose from her seat so that she could see into the lighted kitchen and the two lit bays of the bedroom windows set neatly like a doll's house above each side of the back porch.

Sarah Wilson answered the door and let her in. Sarah was wearing a long black dress with white frills of lace at the cuffs, at her ankles and ruffled at her neck. 'We're so glad you can do this for us, and at such short notice. John's mother has been off colour and, anyway, that's a long story.'

'It's alright, really. Mr Wilson asked me at afternoon break and...'

'But I'm sure you could have been out enjoying yourself on a Friday night, couldn't you? John's still upstairs getting ready. So let me show you round. There's the television;

there's some nibbles in the kitchen, through there, and the coffee pot's fresh this evening. The baby bedroom is first right at the top of the stairs. Andrew's down and, we hope, out for the count. I should be surprised to hear from him tonight. He's been out in the garden until it rained and then he helped his father in the garage by swallowing nails and so on. Make yourself comfortable on the settee.' Sarah sat at the other end of the coffee table and lit a cigarette from the onyx table-lighter.

'He's crawling then?' said Julie. 'He seemed so much a baby when I've seen him with you outside school.'

'Yes, he's growing so fast we can hardly keep pace. It's like watching one of those nature programmes where the plants are speeded up. He's wonderful fun. I can't wait to have another baby.'

'Oh, you're going to have another baby then, are you?'

'Well, not just yet,' said Sarah, stubbing out her cigarette in a pottery ashtray on the coffee table.

Julie felt stupid. Some things were meant and at other times people just used words just to fill in the spaces. She ought to have learned that. As Sarah talked on about Andrew and his fads, Julie put on a listening face and looked at her, really looked at her. Yes, she looked the sort of wife you'd have imagined John Wilson to have: the simple, classy dress. Classic. The way she seemed so much in control of what was happening around her. The posed cigarette, which had a strong, foreign smell; the way the baby was tucked away on time. She had probably been a teacher or something professional, too. And she would sail back to some successful job again when all this baby business was done. Sometimes she'd pick John Wilson up from school in the car, Andrew perched in one of those new baby contraptions in the back and Mr Wilson not taking the wheel but slotting in beside her. He would sit with his briefcase bulging on his lap like a housewife with shopping. How different from her own family's was their life? Julie wanted to ask, How did you two meet? How does it work out like the way you are? Somehow everything would have been fitted together for them—college, careers,

41

their own house, a car, babies—like a plan drawn up, or the plot of a play. Julie was sure she would want it that way too.

John Wilson came downstairs heavily, in a rush.

'Where's my blue-striped handkerchief, love? Hello, Julie, I thought that must have been you. Thanks for helping us out like this. Sarah, love, it was in the top drawer, but now I can't find anything except white funeral sniffers. We shouldn't be too late for the Gilberts, should we? Where's that bloody hankie?'

'He's never been on time, ever since I've known him. Makes cutting it fine into an art form. He was late for graduation ceremony and had to squeeze in behind the Chemical Engineers or somebody,' said Sarah, conspiratorially, 'I'll find the blue hankie for you.' She smiled a fellow-woman's smile across at Julie and went with a sigh out of the room.

John Wilson took a bunch of keys off the mantelpiece and recited a catechism of 'Keys, watch, cuff-links, pen, wallet, diary, no handkerchief,' touching items and pockets as he did so. 'Sarah has showed you everything through there, I suppose?'

'Yes. Thanks. Kitchen. Baby Andrew in the first bedroom. A posh evening then. That's a nice jacket,' she said. It was leather, black, with flaps over the pockets. She guessed it was new, for it gave mousy squeaks whenever he moved his arms. In school he wore a brown corduroy thing with a flapping belt and leather patches at the elbows; his ties were always loosely down, with the top button of his shirt left undone. He had a habit of pulling up each of his socks after sitting at the front table and before starting the lesson.

'Yes, it's my Christmas present, from Sarah, an early one,' he said, looking confused by the compliment. 'One of the leather boys,' he added, lamely. 'I expect she's shown you the supper, in the kitchen under the tea-cloth, by the kettle—crisps and pies and things.'

'Oh, yes, I'll be fine,' Julie said, following him through to the kitchen.

'Yes, there's a pork pie,' he said, lifting the cloth.

'I don't eat much. Your wife, Mrs Wilson, shouldn't have bothered, really. What a big kitchen,' she said. It was fitted in white, with a tiled floor. A string of onions and a bunch of white onion-type things with scaly segments hung alongside a cork notice-board. The board had papers, notes and several postcards pinned up.

'We re-did it, extended it from the side of the house last year,' John Wilson said, reaching over to the sink to tighten a trickling tap. He leaned against the side of the sink unit, 'How are things, Julie?' ' he said, 'You live over on the Ridgeway, don't you? Doesn't your father work at Graham's, the aeroplane plant—I remember you doing an essay about 'The Daily Grind a couple of years back—fourth form, wasn't it?'

Yes, Graham's, that was where her father worked. She began to talk about him, his hours and the way he attacked the garden and other jobs when he'd had trouble at work. She wanted to talk more about her mother, but could think of nothing to say that wouldn't sound trivial. What did her mother do? Work some mornings at the corner shop and skivvy for the whole family. She seemed physically incapable of sitting still; she was constantly doing—cooking, sewing, ironing. She filled in the forms, paid the bills, counted the milk and the papers and reckoned the gas they'd used. Sometimes she'd settle with her knitting in front of an old film, but there'd be hot drinks to make in the commercial break, or sandwiches, or the immersion to put on, or something else to pull her to her feet.

'All mothers get a harder time of it, don't they? he agreed. 'When I was a child we lived with my grandmother and she and my mother used to battle over who would clean the most furniture. They'd battle over meals and fussing over my Dad and me. We certainly ate well—plates heaped, with meat and three veg islands in a sea of gravy. Sarah's been getting me off that and on to salads and yogurt. I'm quite taking to the continental stuff, though. Here, have a sniff of this.' He took one of the white onions and broke off a segment. 'Garlic, a Frenchman's delight.'

'Ugh!' Julie wrinkled her nose over the thing. A cut onion made her cry, but this was different; your nose felt redder; felt as if it could taste for itself.

'It wards off evil spirits, they say. That's to do with the reek of it, I suppose. Oh, no.' He looked up at the ceiling to the sound of a baby's cry. 'Now, if garlic could ward off babies!'

Julie was glad that Sarah would have to sort out Andrew: she felt that she was seeing John Wilson as a different person here. In school everyone stuck to their roles: even when teachers let out some personal detail, or an opinion that was unconventional, you guessed they were putting it on, that it was all part of the act. John Wilson had always been the one the girls fancied. Perhaps it was due to the material they discussed in class—the way a person's life was always close, just under the surface of the novels and poems they had to study. Here in his own house his appeal for Julie was much stronger, more disturbing. Having to talk to her while baby Andrew was cracking open the domestic bliss was making him seem uncomfortable, intimate and vulnerable. All the fussing over the mislaid hankie, and the way he kept smoothing his hair as they talked.

'I never knew how much noise a baby could make, especially at the most ungodly hour of the morning. Well, you'll have the business of a house and kids one day, won't you? Don't make the mistake that we all seem to make though—you have a good time and move about a bit before you fossilise into suburbia, eh?'

Julie wanted to say that she'd willingly give the suburbs a try, but could only come out with, 'I don't know—I haven't thought too far ahead yet. Exams are the first problem.'

'Yes, the trouble with our university years was that we just missed the Great Liberation. We were leaving college and setting up careers just as everyone a couple of years behind us was overtaking in the fast lane—occupying the registry, marching for causes, putting a bit of colour into things. All the things that we can discuss in class today were kicked off then. Risky things, unsettling times: 'I saw the greatest minds of our generation...' all that stuff. I love books more than anything, but I wonder sometimes if we grow up too quickly.'

'You don't seem that old,' said Julie, not really following his drift, 'not like...well, some of the other teachers.'

'Ah, but we all end up being "the other teachers", you see. That's the trouble, we end up turning into the characters we have been acting. No, you lot must go on out there and work out a new way.'

'There's the A levels first,' Julie said.

'Nonsense. You lot are a strong year—you'll come on fine well before the examination. It all begins to click into place one day, you'll see. Would you like to make some tea for yourself? No? Let's see how the boy wonder is doing then, shall we?'

They went back into the lounge and as Julie sat on the settee the other door opened and Sarah entered raising two crossed fingers and then pressing a finger to her lips in an exaggerated espionage movement.

'Andrew decided to sing something between Wagner and the Rolling Stones, but I've managed to soothe him back down again,' she said.

'Can we speak?' said John in a forced whisper.

'O.K.' Sarah replied, in a louder voice, 'but let's make a rapid escape—we're late already. Julie, you'll be alright. He really is safe and quiet now. We have this final flurry quite regularly. His dummy's in a plastic cup by the bed; if he plays you up. a good suck and a rock over the shoulder will sort him out.'

John Wilson helped her on with her coat and she stretched her arms out for the sleeves saying in a posh voice, 'Thank you my man. We won't be too late, Julie.'

Julie felt like an audience; everything they did together was a sort of act. She thought that must be 'sophisticated'. Couples acting as if in a play—even her parents did that. Though her father and mother rarely entered into anything as elaborate, the way they treated each other did fall into patterns; they had their own habits. He'd come home from the dogs or the pigeon club and take an indignant scolding. If he was really in the wrong—losing heavily, or a couple of pints too many—he have brought fish and chips for a late supper or a couple of bottles of ale and pop for Sunday dinner. Once when her mother had complained about her lack of housekeeping money he'd thrown a fit and stormed out to the club, then on to the dog track where he'd blown half his wages. Her father had never held a coat for her mother even in fun. Probably no-one else had either.

When John and Sarah had gone Julie closed the front room door and turned on the television, keeping it low so as to hear if the baby cried. BBC One had a vicar being interviewed about a pop band he was booking for Easter services. BBC Two was a string quartet in a stately home. ITV showed a commercial for a carpet sale—smiling couples gasped at huge rolls of flowered carpets, then sank back securely into deep purple armchairs. She turned the set off and started to look around the room. The coffee table had that day's Manchester Guardian, a selection of magazines and journals. The two bookcases contained hard-back art books and some old novels and poetry. One wall was filled with paperbacks stacked on loose wood shelves supported by bricks. Someone had started arranging these into alphabetical order. Julie traced Abse, Albee, Brecht through to Lawrence whereupon the order abandoned itself to random rows: *Eastern Religions that Have Shaped the World, Traditional Recipes from Ireland, The Rise and Fall of the Cistercians, The Electric Kool-Aid Acid Test*—titles that seemed either weird or boring.

On a low corner table which held the telephone there was a framed photograph of the two Wilsons wearing graduation gowns and hoods. John had an academic cap. His ears stuck out absurdly, Julie thought, he was like a cropped animal, a groomed dog. Sarah hadn't changed much except for the fact that she wore glasses in the photograph. The Wilsons posed with a clear pride in front of some impressive steps and civil columns. Julie thought she would have too. But she wondered why they kept the framed photograph there. Was it for them to look at? Or for visitors? Her front room at home had nothing but her mother's brasses that had come down from Granny Colclough and two cups her father had won years back with his pigeons. He'd given up the birds, but still kept the trophies. Perhaps when Sandra passed through college she'd be lined up with the pigeons.

Julie scanned the wall of books again and settled at James Joyce—an old copy of *The Dubliners* scrawled over with notes and under-linings, *Portrait of the Artist as a Young Man* and then the thickly-bound volume of *Ulysses*. Mr Wilson had said that it was a book for them to look forward to later in life, 'Like climbing Everest.'

'Nine hundred pages,' she said aloud. It felt like holding someone's life. The writing inside seemed strange—bits of a play, old fashioned speech, like Chaucer and Shakespeare, and then the whole of the ending, for pages and pages, as he had described, with no punctuation, had no gaps or sense. She replaced the book, squeezing it tightly into place, then went over to try the television again. Channel One now had a programme about sharks. They cruised a shadowy underworld of bubbles and silence, menacing and self-contained, but with sudden, unpredictable twists. The commentator's voice rose and quickened when they did this. Then, in one of the quiet cruising moments, Julie heard from upstairs a high crying and the sound of the cot moving.

She sat rocking the baby for what seemed like an hour, so long that she was drifting off herself. It was cosy there on the edge of the bed with the round, soft weight of the little boy, the loosening pucker of his lips as, in a deeper sleep he relaxed his grip on the dummy. She swung her weight forward and rose from the creaking mattress to put him back down in his cot. She left the door of the little bedroom ajar and stood on the landing for a few moments to check that he was asleep. On the landing she noticed that there was glow showing under the door of his parents' bedroom.

'Left in a rush,' she said aloud, startling herself with the sound of her voice. She pushed open the door and saw that the strip-light over the dressing-table had been left on. Reaching up for the push-switch she stopped, held by the sight of herself, arm and face raised in the three mirrors. In the centre mirror she looked strange, like some other person. She sat down on the dressing seat. Square on she resumed a familiar pose and expression, though the low light made her hair and nose cast different shadows. She was what she always was, except that here in the Wilsons' mirror she was trespassing. Her face turned into Sarah's face, and then she imagined John's in the side mirror.

She turned away and took in the rest of the room. A high-backed cane chair was in one corner; the bed had a curved cane head and a lumpy quilt thing covered in a flower pattern; thin plum and beige curtains were drawn; between the window and the bed was a low, modern chest of drawers with brass handles like belt buckles. There was a framed drawing on the wall by the door. In it a blue couple lay wrapped around each other, their bodies' odd shape warping the geometric pattern of a thick quilt with blue tree and bird shapes on it. A wine bottle stood on the bedside table, while on the floor three kittens fed from the teats inside the curve of their swollen, sleeping mother. The man had a beard like a young Greek hero in a text book illustration. Both he and the woman were looking directly out of the picture and smiling.

Julie went back to the dressing-table and pressed off the switch. In the seepage of dimly reflected light through the door from the landing she saw herself pulling on her sweater over her head. She unbuttoned the top of her jeans before unclipping her bra. Dropping and angling one hip, she acquired a mystery; she was easily attractive, wasn't she? Like a girl in an advert. Her body now appeared neat and symmetrical. The room was warm enough, but everything about her tingled. Her nipples rose and bristled before her eyes.

She took everything off and slipped under the quilt to lie in the centre of the bed. There was no top sheet, but the quilt was soft and warming. She pulled it up to her neck, then slid her hands to her sides and across the extent of the large bed. She brought her hands back to her sides and lightly touched herself along each leg, starting below the knee and moving up until her index fingers met at her navel. She then put each index finger in her mouth and left a drop of saliva on first one then the other nipple. Her hands stretched back behind her head: under one pillow she touched the buttons of a pair of pyjamas, under the other the lace frills of a nightie.

Just after midnight when the Wilsons returned, Sarah, rushing upstairs to the cries of her baby, found the girl asleep there in her marriage bed.

The Gift

I

Tess was an orphan. Her mother and father were Mr and Mrs Howell. She was their gift. They had lived at 18 Chestnut Avenue for as long as she could remember. As she turned the corner coming home each day from school her feet matched the patterns of the pavement cracks. Nothing in that avenue could change. The street with its line of tall cherry trees stuck out of the pavement, the neat hedges, gates with numbers, none of this had changed since her earliest memories. In the strong summer sun the single surviving chestnut turned over the palms of its leaves like a magician doing card tricks. The spiky fruit would ripen and plump, boys' sticks litter the road, and then autumn would press the fallen leaves to the wet pavement. Patterns. Tess couldn't imagine any of that ever changing; even the neighbours seemed to have stuck to the place, though whether that was out of loyalty to the "Avenue friendship" that Mrs Howell loved to speak of to strangers she met at holiday hotels on the south coast, or simply because they had reached a stultifying, immobilising middle age collectively, it was difficult to say.

There was no one of Tess's age on the avenue now that the sons and daughters had grown up. They were weekend visitors with their young children; or were students seen rarely enough even during the long summer vacations. As a child she'd played on the fringes of the games spilling out of the other side of Brinsley Copse where the outer ring of the council estate's houses backed their gardens up to the trees. But the estate kids would always race too fast on their bikes along the path leaning out to pluck leaves from the lower branches. They'd always break off to play at hospitals or wars in somebody's shed or garden den. Tess would hold back remembering her father's warning about other people's gardens, her mother's disapproving look.

'Come on, Margo, mind the gate,' she said to the large, pampered black cat who was old now and for years had never seemed to jump or move anything like a cat. Tess hated the way the fat thing rolled around under the dining table, insinuating itself during meals. Her mother would lower scraps from her plate down to its mouth with a fastidious forefinger and thumb.

'Is that you Teresa? You're late aren't you, dear?'

'Yes, I'm sorry. I got talking after Maths.' She'd found it painful to call the woman who'd brought her up 'Mother' since the talk they'd had on the morning of her ninth birthday when they had sat her formally on the settee and told her about her adoption. 'God decided not to give us any babies of our own and so we went to the people who look after little babies who...'

'...who haven't any parents—like Mother and me—and then people like Mother and I come along and look after the children and give them...'

'...take them home and look after them and be their new mothers and fathers,' and she picked up her knitting to fidget with the needles and occupy her hands.

'How did you get me?' she'd asked.

'We knew you were for us,' he'd said, looking deep into the bowl of his pipe and avoiding the eyes of his wife and chosen daughter.

'You were a gift, wasn't she, Ron?'

'You are our Teresa,' and rising he'd ruffled the young girl's hair as he passed out through the kitchen to busy himself in the garden.

Tess had felt that moment of touching like a point of real shock; they were not a demonstrative family and kissed each other rarely. Her father's hand, a man's hand, seemed to violate her hair. It tingled, felt like the otherness of a wig for hours after.

Tess began to climb the stairs without stopping to remove her school mackintosh.

'I'll just get some work done before tea. They're piling the revision on me a bit now,' and she carried her briefcase upstairs, right hand running over the raised pattern of the wallpaper as she went.

Lying on her back on the bed her eyes traced the hair-line crack of ceiling plaster from the centre-light to the top edge of the wall. The room was unmistakably hers. A small writing desk in one corner; low bookcase alongside the headboard of the narrow bed; posters covering most of the floral pattern of the wallpaper. There was a surfacing whale rising against a horizon of factory ships. Tess had sent a postal order to the Survival fund after seeing a television documentary the previous year; they'd sent her a poster. Jimmy Connors playing a double-handed shot and airborne. A rock band in purple and red concert lighting with a girl lead singer. Another poster, with notes, of Hamlet the Prince from the Sunday Times.

She felt better lying on the bed and the pain in her back which had started up again during that lunch-break was easing. She looked down at herself along the length of her body. Her legs were strong and well-shaped even under the dull blue of her school uniform. She had suffered a persistent attack of spots on her face and neck which lasted from her second year at St. Mary's up to her fifth. She'd used creams and once even a face-pack that smelt like rotten flowers and earth. The disfigurement tightened her facial expressions and pulled her back to herself. She worked quietly and steadily and accepted that the boys in her class seemed barely to notice her. Then the spots had gone.

Two girls attracted the group of smutty, precocious boys who grouped in places along the windows in Room 15; Sharon, whose breasts were high and full against her tight blouse; and Claire, a short, dark girl whose large, brown eyes smiled at everyone, and who, sitting in the front row in the fourth year, could quite distract Mr Newell floundering in his first year as a History teacher.

Tess had moved into the sixth form and taken History, English and Mathematics, her three strongest subjects. Newell, as her new form tutor had queried her choice.

'All this talk of a broad-based combination,' he'd said, 'when what you need is a language.'

But Maths it was to be. She found the abstraction of the subject was testing her to the limit; but in details the calculations had a directness that she felt safe with. The names of popes, emperors and ministers seemed endless and without real significance; neither Eliot's cool cleverness nor Conrad's tropical storms related to her feelings, the sense of confusion and isolation which swept through her without apparent cause, at a bus stop, in the troughs of lessons and at quiet moments in her room. But the numbers and signs which stood to attention on the pages of her Maths files had a straight-forward certainty which cooled and settled the complexities that arched through her body and spun her mind.

She was safe too because the subject deflected her parents' interest and interference. Hamlet was the only play they'd sat through together, and her father had, in an afterglow of enthusiasm, for 'the culture I missed because of my background', read the play several times. He sprinted through the Lilliputian print of the clumsy omnibus Shakespeare that held in place the unbroken sequence of Book Club editions on the shelf. For her mother the Matriculation she'd been so proud of taking as a girl had shrunk to the memory of the dry bones of grammar and, rising out of them like a dream, Coleridge's Xanadu.

Just like real blood-parents. Tess had assumed characteristics from the Howells: his steady slowness of action broken by sudden moves; her wistful dreaming.

David Llewelyn was always a couple of years ahead of her, and the previous summer in his university vacation he had returned from college, a changed person. His hair, 'rather long', her father noted, was cut roughly back to collar length and he wore light silver glasses that made Tess think of the stiff portraits of revolutionaries in the colour supplement—Trotsky, people like that.

The previous Easter he'd passed his test and now drove an A40 that had been transformed by the former owner's taste for pink and army brown into a bizarre beast, far from the original's sensible pale blue. A change of paint; that was David. That was really David. She had been so struck by the apparent change in him that she had been drawn to him out of curiosity. He was something new; he had perhaps come trailing wonderful clouds from the university. Clouds of words and images that pointed the way to a wider life. After a term of Modern Greats at Oxford he could spin a web of connections between events and forces which up until then had been mere phrases for her in the heavyweight television programmes. Eliot began to make sense.

Standing for the 73 bus one morning late in the Autumn term, under a threatening dark sky she had accepted his offer of a lift.

'Mind the door now, it's got an appetite for the legs of young girls,' he had said and she pressed back into the scarred leather of the passenger seat as he leaned across to pull the door's strap. 'How's the old place then? It seems as if I'd left years ago. After that third year in the sixth the last few months have been such a release, so many different things. They've flown by.'

'It's pretty much the same as always, I suppose,' she replied, and left it at that. He needed no prompting to respond with details of his new life up at college and the ten minute drive was filled with names of dons and fellows, The lexicon of Oxford—Brasenose, Bumps, Bodleian, The Bear, Balliol. And rowing: Tess was impressed.

Over the following weeks of the Christmas vacation they met frequently and Tess was drawn into the world of the Common Room and Quadrangle, of the friendly uncle porters, the bicycle community, the river that wove the whole patchwork of history, learning, class and tradition into one heady, fine cloak of success and belonging.

That vacation they seemed to move in relation to each other, whether in the Avenue, or down town; in the local library; once even, in the bus station when the Austin beast's suspension was being patched up. They'd meet and chat, and then talk—perhaps without direction, but always seriously. Often they would wander around the central square of shopping streets that shaped the town and end up at The Simple Simon, a new snack bar, all pine and vinyl and steel, that was in the new shopping precinct.

'Two coffees,' he'd order, as if the girl serving just wasn't there. He never said please to her and on their first couple of visits Tess thought of remarking on the fact, in a light, jokey way perhaps. But then it seemed to fit in with the other things he did. He somehow managed to speak about other people, even his parents, as if they were moons circling the world of his college. His records, his books, his car. Dull but necessary; that's the way he treated the concerns of others.

Except Tess quickly felt herself to be part of the real world as David saw it.

'They've been good to me in their way,' he talked always of his parents as if they were dead or had moved to another area, 'But I can't really talk to them.' He stressed the 'really' with the fingers of his right hand spreading, then bunching into a fist.

'My father and mother are alright too, in their way,' she stirred the remains of her coffee, 'but we never talk about really important things. They just switch off,'she said. She wanted to add, 'not like talking to you,' but thought that it would sound simpering. Lifting her head up, she caught the full look of his eyes and then it didn't seem to matter that she'd been on the point of talking about her adoption. Her sharing of that discreet fact would have been too obviously dramatic, no matter how she phrased it. It was not necessary to be interesting, or remarkable in that way, she was happy to be his audience.

'Let's go over to Bryant's Books and catch the next bus,' he said, his hand coming to hers and taking the spoon away, back down to the saucer.

II

'I think we could stretch to a new dress, don't you think, Mother?'

'Yes, Ron. You could do with a new dress, Teresa, something pretty. I don't think you've had anything new since your last long one, with the green frills, for that party at school.'

It was true, Tess' wardrobe was filled largely by her mother's reluctance to clear out tired or outgrown clothes. She had three school blazers: it was like a series of exhibits marking her progress through puberty. Her mother had been of no help to her. At thirteen she still wore a vest, her breasts jiggling inside her blouse as she ran for the bus in the mornings. And even then it had been her father who had raised the matter. Over the dishes at the sink whilst Tess was replacing the cutlery in the sideboard drawer she'd heard him say: 'Shouldn't Teresa be wearing some underclothes, Betty? You know, at her age.'

'Well, she's never asked for a bra or anything. But perhaps you're right.'

Her first period had been a trauma; in the holidays, thank God, but she'd rushed from the lunch table and hidden in her room. She sat hunched on the edge of the bed, her body working its chemistry while she stared down and let her mind wander among the curling patterns of the carpet.

Her mother had glossed over the incident: 'It's only nature working its ways. We have to put up with that.'

But back at school the following week Sharon Brown had explained it fully through one lunch-time to a huddle of girls. For a while these talks about their emerging sexuality drew them together, but later that term Sharon began to meet a fifth form boy down in the Public Library and the group splintered again.

The invitation to tea was David's parents' idea, or rather, his mother's. Ruth Llewelyn had barely spoken to the Howells; she felt they had little in common, and besides, their cat was a real nuisance, stalking through her neatly turned flower-beds and leaving its 'messages'. Still, the girl seemed quite pleasant and David's ties with the Avenue were to be considered now that his college was clearly the centre of his world; she might bring him back to earth.

Tess walked self-consciously up the road to the Llewelyn's. The new dress was cornflower blue with abstract flowers of white at the neck and the hem. She had felt so suave extending her arms in the boutique's full-length mirror to show off the flared sleeves, but in the evening's dank air, jammed into her plain coat, they seemed to constrict her arms. The flowered hem poked below her coat and she felt sure that she looked ridiculous.

Mrs Llewelyn opened the door with a smile and a voice loudly familiar: 'Do come in, Teresa, or Tess is it? What a lovely dress,' and she slotted the coat neatly onto a hanger in a cupboard.

They had built a cloakroom just off the entrance hall and had extended the basic Avenue semi-detached style on both ground-level and upstairs. There were carpets throughout, flock wallpaper and patterned curtains, the doors with brass handles. Tess sank into the large settee and had to angle her head forward uncomfortably to follow Mrs Llewelyn's facial language as she talked inconsequentially of the season, their garden and the promise of snowdrops and daffodils in the new year.

David came in wearing a pair of jeans and a lumberjack check shirt. Tess felt stupidly overdressed.

'Been having a bit of trouble with the carburettor,' he said, holding up an oily hand but it did nothing to lessen the mixture of discomfort and irritation she felt. Why couldn't he have left the thing alone for one afternoon? Hadn't he realised that she would dress for the visit? But once he began to talk the conversation took on reality, a purpose to which his mother's polite chatter had been no more than a prelude. What was to be done about the army and Ireland? A friend at College saw the Baader Meinhof gang as urban artists of violence. And where was the Centre-left when the streets caught fire?

'A bored, disillusioned set of well-to-do children. They've grasped at a set of pseudo-political slogans just to gloss over their simple need for excitement.' Then he developed the point, talking of 'historical necessity' and the post-war generation.

It excited Tess that he should talk at home as he did at the university, or over coffee with her. Mrs Llewelyn contributed little but appeared to be listening, holding the newspaper at bay whilst she put on her glasses in order to look at the front-page photographs of the siege and the trapped terrorists. At home Tess could not imagine such a topic being extended beyond her father's tongue-clicking and well-worn line about the death sentence and her mother's 'Terrible', their respective stock responses to bad news on the TV.

Mr Llewelyn arrived with a beep of his horn and whilst David manoeuvred the A40 to allow the larger saloon into the drive, Ruth Llewelyn took Tess into the dining room and through the metallic, smooth sliding doors, out onto the patio. It was such a well-tended garden of curved flower beds and a vegetable patch, freshy dug over, near the bottom hedge.

'It's been so mild, the roses have lasted right through the winter this year,' she said, and taking a final deep red rose in her hand, she deftly snapped the stalk. 'For the table,' she explained.

III

David walked her home slowly down the Avenue in the dark. He didn't hold her hand; she didn't mind, and anyway she felt a quiet scorn for those couples in school who seemed cemented together as they paired and scattered to the edges of the grounds at morning break and lunch-time. At the end of term she'd had an embarrassing confrontation on prefect duty one break-time in trying to manoeuvre a couple of fourth formers out of the Middle School block. Whilst the girl, a loud precocious creature called Maureen, slowly put her blazer back on, the boy had turned surly and might have even threatened Tess. His eyes narrowed and fists clenched at his side, Tess had been stopped in her tracks. The thought of becoming involved in that sort of scene, the boy Darren, wisps of manhood on his upper lip, grappling with her, perhaps ripping her prefect's blazer and that slut Maureen goading him on, made Tess uneasy for days afterwards.

David seemed positively brusque with her until they reached her parents' gate. Instead of opening it he stopped and leaned back against it, engaging the latch.

'Let's go for a walk,' he said. 'It's early and I know it won't rain.'

'Your father swore it would, after he'd washed the car.'

'That's the weaker of the two stock jokes he's told as long as I can remember. He talks in clichés; he's tired, worn out.'

Tess thought this was harsh. Still the man was his father, not hers. They walked down the road and through the sparse cover of Brinsley Copse, each tree dark and mute in the dregs of the day's light. David stopped at the trunk of a great oak which served as a focal point in the wood. He planted his feet apart there on the bare earth that was worn smooth by the years' running feet and skidding bicycles.'Tess,' he said, nothing more.

And she walked to him, right up to his body so that kissing her was his only way out. And thinking afterwards, what really surprised her was her stupidity in believing that it was she whose initiative it was; for how could she not have gone to him, letting him stand there like an actor losing his lines in the shabby climax of a bad film.

Her first real kiss; and how good it was. Not furtive, hurried and tense, as she had feared, but with her mouth relaxing and widening to his. The taste of his tongue like some strange live meat. Turning her round he pressed her against the tree so that she felt the rough relief of its bark printing the moment into her back, and then that sensation replaced by the feel of his hand slipping through her dress to take her breasts.

That was the first time that she had felt as if her body were not hers. Heroines in books and films had always reacted against the violation of their flesh, but that hand caressing her breasts enlightened her. Your body was not simply territory to defend; it was to be offered, and winning (what exactly, she was not sure at this point) was possibly by that sharing. As he pulled his hand awkwardly out of her dress the edge of his sleeve flicked across her nipple, so that for seconds she seemed not to need to breathe.

They spent almost every evening together for the remaining weeks of the vacation. He met her from school and under a patchwork of excuses and feigned academic interests they were able to get away from the stifling Avenue in his car. Always they would leave the film or concert early and squeeze into the chilled, soft leather of the old Austin.

At a party thrown by the head-boy she went into the back-bedroom with David and she would have let him do it there under the paisley-quilt, the top blanket scratching her bare shoulders. But the stairs drummed constantly with footsteps and giggles, the house rocked with the noise of the boys playing at being loudly-drunk students.

IV

The train was no more than a few minutes late and she knew that she would be able to meet him at their agreed time. Somehow she had imagined a compartment; a door with blinds and perhaps another occupant, an old woman possibly, and they'd talk inconsequentially about the countryside rolling past the window. The woman would reminisce about her dead husband. Tess would talk about David and her journey to Oxford; she'd sound the modern young woman with her freedom and boldness. But the carriage was one long corridor and no-one sat across the table from her. She flicked through her novel, but hardly saw the words or remembered the characters' names.

Her mind ran through the scene with her parents when she'd told them of her trip. A weekend at Oxford in one of his college's guest rooms was perfectly proper. And wasn't it educational, I mean Oxford? The widening world: her future. It hadn't been a confrontation really. Their natural, instinctive objection could not have been raised without their referring specifically to the propriety of the stay. The threat to her virginity, implicit in their fears, was too personal, too embarrassing to be mentioned. Her mother fussed about clothes and the rail fare while her father had shown a particular concern for her homework. The thing became a twelve-year old's jaunt to the zoo with the school trip. What they ignored ceased to be a problem. David was such a nice boy, the Llewellyns a good family, and after all it was Oxford, Lincoln College, Oxford where John Wesley had studied and which had a library, or was it a chapel, built by a famous architect.

It was Tess' first ride in a taxi and she hurried away from the car, fussing with the clasp of her case, leaving the driver with a generous ten bob note to cover the tip she thought you had to give.

'Mr Llewelyn? His sister? Come along miss, I'll take your case for you.' She followed the porter, a cheerful man in his late fifties, out of the lodge, around two sides of the quadrangle.

She immediately sensed the appeal of the place. Lines of small-framed windows, ivy-fringed, looking down onto a cropped, uniform lawn. The stone smooth, beige and stately, taking what worth the January noon-sun could offer. Everyone seemed to walk with a purpose, arms full of books, or sports bags. Coming here one was elevated, plunged into a tradition and a set of values which altered one's life.

'Just up the stairs now, and we'll find number 24. There'll be just two guests for the weekend; Mr Andrews's cousin is visiting too. Anything you need, just call for the porter. It will be me or Clive—he's the young handsome one.'

'I'm supposed to be meeting David, Mr Llewelyn.'

'Yes, Mr Llewelyn left a note to say that he's with his tutor until two o'clock and that he'll be straight up to welcome you as soon as he can. You go in and make yourself comfortable. There's a kettle and tea over there on the desk and the milk's in the pantry fridge at the end of the corridor.'

Through the panes of the window Tess peered out at the quad and the wisteria-covered walls, everything fitting together to complete an entity, an enclosed sense of belonging. The security of the college was projected out along the sky-line for there were towers and spires against the growing clouds and they proclaimed the true nature of the town. What office-blocks there were seemed incongruous, standing uneasily among and above the old colleges.

'We're going to a party,' said David, as he breezed into the room. 'A friend of mine, John, over at Christ's—we play squash together. Did I tell you I'd taken up squash?'

It was six hours later that he kissed her. After the dinner at college, the drinks with a group of bar-philosophers at The Carpenters, all wood panels and inscribed pewter tankards, with the night air chilling, scything through coats, his arm at last round her, at the pillar of the lodge-gate he kissed her, and walked her by the hand round the angle of the quad, to his room.

David wasn't fickle, that wasn't it. Rather, he turned like an exhibit, a ceramic: a facet, a fact, another facet, and each time giving his whole attention, concern, his love even. Nothing blended in his life though; he lived in a number of directions, on a number of planes. Coping with one aspect of his life at a time, he maintained a carefree manner. Family, friends, college, sport, fulfilled the compartments of his world by turns.

Tess fetched her case over the following morning and they hardly left his room for the next two days, dodging porters and other students. Cramped in his narrow bed she was pressed to the wall and could barely sleep. He seemed to be able to sleep anywhere, an arm and leg draped over the side of the bed.

Each time when they'd finished making love they talked: he about his growing up, more and more about the furtive early exploration of puberty, crushes on girls, shaving with his father's razor when his parents were out of the house, strange and banal rites of passage. She listened but gave little away about her own bodily anguishes. David drew nothing intimate from her. Her body she shared; something lonely and incomplete was moving to rightness. Sharing her fears would have meant losing everything. As he slept she lay still and paraded her secrets for herself. His wiry spectacles perched on the bookcase, staring.

At the station he said, 'See you soon.'

Goodbye, David,' she said. She half-dozed all the journey home.

V

The aching sharpened into real pain shortly after supper that evening and she excused herself from the washing up.

'Don't you want to see the serial later? It's the last episode of that Mrs Gaskell thing.'

'I've a really bad headache, Mum. I'll have an early night and try to shake it off for school tomorrow,' she replied, and made her way up the stairs, promising to take some aspirins.

She'd been having twinges throughout the day, since the morning's gym lesson, though she'd flipped a shuttlecock around with feigned enthusiasm. But something was obviously happening to her now.

She had told no-one about it. For weeks she had barely thought of David. It was like the chapter of a book she'd finished. The Easter vacation had passed and he had made a brief appearance at home, staying a single night and driving off the following morning for a course in London. It didn't shake her that he hadn't called; the Oxford weekend was months back and apart from a letter she'd written to him on the Monday following her visit, Tess made no attempt to contact him. He had not answered her letter. What had she written? She couldn't remember: something about how she had known that she would sleep with him, and that she had wanted to for a long time. But it had dribbled out inconsequentially at the bottom of the page with something about train-times and the journey home. There was no mention of love or anything like that. She had returned to the routine of the school term and the preparation for the Summer exams. There was no place for David in that; she wanted to clear everything out of the way and simply do the examination work. The long Summer holiday and then college for herself, not Oxford, but Bangor or Reading perhaps. There would be time enough for the bother of living then. No-one had told her, but when her third period failed to come she had to consider the possibility that she was pregnant. Her waist had thickened but an aunt had sent a fisherman's smock for Christmas and she lived in it; she wore loose jumpers and had bought a pair of jeans several inches larger than usual. At least she hadn't been sick; in fact her appetite had strengthened noticeably. If she'd been sick they might have guessed.

'I think our Tess is having one of those late growth spurts. She's eating like a horse.'

'Leave her be, Ron. You used to go on at her for not finishing meals.'

'I've always liked lamb,' said Tess, pulling her chair tighter to the table and making an effort to sit upright.

She became very conscious of her breasts which seemed to tingle when anyone looked at her. Surely it was obvious to everybody? But her parents had never really looked at her, not face to face. Even when the conversation turned to something personal her mother would be over the sink or busying herself at the cleaning. Her father was jolly or broody by turns. Both were an act. Tess couldn't believe that anything really touched him.

That very evening she'd wondered if her mother had something on her mind, but Tess's excuse of a headache had drawn her concern and she was content to talk about that.

'You're not worried about those exams now are you? We both want you to do well, but as long as you do your best, that's all we ask. A university girl, eh?'

Tess had smiled, reassurance, but her mother persisted. 'It's a pity that David couldn't come home more often. You liked him didn't you? Such an interesting, confident boy, too. Perhaps he'll help you revise?'

'He's very busy himself, I should think,' Tess said.

Just after nine o'clock she felt a twinge more painful than the feelings which had prodded through her body progressively during the day. She noticed that the alarm marker was near the hour hand and stretched across to the bedside table to press down the stop button. Her shoulder and upper arm slid back along the pillow uncomfortably. It was wet and cold. She realised that she had been sweating heavily and longed to go and stand under the shower in the bathroom. The water ran through the pipes like messages though and her mother was sure to come up and fuss about towels.

She pulled the blankets tightly around herself and shivered.

The stuff came in clots. It was not like the film they'd shown in the fourth form, a joyful pain like pushing yourself to the limit at a sport. Nor was it simply shedding a skin like a snake; she felt as if she were coming apart, somebody unpicking the stitches of her body. Partly lying, partly sitting with her legs over the side of the bed, she wrapped an old dress and a thick pullover she no longer wore around her thighs to take the mess. Was she having all her periods at once? The pains which pushed down through her were more like waves than those monthly cramps though; like waves, but irregular, out of sequence so that the tide beat against itself, surge and pull, leaving troughs of cold hollowness.

She didn't cry out; instead her breaths came slowly, fiercely like a marathon runner's, but without the conscious control of that pacing. She seemed suspended between the throbbing in her body and the bellows in her lungs. All her body's rhythms were clashing and she felt as if she would have to call out. She blacked out to the awful vision of her mother and father forcing their way in through the door. But no-one came. It was her imagining.

The soiled and bloody clothes she bundled and pushed under the bed. Edging around the bed she stiffly made it to her wardrobe by holding onto the work-table with its text-books and files of notes. She bent with difficulty and tipped her new shoes, a Christmas present, out of the cardboard box. The foetus—'It isn't a baby. Not a baby,' she said to herself, seemed absurdly heavy as she moved it in her cupped hands like water. Neatly laid in the tissue paper it could have been the blind form of a young animal. It was an animal pity that she felt as she looked down at the blue-tinged flesh in the box.

'I ought to say something,' she thought, as she picked up the lid. It had 'Hardy's Quality Shoes' and an insignia of a shield with a deer's head inside.

She said,

> 'Not in entire forgetfulness,
> And not in utter nakedness,
> But trailing clouds of glory do we come
> From God who is our home.'

She didn't see what God had to do with anything, but she liked the rhythm of Wordsworth's lines and the 'trailing clouds of glory' sounded as if it could have come from a hymn.

She pressed the lid down as tightly as she could and fixed it with sticky tape. The box slid back into its shelf.

Then she turned out the light and lay in her bed. The stars shone dully through the gap between her curtain and the wall. The hands and face of her alarm clock drew light from the sky and flickered.

She closed her eyes and stared up at the lids' black insides. A screen blank, as when a picture has just flickered to its end. Her mouth tightened and she hummed fragments from the lullabies she could remember.

Umbrella

The drone of the Country and Western singer faded as the news jingle began.

Want a woman like you
To keep me from feeling blue
Want a woman like you
What can I do...?

11.30. She flicked off the switch on the stereo deck. 11.30—that gave her fifteen minutes to get Richard and his pram into the car and make it to the school in time to meet Alun. It was his fourth week at the Infants and she was having to bring him home for lunch during that settling-in period. It was a chore, but in a sense she welcomed the shape this gave to the day: a lunch-break neatly bisecting a morning of housework and an afternoon of shopping, then preparing the evening meal. Sometimes, if the weather was fine, she'd set off early and wheel Richard in his pram down the road and across the park to the school.

Her days were packed tightly, like a parcel, held together, labelled and waiting for Colin to open on his return from the Bank. She liked it that way and kept it tight by working her way steadily through the circuit of jobs that made up the core of being a housewife. She hated the word 'housewife', but in the six years since she'd first become pregnant and given up her job at the Midland, the notion of an ideal housewife had been established in her mind. She wanted to care for her children, had become jealous of their attention and dependency when grandparents visited. Grandparents had the best of it; they got the games and the giggles and cuddles and missed the splintered nights and early morning stink of nappies.

She leaned over the pram at the foot of the stairs and felt under the plastic lining of Richard's nappy. Dry, thank God. She stood there over him, studying him. His eyes remained closed, beautiful, almost translucent like butterflies' wings, his head to the side, resting against a clenched right fist. He was soft and precious, though in sleep he could be distant, like a vessel on its own true course, but barely appearing to move.

These periods of sleep were like oases in the day. She liked to come across that peace almost by chance—ten minutes, perhaps half an hour when everything was in place, the house was all hers and her time was hers alone. Her body was hers and she would close herself in on herself, turn off the housework music that poured from the radio like sudsy water from the hose of the washer.

She'd pick up a book, find her turned-down page and read. She liked the ritual of turning down the top corner, marking the spot she'd reached. The branch library was just a mile away and she could fit it in on her way back from the shops. She had never read so widely before. But she'd made a rule for herself—no Romance—she wouldn't be seen dead hovering around the sloppy section. No, she'd decided to read anything but that stuff. She picked up books at random—Science-Fiction, American Precinct Murders, Biographies, around the world yachts-people and once even a smoking-sixgun Western. She tasted each writer and style —savouring the unpredictability. It was like choosing from the tea-cakes on visits to her rich Aunt Josey's when she was a young girl. The house had been huge and old, mouldering away as if it would sink into the unkept garden. She remembered Aunt Josephine as gnarled and witch-like with silver framed glasses perched on her hooked nose. There had hung everywhere the old woman smell of dust and camphor mixed in with the sickly-sweet cakes that would magically appear like a tower of temptation on a silver stand. It was strange, the whole memory seemed to her now shaped as if she'd read it in a novel.

The picture of the Tower of Babel that hung in the entrance to the library always reminded her of a heap of chocolate eclairs and macaroons, or her Aunt Josephine's treats. There would be a time when the boys were older when she could think about work again. And perhaps time to herself—to read, lunch with the ladies, spend time at the hair dresser. That was life wasn't it? Putting up with chores and duties and dislikes for the sake of the wee things.

She flicked up the pram brake with her foot and leaned on the handle to move Richard out of the hall and through the front door. Half way into the front room the hood lever jammed against the door-frame.

'Damn it, damn it.' She glared at the lever. It happened time and time again, the angle of the pram catching exactly the same spot so that a groove had been worn through the paint and notched into the wood. She pulled back to the stairs, straightened and squeezed through.

She pushed across the front room then, took her coat off the lobby's hook, checked that her bunch of keys was in the pocket. The see-sawing as she tilted the pram over the front step and onto the path caused Richard to waken, but she settled him back down with his dummy and pulled up the hood against the freshening October wind. She stopped the pram alongside the rear door of the old Austin 1100, and flicked off the side catches, releasing the body of the pram from the carriage. Then she had to go round to the driver's door, which was the only one that would take a key from the outside, and lean across to flick up the rear handle. Spots of rain appeared on the side windows. Her eyes caught the digits on her wrist-watch—11.34. That gave her about ten minutes. In pulling back the driver's seat she banged her knee on the steering wheel.

The traffic was light and she crossed Colbrook Road to use Drover's Lane, skirting the west end, affordable, but still safely included in the best catchment area. Location was so important, Colin maintained. He'd drawn up a list of priorities when they'd bought the house. First, location, then size, garden and garage and finally, decoration and fittings. All these things determined your price.

He'd written his priorities on the first page of a notebook, then the mortgage possibilities (with the bank's significantly reduced rate, as they were both employees) and then on successive pages the points pro and con the two dozen or so houses they'd viewed. Colin needed to record, plan, get things down into columns. He was the most ordered person she'd ever met. It was his strength.

There was a carpet store across from the school gates and she managed to snatch a place in the car park. A large board loomed over her proclaiming 'Customers Only— Others two pounds per hour' but this was nothing compared to the greater threat of the traffic warden who walked the yellow line that circled the school and so most people used the carpet place.

As she pushed Richard over the crossing she smiled at the lollipop-lady who glistened like an Eskimo and mechanically greeted everyone with a resigned smile and 'Bloody rain again!'

Beyond her, the traffic warden paced the line like a camp guard. He was tall and lean, watching eyes pierced through his wet glasses like some tired bird of prey.

'The beginning of term purge, Alice,' remarked a woman in her thirties from under a coloured golf umbrella.

'The old sod's bagging a brace of mothers to re-assert his control over us,' replied Alice, 'He'd be naked without that pencil and notebook, wouldn't he Rachel?'

'My God! Can you imagine him naked?' asked someone wearing sky-blue oilskins.

The coloured panels of the golf umbrella twirled and a voice replied, 'Not me, Yvonne. After all these years of being the dutiful wife and mother at home I may be prone to fantasies, but not in my wildest dreams would old Hawkeye figure in his birthday suit!'

The same faces, cars, changes of clothes. One quickly came to recognise the women on the school run. About half of them drove Minis, Fiestas, toy-town Fiats,—second cars to back up their husband's firm's Cortina or leased Rover. Perhaps they weren't as yet a 'set' but they seemed to gravitate to each other in their Oxfam chic, their lacquered toe-nails winking from open-toed shoes. Alice, Rachel, Yvonne, Caroline—to her they were faces and voices with names. There was to be a P.T.A. evening scheduled for a fortnight's time and she'd got to get to know them better then. Or would she? Would the conversation extend beyond kids and teachers? She could see it—Colin would be bored with the small talk but she could just imagine his looking them over, weighing them up during conversations. He'd catch his bottom lip under his front teeth, posing with one hand in his pocket and the other fluttering like a bird, looking concerned and witty—a real charmer.

He'd been like that when they'd first met. He was sharp at the bank and she'd been impressed. His promotion to chief cashier had brought them back down the coast, though since then he'd seemed to lose impetus. He no longer talked of running his own branch. After the first year he'd lawned and arranged their small garden; in the second year the house had been redecorated and now he seemed to be often at a loose end. He'd taken to spending a couple of evenings in the week up at the Horse and Plough. He was even talking seriously of taking up golf.

The bell sounded and the waiting mothers drew closer to the gates. The children came from their classes to the school's front door and, buttoned up by their teachers against the rain, they were released into the world like a succession of bright seeds as respective mothers' waves were acknowledged.

Alun scurried across the tiny yard and catapulted wetly into her arms as she bent to greet him.

'Did you have a nice morning?'

'Mummy, Mummy.'

'Did you do anything nice?'

'We saw 'Play School' on Miss's television and I painted Daddy. Is it a sweets day, Mummy? Is it?'

She promised him a visit to the corner shop they would pass near the library on the way home for lunch. She still had several chapters of her John Le Carré to finish, but the Arnold Palmer book on golf she'd taken out for Colin had become overdue. She hadn't seen him reading it anyway; not that he'd ever been much of a reader. She went through the performance of loading the children into the car—squashing Alun up against the outside door and then lifting Richard's pram top onto the rest of the rear seat. 'Shh, he's asleep, let's try not to wake him.'

Hers was the last school car to leave, but the roads were still clear in the lull before the lunch-time crowds from town. She was at the library in a matter of minutes and, leaving the two boys in the car, hurried inside to settle the fine and renew the golf book.

When she returned to the car Richard had woken and was bawling. He must have begun as she'd shut the car door for Alun had been upset by the crying and was himself close to tears.

'He won't stop crying, Mummy. I talked to him but it wasn't any use.'

'Come on, love don't worry. Your baby brother's got hungry, that's all, and crying's the only way he can tell us. We'd better give him his dummy and get him home straight away.'

She checked each of the doors again and set off for home. At the junction with Drover's Lane she was forced to edge around a car parked awkwardly near the corner. She'd almost committed herself to the turn when a sports-car suddenly materialised forcing her to tread sharply on the brakes. Alun was thrown forward against the front passenger seat and bumped his nose.

As she turned to soothe his yells and to replace Richard's dummy she burst out with 'Bloody hell!' How stupid—it wasn't her fault—it was that stupidly-parked car. She felt like getting out and giving them a piece of her mind, but the thing started up and pulled out around her. She glared angrily at the driver, but the other woman stared straight ahead and the man alongside her turned his face to look away. She noted a coloured umbrella in the back window of the car as it accelerated away down the lane.

'It's Daddy!' shouted Alun, 'Daddy! Daddy!' He bounced up and down on the seat and waved.

'It can't be Daddy—he's at work. Sit back in your seat now when I'm driving.'

All the way home she had that stupid golf umbrella in her mind, and the man's head seen fleetingly, but repeating itself over and over like a re-wound film.

Some Kind of Immortality

This is the second time with this one—let's call her Alice—belts and braces, she needs to make sure it works. Though, for my part, there's never been a problem. And this will be straightforward. She's not unfanciable, thirty-five or thereabouts, around my height, auburn hair swept back and held by a tortoiseshell clip, business-like, neat. Lap-top Googling away on the coffee table to indicate that she's busy, end of a working day. No offer of coffee this time. On the bathroom shelf above the closed toilet lid on which I'm sitting are copies of National Geographic, an old Private Eye, Gone Girl with a page turned down two thirds of the way through. And a copy of Playboy; thoughtful that.

A teacher? Possibly, but I have seen no pile of exercise books, on the previous visit or this time. Middle-management, I'd guess, stalled in the middle of a management career, same rung on the ladder for long enough to think that the ladder may not really be there. This semi is on a socially-rising avenue in Highthorpe, new reg. Audi 3 on the drive. No problem with my parking just around the corner and walking to the door, my car will be untouched on my return. Which, ah, ah, will be within the next ten minutes, as she is not, I take it, one for small-talk; nothing that isn't on my form. Nice curve to those jeans: no need for Miss January. Thank you Ma'am.

It's a service—no, I mean that—a service. I'm discreet and only go free-lance because of the restrictions of the agency. Restricted rights; lots of form filling; all a bit cloak and dagger; ten donations, maximum. Their office is above one of the estate agents on Montague Street, a small plaque —'Family Matters'. And when your turn comes Gaynor is sitting behind a desk, always with an angle-poise over her papers whatever the weather, winter dark or summer shine. One of those indeterminate ages—think Dame Judy as 'M' circa *The World is Not Enough*, Pierce Brosnan? Certainly before Daniel Craig, anyway.

And Family Matters is better than the HFEA, though Gaynor is registered or something and going by the forms I had to fill in all over again, she takes care. But she draws the line after after ten, though I feel, I know, that I can and should go further. And don't get me wrong, I stick to the no alcohol or sex regulations so many days before. Or pretty much stick to them. It's not that straightforward if you have a life-partner, or a live-in wife. Which is where I am now.

I am upfront as far as possible, leaving the women my mobile, or a mobile at any rate, because I care about the success and the consequences, the children. I'd like to think that in years to come, for years to come, I could stay in touch. Though that's unlikely, isn't it? And I know that the ten-only rule is so that years down the line no two half-siblings could meet and marry and risk serious problems with their own children. I am fully aware and take lots of precautions: I keep a record of dates and addresses, contact numbers and I am wary of going to donate in the same areas of the same towns. I can cover the whole of the Midlands; sometimes, with an alibi, further afield, and, well, do the maths, it's unlikely, isn't it? Also, I leave the birth to them; how could I do otherwise? I missed Alex because I was in a meeting in York, but was there for Rachel, though what use I was I still don't know. There's been university research in London arguing that the mother would rather have another woman—sister or friend—than her man. I'd be difficult to explain away, wouldn't I?

To my mind, the woman is always the mother, by law, but the father is only the *father*. It's a one-way, unbalanced system, and this way I can keep control to a greater extent, maintain some rights, an extended interest and possibly a commitment.

The forms and the websites are clear and cold: height, hair colour, nationality, race, education. And I've ticked enough of the boxes. I mean, who would choose 'Baker' or 'Construction Worker' when there are any number of 'Postgrad. Researcher', 'Law Student', 'Naval Officer' and the like. Why would she not choose a professional?

As for my side, I do ask for a photograph from the client; I'm not George Clooney, but I reckon that I have attributes—tall enough, healthy enough, a half-decent degree, followed by a career, of sorts, and I look a bit younger than I am. What's not to like? And, so far, they seem to like. But I have to judge them too: I'll not be wasted on an—and you may not like me saying this, but how else to put it?—ugly woman. And there's no STD problem with me; I'm a devoted husband and father; I have no need to take on the whole business and am happy filling a pot.

I've been discriminating; and I give an honest service. Never more than once a week, if that; no 'second pressing' of the vintage from me, though there are on-line boasters who reckon to fire hits off like a Gatling gun in a Spaghetti Western. I'm more of a Seamus Heaney childhood frog spawn bloke, and that image, harking back to that poem we did in school, is my way of dealing with it,. Lots of minute dots becoming tadpoles, and enough of them swimming the right way; that's been my way of visualising it.

So this one, Alice, is it—well, Aston Villa she will be filed under, month, post-code, date of success, date of delivery—'A: Jan; CV33TB; 22/3; Nov.' in my lap-top's 'United Fixtures' file, because Jan would never open that one, or understand the relationship, or blatantly obvious non-relationship, between those listings and the football club.

Of course, the money has to be sort of laundered. The official set-ups can cost these women well over a thousand quid, more for certificated Oxbridge types. There's even been an 'egg broking' company targeting Cambridge undergrad. girls for their eggs—almost a grand a time. That's each, not in half dozen boxes from bloody Waitrose. Then there's the on-line 'Oxford graduate sperm donor', that's the sort who can't even spell 'guaranteed' on his website. It's a bloody minefield out there in the wider sperm donor community. Since a few years back when they ruled that donors had no right to anonymity the flow has nearly trickled out, as it were. Women are forced to go abroad, like the States, and that costs and who knows? British is best, right?

Stem cell research can end up producing a baby with two mothers and a father, or whatever whacky combination you choose. Talk about a split personality. IVF I don't have a problem with; but check the websites. Again, there is a premium on Oxbridge eggs; think Eugenics, *Brave New World*, *The Handmaid's Tale*, Margaret Atwood eat your heart out—the future's here, baby!

At Family Matters I only came across a couple of blokes in reception and we all kept our heads down in the car mags. Or with our heads down, following the swirls of the carpet. My sort of age, though I noted an expensive pair of brogues and designer suit on one of them. No, it's on-line that you get the wide, wonderful wacky world of the donors. From the earnest graduate students to the frankly bonkers supreme white race types, thinly disguised and some not disguised at all. Didn't the Nazis have breeding brothels—Lebensborn, the blonde, blue-eyed fountain of life? I heard that geneticist guy Steve Jones talking on the radio once; he got really animated about Crufts, race horses, all those pedigree animal breeding businesses. He said that it was unnatural, perverse and against the normal workings of the world. The natural order was that there should be no restrictive order, inter-marriage, sex across all the cultural and racial divisions. Mixing up the genes kept all the lottery numbers in play. At uni. one of our history lecturers claimed that if Hitler had kept the Jews and their brains on his side, instead of destroying their bodies, it would have been no contest and we'd all be speaking German now. That stirred the class and woke up a few at the back.

Who knows who they are, really? Steve Lee in the next office to us has traced his family tree and come up with Romany connections. Another lot who fell foul of Adolph the failed painter. They are not from Egypt, of course, but from tribes of people going back centuries in northern India. He said someone has researched the gypsies in Wales, where there's a lot of them apparently, and found that their DNA was more Indian in characteristic than most people in India. Not so much to do with the randy squaddies of the British Army in the days of Empire, more to do with the closed communities of the Romany who rarely married out. Problems there, of course.

Who knows who they are? What about centuries of mistresses kept by our kings—dukes and favourites who were well looked-after? We're all a bit royal, perhaps. I once read a piece about the painter Augustus John—seems he could not walk through Soho without stopping to press a shilling into each child's hand, in case they were his. How many children had Lady Macbeth? How many children had Lucien Freud?

Last time we took the kids down to London- the Eye, the Zoo, the moat of poppies at the Tower—Jan, who is in social services, also wanted us to go to the Foundlings Museum in Bloomsbury. Unwanted babies were left in the gutter in eighteenth century London until this childless sea-captain Mr Coram set up an orphanage, supported by concerts by Handel, paintings by Hogarth auctioned, royal patronage. There's an exhibition of the tokens which mothers left in the hope of later recognising and re-uniting with their children. But that never happened. They were all sent to be wet-nursed in distant villages like Hampstead and Dulwich and given new names; the girls went into service and the boys to the navy or the army. It's all a balance of ordering and chance.

'Bastard' was a legal description in this country until 1969. If my mum had got caught at university I'd have been a bastard and probably given up for adoption. 'Think of your future, my dear, your career.' I can just hear my in-laws counselling common sense. All those poor buggers shipped out to Canada, Australia, many of them poor and many of them buggered too.

In the museum café the walls were decorated with the names of famous orphans and foundlings—Moses, Oliver Twist, Superman, Romulus and Remus, Nelson Mandela, Keats, Tolstoy, Satchmo, Marilyn Monroe, Steve Jobs—all four walls covered with kids abandoned or bereft. So what's the problem: my ladies are guaranteeing at least one loyal, desperate, concerned and focussed parent, aren't they? These children, our children, will be fine. They are not orphans and no tokens will be needed to secure their future; they have the welfare state, not to mention my genes.

I've made this pact with myself: I'll go on for another three years, Alex will be going up to the comp., then Rachel won't be far behind. And as for telling Jan? Perhaps some time way in the future, when our lives have run on a bit, but it would have to be the right moment and I can't see what or when that might be. The money I make is in an account for the kids and will help with their education—should be a few useful grand by then. Seed money, you might say. And I don't do the sex. Tried it once and carried the guilt for too long afterwards: this way it's more rational, I'm at a distance and if I hear nothing more, well, I can handle it. The sex was in Solihull—Wendy—Wolves, as it happens—and I was tempted to swing by there for months afterwards. That way madness lies.

Swings and roundabouts, schools of thought, playgrounds, the egg and sperm race.

I'm wandering, making a life and killing time. It's been half an hour and I should go back out to her. Flush and splash. For six hundred quid they expect a bit more than five minutes, though that's what it takes. I shall emerge with the treasure between my right fore-finger and thumb, the pot of gold, the Milky Way, her future. It's at this point that, yes, it's starting, always the Space Odyssey theme in my head. I'm a rocket man and his capsule, squeaky clean courtesy of her Gilchrist and Soames on the sink between two perfectly polished taps. She has my mobile, the one that sits in my desk drawer at the office, but I expect to hear nothing from her for a month, if then; no conversation. It will work, it always has. Thank you. And thank you, love.

The Round

Glanmor's Golf Club was one of the main outlets for the small seaside town's sportsmen. If you were too old for the fierce brand of rugby distilled in this western outpost of the cold, rain squalls spiriting in from the Celtic Sea to muddy your boots; and if you couldn't swim, or fiddle with the ropes and swivels of the sailing dinghy, then you had to be a golfer. Though the club, unusually for those days, encouraged youngsters too. When his parents had moved down into Dyfed, Rees, who was fourteen, had picked the game up at school and even had a few free lessons with the old professional, whose daughter was in his class. Within a year he'd managed a string of cards and was given a 24 handicap by the committee. Encouraged by this, he'd put his name down on the competition list for the Rabbit's Tail annual cup. School finished on the previous Friday, so he'd come in on the bus to practise for his first round match the following weekend, and because the competition draw was to be made that afternoon.

The course was busy though, and he decided to sort his clubs out while the first tee cleared. Throwing a ball like a dart he aimed at the opposite locker in the cool changing room. Bounce, thud, and back in the fingers. Timing—that was the key to all sports: penalty-kicks, striking for the ball in the scrum, ace serves—timing. But saying it was easier than doing it.

He'd got into a rhythm and had become quite absorbed in the feat, counting up to twenty odd when the changing room door opened.

'Hello.'

His missed the rebound and the ball scuttled under the clothes rack.

'Hello—young Rees isn't it?'

'Hello Mr Bailey.'

'Rogers. It's Rogers.'

'Oh, yes. Sorry, Mr Rogers. I always confuse you with Mr Bailey. You always seem to be partnered when I've seen you out on the course.'

'Inseparable sufferers we are—the Four Horsemen of the....whatever it is. I'm afraid Glyn Evans isn't too well. Tummy trouble I think. Old age is handicapping us all, you know. The call of that great 19th hole up there in the clouds—that's where they get the sudden death finish from, isn't it ? Would you like to make up the four then? That's if you're going out.'

'Why yes, thank you. I was going out to practice and a round of proper golf will set me up fine. If you think I can keep up.'

'Of course. That's the spirit—the enthusiasm of youth. Get yourself ready and meet us on the first tee in about five minutes.' And he was gone, out of the door, spikes clattering down the corridor.

The Rogers-Bailey pair and old Jimmy McAllister were out on the first tee loosening up, aiming at target daisies.

'Here he is boys,' said McAllister, 'Let's toss for strike.'

'Tails, and it's our honour...we're off!' said Bailey, planting his tee and starting to line up his drive. His back-swing was like a slow-motion film, or those frozen movement photos in golf manuals. With apparently no effort, his ball sailed steadily over the rise of the dune, and out of sight, down into the heart of the fairway's first undulation.

McAllister's rather jerky swing resulted in just as satisfactory a shot, the ball clearing the sand and hooking slightly down the left side of the fairway. Pop Rogers complimented him with a 'Ho, ho, tacking his way through wind and wave as usual. You picked the right partner there, young Rees!'

Rees rummaged in his bag until his hand settled on the cellophane of his one and only new ball, a birthday present from his gran. Mr Rogers coughed pointedly at him. He coloured and stopped the rustling as Pop Rogers took aim and swung easily and firmly through the ball. He stopped short of a full follow-through and slid the club down through his hands almost before the ball had risen; then he stayed leaning on the flexing driver to watch his shot fade strongly to the right of the fairway to settle, Rees thought, in same patch of rough he'd hacked at with regularity at the beginning of rounds over his short golfing life.

'Damn wind,' said Bailey, but his partner shrugged and invited Rees to start.

'Off you go, lad—show us how to do it.'

Rees decapitated a couple of daisies with his practice swing and, re-assured by this accuracy, set his ball on a yellow tee and lined up on the marker post one hundred and fifty yards away.

His left knee had wavered. Yes, that was it, his knee had moved, bringing the left shoulder dipping down too far. He looked down at the half-plugged position of his ball, nestling in the fairways's protective bunker, shaped like a huge kidney. His drive had ballooned, held on the breeze and fallen like a dead duck.

Closed stance, hands further down the grip, head down, he told himself. But it took him four hacks to force the ball out. Having waited patiently for him, the three old men proceeded to hit the green or its fringes with practiced unconcern. McAllister laid up a long putt for the half with Rogers, but Bailey's putt dropped for the hole.

And so it went. Rees and McAllister went four down by the ninth tee. McAllister had taken the short 4th and halved a couple of others. Rees was a passenger. His drives splayed like water from a garden hose and the two holes he'd played reasonably well had been lost to pars by one or other of their opponents.

'Steady does it boy,' said McAllister on the 9th tee, 'we can win this. They always slow up after the turn and get tired. Glyn Evans and I usually come back at them from now on.'

And so it proved: McAllister holing a long putt from off the green. Only three holes down now, they walked to the 10th tee. The second half of the course was stretched before them. It snaked its way back towards the town. The view was so fine: the beach which bordered the course ran back towards the town and its bright hotels and shops, and beyond the sand, the sea washed flat to the Island and the horizon. The waves, peopled with holiday children, lapped the game clean from his mind as Rees looked ahead at two golfers playing down the 12th fairway. They were evidently lost and were mistakenly aiming for the 9th green which the four of them had just left.

'Look at that daft pair—bloody visitors!' said McAllister, as he stepped back from his drive. He shouted, 'Fore!' and they scuttled self-consciously out of his line of fire.

'Off you go, partner.'

Rees's drive was again much steadier. Try less—succeed more; that's the mysterious nature of the game, he thought.

'Glad those idiots didn't put you off, lad,' said old McAllister, as he turned to glare at the pair behind them.

Rees had often met a visitor at the club, or picked one up out on the course and played them home to the clubhouse. Some were interesting people too: car-workers from Birmingham—flashy Jack Nicklaus clubs and no idea: two Scots with cheese-grater accents who told him of the great golf in Scotland; and a young man in his twenties who had a glass eye and relieved Rees of possible embarrassment by giving him a shot a hole and still finishing him off at the fifteenth. Golf—an education.

Which was why now, walking from his second shot on the 10th, he began to consider his present partner. McAllister was a disappointment. As a character that is. Consider his background: born to Scottish parents in wreckers' Cornwall, at sea since a lad and already an engineer serving in the Middle East and Atlantic when the war broke, and then torpedoed, three days in an open boat and limping home to a post-war job as harbour-master at Glanmor. Torpedoed: what did three days in a boat on the ocean do to you? Then retirement and golf. Rees gleaned little more than bare facts to add to what he'd heard of the man. After a war, what excitement some people had had in them was, perhaps, exhausted.

He was certainly taking his golf seriously for, as Rees reached the sandy hillock which protected the valley of the

83

10th green, McAllister was in the rough bunker of the upward slope, trapped by his ambitious second shot to a green no longer within his reach. There he was, shuffling his feet for position in the sand, hands down the grip and stern-faced concentration. Textbook stuff. But as he lined up his shot the wedge he was using slid into the sand, leaving itself in clear contact with the ball, which he then proceeded to stroke cleanly to the heart of the hidden green. McAllister looked up at his partner as he turned to replace his club.

'On for three?! Where are you lad?'

'Just off I think, for three—but our opponents, the mighty Bailey and Rogers are both thereabouts for three.'

The old engineer wiped the sand from his wedge and slotted it carefully back into its place in his bag. There was no mention of the penalty stroke his touching the sand should have brought as they walked down to the green together.

'Nice recovery, Jimmy,' said Bailey.

'You play up, Bob.'

And Rogers putted up dead, accepting the 5, which Rees matched after his two putts. But there was McAllister, with the same stern-faced concentration he'd shown in the bunker, sinking his 12 footer and picking his ball out of the hole with a clenched fist. He claimed the hole with a par four.

'Sorry boys, I don't usually sink those, do I? Still, that pulls your lead back a bit.'

'But surely....' began Rees.

'Don't worry, we'll pull the others back, boy,' continued McAllister, as he marched on to the next tee.

'Sink any more like that and we'll confiscate your putter,' retorted Pop Rogers. 'Anyway, we'll see about that. Your favourite hole's coming up, Jack—let's see you perform.'

'It's only damn hole I can still reach!' replied Bailey, as they started off for the 136 yard short 11th.

Rees was confused. Hadn't the Scotsman cheated? Perhaps it was because the man was aged and missed the odd thing these days—wouldn't Rees himself be a creaking golfer in old age, forgetful and creaky? And how serious should games be anyway? Three old men and a schoolboy, driving off to the postage-stamp green of the 11th—out for the sun and sea-air, punctuated by the sound of metal against whatever it is they use to cover the twined miles of elastic inside a golf ball.

Rees and the old sea dog fought back well and by the 15th were truly back in the match.

'One down, boy,' said McAllister, with more seriousness, 'Off you go, and watch that gorse over to the right!'

McAllister seemed to ignore the view and, judiciously, the scrub and bush menacingly lining the brook which moated the fairway. 'Head down and steady swing,' he murmured to himself and the listening world. He sent a low drive cleanly down the cropped green of the narrow, dog-legged fairway. Rees felt an odd sense of disappointment. As he tee-ed up his own ball he could feel the scars he'd made on it. The wonderful view which had previously lulled him away from the pettiness of the game now closed in around him. The fairway became a diminishing green target, threatening and irritating his composure, so that hissing produced a wild slice.

'Keep an eye on that one!' warned Bailey, one hand shielding his eyes like a classical sailor. Rees could imagine him on the bridge of a destroyer, the prow of a whaler.

'Watch it lad. That tree's a good mark, I think,' offered Rogers.

But as Rees was scraping around for his lost ball in the rough to the left of the fairway it happened again. McAllister's second shot was caught in tight rough some twenty yards off the green and was matched against Rogers' ball sitting well on the apron of the green for 3. Rees saw McAllister's shoe nudge under a tuft of grass to move the ball up and into a lie that tee-ed it up for a clean hit. Rees stopped in his tracks and just stared. McAllister looked up and with a forced smile said, 'Get this one on and I'll have a putt for it, eh lad?'

And he did. McAllister and he couldn't lose the game. They were on the 16th tee and dormie 3 up so they'd at least get a half after that appalling start. In fact, they looked likely to take the game, for their opponents were fading.

He's crazy—thought Rees—he really is?! He certainly saw me when he was cheating. But it had had no effect. It was as if McAllister had looked through him.

McAllister and Rees went on to win the game on the 17th, but after the final hole Rees excused himself from the offer of a shandy and went straight to his corner of the locker room. He dropped his clubs with a clatter into the locker and sat down on the bench to fumble with the laces of his golf shoes. One of the spikes was wearing through the leather sole and had begun a blister on his left foot; the knot he'd tied in his lace had seared the top of his right foot. Rees felt miserable. With a burst of anger he swung the shoes up to his locker shelf, scraping them against the door. Giving the three men time to leave he went up to the bar and set up a few snooker balls which he began to pot.

Rogers came in. 'Haven't you had enough? Wish I had that youthful energy still.'There was a time when we could squeeze 36, even 40 holes into a summer's day.'

He turned to look at Pop Rogers. 'I'd rather play snooker really—apart from the fresh air and the scenery, the sea shore,' answered Rees.

'Be perfect to have an outdoor billiards hall eh?'

Rees smiled appreciatively. 'You'd have to allow for wind direction when you lined up a pot though,' he replied, weakly.

'Yes indeed. Look, lad,' said Rogers, coming over to the table, "Don't worry about the game today.'

'Why should I? We won didn't we?'

'I think you know what I mean. I saw him too, you know.'

'But it was two holes he cheated on, and maybe more!'

'Quite possibly,' admitted Rogers.

'Then why...'

'Because we accept it. We have come to accept it, I should say. It's not Nicklaus and Palmer in the Open, is it?'

'You mean he's done it before?'

'I mean he does it—it's part of his game—the nudged ball in the rough; the handful of sand and ball thrown out of a bunker; the ball marker inched forward on the putting green, he's done it ever since we started up our regular games.'

'Then why do you play with him?' interrupted Rees.

'Look David—funny, we haven't called you David all day have we? Look, you are young with the whole of your life ahead of you for you to make a mark with. Jimmy McAllister has lived his life, yes, and lived it with interest and no small amount of excitement. But now he and I and Jack Bailey and Glyn Evans have our lives shrunk to the size of... the size of this,' and he picked up the blue ball. 'So if we want to pretend it's the British Open Championship once or twice a week, then that's alright. And if Jimmy McAllister wants to win that badly, then I for one don't mind his cheating. That's why we say nothing. Alright?'

'Alright. Not that I would say anything, either, Mr Rogers.'

'No. Well, see you next week perhaps? Must dash off now or the missus will cremate another dinner.' Before turning to the door his hand sent the blue ball rolling directly to the far top left pocket where it sank and rattled in the bag.

Rees potted the cue ball into the same pocket and clipped the cue back into the rack. Out in the corridor he saw that on the notice-board the Rabbit's Tail Cup draw had been made. He ran his fingers down the first round list and read -

D Rees plays J M McAllister.

David Rees took the pencil that hung alongside and put a line through his name. He wrote 'SCRATCHED' in large letters in the margin. He felt something in his stomach, and looking at his watch saw that it was approaching tea-time. He felt hungry. Then he walked out and went through the car park, breaking into a slow jogging run with the bobbing suggestion of rugby jinks and feints, Cliff Morgan, all the way down the long drive to the bus-stop.

The Eighth

A mid-October evening, five-thirty with an hour or so's light left, when I park the car at the little railway station and cross over the line through the swing gates to the path that runs to the beach.

I am a country member so I can play the course with all the rights of a full member: I choose to come on at this point between the seventh green and the eighth tee just to the right of the public path. The eighth hole follows the line of the army's shooting range and then bears left a little towards the beach. The ninth tee is some forty yards through a gap in the dunes and plays back along the line of the beach to a green close to the public footpath again.

It's an awkward, challenging couple of holes to start with, as I choose to do, coming on to the course half-way round, but I like that corner of the course, striking up towards the Point, then turning back to face the town and the length of the beach with its views across to the island and the town and, beyond, the stretch of the coast all the way to the Gower. It's quiet of an evening, the furthest part from the clubhouse and usually clear of other golfers; by this time already making their way back over the closing holes to the promise of a pint at the nineteenth.

Just at the point where the Coast Path turns up alongside the shooting range, and the public path swings on to the beach the M.O.D. and the National Parks people have put a weather and vandal-proof map of the area with bird species and general instructions about how to find the First World War practice trenches up on the Point. It's not that easy and the instructions are hard to follow, once you are up there with the hillocks and humps of the headland, the clumps of gorse and wind-swept twmps. They could be the hard-dug trenches from which young men rose and charged with fixed bayonets at the lines of sand-bagged dummies, imagined as the Hun; or they could be the cattle and sheep smoothed hollows out of the prevailing westerlies from off the Atlantic. Could, in truth, be anything.

I sometimes think of them as I fiddle over a tricky putt, or find the air noisily stitched behind me as the rapid fire gun drills are completed over on the range. Sometimes I think of David Lloyd George playing the course in 1909 when he was Chancellor of the Exchequer. Though back then he would have stopped short of this point, for the course would have turned back on itself long before.

This evening the light is fading fast and the sun is low to the west of the village on the hillside. Three scuffed shots have brought me to the edge of the green where I bend over a putt. And then I am aware of sounds behind me— voices and some barking. Two men and three dogs are coming up the middle of the fairway some eighty or ninety yards away. All that beach and the dunes, but these people bring their dogs on to the course.

Excuse me, but the beach is over there. This is a golf course!

One of them, the older man stops and shouts back something which is lost on the wind. The other stops and then, waving his arm, strides towards me.

'Let it go....' the older man says, using a name I can't make out.

But the other continues towards me, followed by two of the dogs, and saying something like, 'No, I've fucking had enough!'

I turn away to the putt, hoping that he will walk on. But one of the dogs, a small, brown yappy thing, has come on to the green and another, a black terrier type, barks again.

This is not acceptable. This is for golfers. It's a golf course.

'We can walk our dogs if we want to: we got the rights. There's no law...' He is right before me now, so close that I can smell the drink on his breath. He is two inches taller than me, perhaps early twenties, with booze-filled eyes.

Look, dogs are for the beach. This is a championship course and there's a big competition tomorrow and dogs run through the bunkers and damage the course.

'These dogs are doing no fucking harm, mate!' His voice is slurred and lubricated with spittle.

89

The terrier has wandered off in the direction of the older man, who has also lost interest and is turning left between two dunes and walking towards the beach. The brown dog sniffs at my ball and then takes it in its mouth. This is a comedy sketch, I think.

Yes, well, your dog would appear to have taken my ball.

'Here. Come here.' He catches the dog by the scruff of its neck and extracts the ball, wiping it on the sleeve of his coat.

Now, if you would please replace my ball, I will putt the hole out and we can both be on our way.

He drops the ball at my feet and takes a step backwards. *A right to left borrow- fifteen feet…*As I line up the putt I realise that my hands are shaking. Nevertheless, and by now rather pointlessly, I send the ball into the hole. I walk slowly four or five steps and pick the ball out of the cup. *Pretty good.* The dogs have gone off the end of the green and are snuffling towards the gorse. My audience of one seems bemused; he's been shuffled to the side of the stage and has forgotten his lines. If I walk on he will surely give up and go away.

I replace the putter, sling my bag over my shoulder and move off.

You enjoy the rest of the evening and I'll enjoy mine.

*

You enjoy the rest of the evening and I'll enjoy mine.

'What? You taking the piss, or what? You fucking being clever…'

Look, it's a nice evening and the light is going fast. Why don't you walk your dogs over to the beach and I'll continue with my game. You have a nice day.

'Fucking what? Nice!' He follows after me and I have to turn. I have to face him. Who knows what might happen?

'You think you're better than me!'

Look, let's just get on with what we are doing. I'm just playing a bit of golf…

'Who the fuck d'you think you are? I'm gonna break your nose. Fucking break your nose.' And he comes across the green with menace.

No, no, I'm not better than you, I just want to get with my evening and you...

'Had enough of this. I'm going to do you, mate.'

No, no, I'm not saying anything. Let's just...

'I've got fourteen charges against me, so what the fuck.' He's right up to me again. No more than a foot or two away. I'm shaking and it's all I can do to keep coherent speech going.

I'm no better than you. I started out in a council house and...

'Your sort are always pullin' it. I've taken enough shitty...' and he raises his fist.

I hold out my hands in the submissive gesture. I must have looked like Christ in a children's illustrated Bible. Suffer the little children. *What's the point? What would that prove? I'm a sixty year old grandfather!*

Something flickers behind his eyes. He stops. I turn way and walk as steadily as I can on down the path to the tenth tee.

From the tee you get the whole sweep of the beach, two miles or so curling back to the town. I am alone. I tee up the ball and hit a seven iron remarkably straight and true on to the snaking fairway. By the time I am walking towards it for my second shot I can see that he's hitching himself over the old rusty gate at the end of the unused path and onto the beach. I prop my bag on its legs and take out the mobile phone. 999.

*

'I've got fourteen charges against me, so what the fuck.' He's right up to me again. No more than a foot or two away. I'm shaking and it's all I can do to keep coherent speech going. If this idiot is going to hit me then I should defend myself—that's my right.

And I've got fourteen clubs in my bag...

91

I swing the bag off my shoulder and pull out the putter. I hold it in both hands as if it were a fairway iron and, feet squarely apart I raise it like a Samurai sword. The Ping *Karsten Anser* putter is beautifully weighted—a firm grip which allows you to direct the weighed head through the ball with control and accuracy. A lot of the tour professionals still use this club. He backs off and, swearing again, walks away.

*

And I've got fourteen clubs in my bag. I swing the bag off my shoulder and pull out the putter. He takes another step towards me and I swing it at his head before he has time to throw the punch. It catches him just below the ear and he lunges past me to crumple to the grass. An adrenalin rush —feelings on the cusp of pain and triumph. I stand over him and raise the club again, in case he should get up and attack me once more.

*

I stand over him and raise the club again. I swing and hit him, hard with a chopping movement, quite deliberately, like lining up a putt, once on each leg, just above the knee. He seems barely conscious but winces with each blow. The putter is unmarked, though somehow I expect there to be blood on it. I wipe the blade anyway on my ball cloth before replacing it in the bag and walking on to the tenth tee.

*

I wipe the blade anyway on my ball cloth before replacing it in the bag and walking on to the tenth tee. The Ping *Anser* is an icon. I Googled it earlier this year after the kids had bought me a new one for my birthday. Karsten Solheim developed it in the late fifties in Arizona and brought out the refined *Anser* in 1966, four years after I'd taken up golf as a schoolboy member on this course. If you've hit the ball squarely it 'pings' as if answering you. It does not 'ping' an answer when you hit flesh.

Should I go back and check on the man? Surely his older companion will be coming back down the beach now to find him? Perhaps not, perhaps they had just met in a pub and the drunken lad had tagged along with the dog walker? But he had taken the ball from the dog's mouth as if he knew how to handle it. How long had this encounter lasted? Was it likely that the man would return? Would he not have given up on the drunk and moved on? Who could blame me? Self defence?

*

Who could blame me? Self defence? A sixty-six year old retired professional assaulted by a drunken young man with a criminal record. Untouchable. It's a free hit.

From the tee you get the whole sweep of the beach, two mile or so swinging back to the town. I am alone. I tee up the ball and take a seven iron on to the snaking fairway.

As I walk on I realise that there could be tabloid front pages, hounds and hacks, 'heroic golfer hits back'—upset families, the distractions of lawyers and court appearances. The lad is from a broken home, a shitty background, school failure, never had a chance.

'One further question, m'Lord—Can you explain why you struck two further blows when your attacker, as you describe him, was already prone on the grass at your feet?'

*

By the time I am walking towards the tenth fairway for my second shot I can see that he's hitching himself over the old rusty gate at the end of the unused path and onto the beach. I prop my bag on its legs and take out the mobile phone. 999.

Police. 077739843563 ... I have to report an assault. At the far end of the golf course....the west end... the furthest before the cliffs...sorry I'm a bit shaken. I have been attacked.

I turn away and begin to describe my position to a man who does not know what I mean, who is sitting in a call centre in another town, perhaps another county; who is probably not a policeman. I tell him that there are two of them with three dogs, smallish dogs, walking towards the town end of the beach, I say. *The beach is two miles long. If you send a colleagues, they should know that there are three paths giving access to the beach and....*

*

I have been attacked. From the beach side of the old gate he looks back at me. I raise the phone to show him that I am not letting this rest. He shouts something and clambers back over the gate. He starts to run down the path and onto the golf course again towards me. I cut short the call.

*

I cut short the call.
Put the phone in my pocket.
Take out a four iron.

The Way Back

Pugh squinted through the wedge of his crossed shoes—a stone circle by Rauschenberg; Leda turning wistfully from the Swan; Leonardo's drawing of a giant cross-bow, a great engine of war cocked back ready to hurl its shaft into some stone wall; below and to the left a miner strutting across the wall, twisted side-on to the shoulder bulged in profile, narrowing down an arm like a piston. Postcards and posters pinned to the wall.

The noise of feet down the stairs and along the corridor signalled the hour and Glyn flexed his legs to bring the feet down from the edge of his desk. Mid-way, caught in an absurd position, between slouching in the low chair and hinging himself up with enough momentum to stand, he held the position for an instant, imagining how some of the students passing might look in and see him as a figure landing clumsily from a height. But no-one looked in and the voices passed by, blurred and greying in the dulled noon time of a bad March day.

'Er, come in,' he answered the knock with an almost convincing tone of surprised reverie: you should study in a study. But the Yale was engaged and his pose was broken by the necessity of rising to open the door. It revealed a young woman of 21, too boyish in her check shirt, wearing her hair cropped, to be thought of as a girl, but with an open, smiling face which sent Glyn back into his room bumbling about, setting the chair opposite his desk to rights and shovelling unnecessary books up to the far end until they stockaded his phone.

'Excuse the mess, Jane. There is a sort of order here.'

'Underneath it all, no doubt, Mr. Pugh,' her tone was friendly and familiar for her final year dissertation meant that their tutorials brought her regularly to Glyn's pokey study on the Arts Block's busy ground floor at mid-day on Thursdays and they had a good working relationship.

The work was going well, but her approach to the poetry of R. S. Thomas was simplistic, seeing the man as some romantic recluse, peering out at the small tragedies of the North Wales hill folk like an eagle, head bunched into moulting neck-feathers, beak curled round on itself as if aiming at its own breast.

'But what about politics, Jane ? The suspicion of the English, and their eventual canonisation as Lucifer's mechanised aggressors bludgeoning the Celt and Celtic nature into a uniformity that's the real bloody pain of Hell.'

'I plead innocence and ignorance of all that,' she replied, with a smile.

'And you from Middlesex acres of the Fallen.'

'Staines,' she said.

'Damned by your own admission.'

'What's in a name?'

'Enough!' and he held up both hands in mock surrender. 'But you will have to watch your approach you know. Sticking to sensible limits for a 5,000 word essay is essential. And with Thomas, this one as much as his name-sake, you've got to avoid distractions. Here's a mystic with his feet in wellingtons and wearing a grey suit.'

They both laughed, Jane easing back into the low arm-chair he'd sneaked from the staff room in the Christmas vacation, one of her legs, in jeans fading into the right shade, hooked over the end of the arm-rest.

'D'you know, Jane, all we need is a kettle and some coffee and we could have really productive sessions here.'

'Remember what happened to Miss Jean Brodie though.'

The phone rang and Glyn, before he could get out an 'I'm in my prime,' ploughed a hand through the books to lift the receiver.

'Extension 219, Pugh here. Hello Liz. Yes, well a tutorial really. No, that's OK. Yes. And when did they call? Hospital...Gwili...last night. And they were sure it was the heart? Well why didn't they phone before? O.K. I'll get back and decide then. Bye, love.' He replaced the receiver, clumsily failing to fit it cleanly back into the cradle.

'Look, Jane, I'm afraid I'll have to cut our hour short. My grandmother's been taken ill and I'll need to get home and possibly travel down to Caer. Anyway, now you can ease that hunger with an early lunch.' He managed a smile as she patted her flat stomach.

When she'd gone, Glyn took a minute in his chair. On the largest wall were Alun's splashed paint shapes from play-school, and next to the window his favourite : almost becoming figurative, blue, mauve and yellow in a large blob, and underneath, a sheltering shape of paler blue. Paint trickles from these two like legs and beneath an ochre sun, finger marks becoming flowers in the hands. Rorschach. A student that week had seen it as St. Francis of Assissi. On the side of his filing cabinet an l.p. sleeve of Thomas reading his poems: the vicar, hands joined across his waist, low and to the left of a photograph filled with sea and an horizon island humped in blue.

Jangling his keys, car, office, house, on his way to the car-park, Glyn registered that in his room he must have seemed calm and sensible.

He cut across country, using the narrow lanes of the Vale with their high hedges reminding him of Pembrokeshire, to reach the main road west. From Cardiff the A48 pushes beyond Bridgend with stretches of three-lane highway which draws out the most maniac driving from people. The fatalities among time-cutting commuters and over-loaded holiday-makers escaping to the West makes the route a battlefield, so he kept to the limit.

To his right, in a field adjacent to the road, the area's T.V. transmitter thrust a huge needle towards the low clouds, threatening to burst them. Glyn's eyes turned from the back of the tanker which had forced him to change into second gear and traced the lines of the aerial's supporting cables down to their bolted hooks and sunken concrete cubes in the meadow grass.

Back in the house his son, Alun, would be sprawled on the carpet or settee soaking in television images, resting

97

before an afternoon chasing and kicking and fighting in the garden. Liz would be getting Bethan down in her cot, fingers crossed for an hour's relief, time off from being Mother before the afternoon swung on towards tea-time.

This ordering of the day into tasks and meals, the organisation of each day, each week to roughly the same pattern was one of the things that Glyn sometimes felt was grinding him down. The easiest thing was to let oneself be carried through the year like that; putting all the small acts and decisions into order. That way the pains were small too. You had to live with the claustrophobia of such a life, house-tied, time-tied, family-tied. That was what had caused the first and only period of conflict between himself and Gran. He'd been granny-reared.

They'd lived with her from the beginning—his beginning, for as an only child he'd always had difficulty in imagining his parents living without his presence, just as it now seemed that Bethan and Alun were the gravitational laws without which his life with Liz would fail to make sense. And with his mother going out to work and his father putting in overtime and his back shed fiddles it had been Gran who held the time-scale in his childhood with her meals. Though he could genuinely remember ration books and toast and dripping, the terraced council-house which seemed so pokey and shabby now, had fitted snugly as any home around any child.

There were, though, constant quarrels and bickerings with the neighbours; four years ago, Gran had spoken to Mair Evans for the first time properly since five-year-old Glyn had ended a fight with Mair's Alwyn by sending a broom-handle past Alwyn's head and through the Evans' back-door pane. After twenty years of sour memory the two women had come together over their bins and talked of Mair's Ron, dead a month back, two years short of retirement. Liz thought that Gran's concern with the movings of Nott Street, the way she seemed to be able to swivel and catch the passing of anyone on the pavement beyond her low privet hedge, was a raison d'être, some tangible function of involvement in life, as hers was becoming smaller and tighter.

'That's why she's glued to *Coronation Street*, *Crossroads* and the rest of the soapy shows, isn't it ? It's sublime. An all-seeing camera beats the slit between curtains doesn't it ? At eighty-six d'you think she'd be as sprightly if she'd no-one to peer out at and nothing to complain about ?' argued Liz.

'Well, I'll only really start worrying about Gran when she doesn't know what Mrs. Rees' social security cheque is and who's the real father of her Ruth's youngest.'

The old woman's omniscience in her niche of the universe was one of the features of her character. Glyn had never felt deeply involved with the bulk of the members of his family. He would tell apocryphal stories about them over meals at friends' houses, or whilst teaching *King Lear* —'Nothing will come of nothing,' or in a lull in the Friday lunch-time bar. It was a convenient safe fiction as he lived a two-hour drive from the town of his childhood; and anyway, wasn't a colourful, close family background the one shared Welsh heritage?

He pushed the throttle firmly down and drew away from the tanker and its tail-back as the dual carriageway carried the traffic at speed towards the dull-reddish brown pall in the sky over Port Talbot.

All that cosy fiction was slipping away now. She was ill, in grave danger, found collapsed on the path by the privet hedge at dusk the previous evening. A neighbour, old Mrs Matthews from opposite, seeing the front door of No. 34 open to the evening's damp, had wrapped a raincoat over her bony shoulders and, torch in hand, crossed the road to check. Gran lay prostrate after a heart attack and the cackle of the *Opportunity Knocks* audience was coming from the corner of the front room.

Glyn's first kiss had been interrupted by Mrs Matthews. It was 1959 in the Palace with a plain girl who limped and hardly spoke a word. He'd been left with her by Bryan Williams who was nearly fifteen, wore suede shoes, could click all his fingers. He fancied her sister and Glyn was a convenient partner.

Mrs. Matthews patrolled the aisles at the Palace like a beacon of vigilance against penknives in the upholstery and groping hands in the dark: the torch lady.

Glyn had no experience of death. His English grandmother had died at the tea table on a visit to Wales, but he'd been a young child, four at most, and that had been a strange dream—running to Mrs John's back door and babbling for help. She was beyond help though and had faded out of his life as surely as if the train had carried her back to that mill town in Lancashire.

Gran's sister Rosie had died in the back-bedroom; two deaths in a childhood. She'd become too ill to keep herself in the rough-stone Pembrokeshire small holding and had been persuaded by his father to come up to the market town to rest and recover. Glyn remembered the journey, in an old Alvis built like a tank, the warm softened seat-heater against his bare legs; her moans and grunts coming from the layers of blankets across from him in the back seat. He had left a new Dinky armoured car in the foot-well sunk into the great car's floor behind the driver's seat. The well was his secret fort on the journey down, and for twenty winding miles back home he'd worried whether the khaki car would be still there, whether Rosie, who smelt of farmyards and bran, would have trod on it.

Away from the geese, the fields and her pining collie, she quickly lost hold on life. Her breathing creased the old parchment of her weathered face, narrowing her eyes and slackening the folds of skin around her neck. When she died they kept him from the room until the men had come for her. Her wooden clogs stood like sentries at the foot of the bed.

Six years back, just after he had started teaching and was full of the new Creativity, Glyn tried to write a poem about the tough old woman. There was no suitable ending though, and the mutual irritation there had been between the leathery farmer's widow and the milk-sopped town boy drove cracks through the structure of his writing.

In health Rosie and Gran could have been twins. The move to town had softened Catherine though over the years. As a girl in her late teens, she had left Jobstone farm, which was obviously doomed to pass out of the family with her father's death; she and her five sisters had lost their older brother to the lure of farming fortunes in Canada —'A hundred Acres to All Who Emigrate'. He came all the way back to sell-up the place and settle the family affairs. Gran had gone into service. Living in the minister's house as a housemaid had been harsh and illiberal but the Great War had re-shuffled society and three years after the end she escaped by marrying a Berkshire man, Ralph, brought into West Wales by work on the Great Western Railway.

He died a matter of weeks before Glyn's birth. 'A life for a life,' she'd said, peering out of the small panes of the front room window at the drifts of snow: Glyn's father remembered that. It was one of the coldest winters on record. People froze to death, their heavy, black cars smothered in huge drifts of snow. The thaw revealed hill sheep in crevices and beneath hedges as sodden heaps of dirty wool.

Further west, beyond the great steel works, the slag-heaps of the mines, only an Indian file of high voltage pylons marred the rich green of the fields. Glyn drove down towards Garw. Four miles and two spread, rolling hills away from Caer, past the old mill beside the bridge.

When he was eleven or twelve, he would ride there on the new bike given to him for passing his eleven-plus. The school holidays seemed to stretch open endlessly in the sun. The hedgerows were full of birds and wild herb smells.

It would have been good to have had a grandfather then. A man with time to spare, becoming crotchety perhaps, but on hand to help with fishing ties and punctures.

Sentiment, he thought, I don't ever remember missing him. What vague feeling of loss there had been was due to the prompting of the grown-ups around me. 'A shame the old man died, you'd have had some times with him, Glyn boy. Knew all about railways. Well, he travelled every mile of the G.W.R. Every mile.'

But Ralph Pugh had remained that slightly out of focus, portly man in the side-board's photograph, with his younger self in a group picture in the hall. There were posed the bell-ringers of St. Mark's and his grandfather next to the slight figure of the vicar who was one of Toad Hall's weasels, imagined the boy Glyn.

Around the roundabout and slotting into the line of a dozen or so cars held back by lights. The council had worked on the bridge ever year of Glyn's life, and every summer the stream of holiday coaches, cars and caravans had swollen to grind down at the road's surface and throb through to the huge foundation slabs buried in the silt and centuries of the Tywi.

The town was clustered on the far side of the slow, wide river, like a growth of buildings with the bridge as its stalk. Glyn remembered coming back to Caer after three years away from Wales, he in his mid-twenties, and for the first time realising how small the place was and how fine; the way it held to the hill running up from the river with a rightness that was a form of beauty. The sleepiness of west Wales that had irritated and exasperated him and his fellow sixth formers was now what the world craved for, getting away from the loud, pressing matters of the world. The projected motorway would mean a fast lane from London to the Irish Sea linking the colour supplement city of their early '60s dream with the harsh, vital coastline they'd taken for granted: Carnaby Street to Caldey Island.

To the North-East the river wound up the broad valley to its source in the mountains. Gwili and the hospital lay in that direction, but when the traffic began to flow, instead of entering the one-way system and bypassing the narrow shopping streets, Glyn swung the car left to the West.

He had phoned through to the ward from home whilst Liz packed some sandwiches and a flask.

'She's comfortable, and doing as well as we can expect. It's been a great shock to her system and——And her independence?' said Glyn.——'Yes, Mrs Pugh is a strong-willed woman. She's taking food and sitting up now. Visiting hours are between seven and seven-thirty.'

The staff nurse had sounded young, but confident in her manner. Coming all that way from the other corner of Wales, he could, she was sure, ignore the strict hours and pop in on his arrival. At eighty-six Mrs Pugh was in less danger there, tucked and resting in bed, than lifting and bending to her chores at home.

Somehow, arriving at Caer, with the sun finally breaking through the turning clouds, he felt the need to take in some of the memories of the place where he'd spent the first thirteen years of his life. He would give himself a half-hour and then drive over to the hospital to arrive after tea and before the visitors.

The curve into town from the dual carriageway going on to the west pulled up towards the mart and Nott Street. To his left was the park where he'd spent almost every summer from the time he could run. There he had perched on his father's shoulders and watched the cycle races, afraid for the lean, wiry riders in their skull caps that reminded him of skulls, strapped by the feet to their pedals and pushed off at the timed start by men in cloth caps and raincoats. Then thrilled by their cambered speed; there was always the guilty hope that there'd be a crash coming down off the last slope. In that park he'd learnt to tackle, the round ball and the oval, and lastly, to smart-talk to the gang from the Girls' Gram, who met the lads from his school (as if predestined) on neutral ground; a Garden of Eden with swings, a crumbling band-stand, benches peeling in the sun and rain.

Those last two summers before they'd moved to Rosie's old house in Pembrokeshire were formative, his body expanding and contracting by turns in a new awareness that excited and bewildered him. He'd moved away from the family, further into himself. His father had taken to drinking more heavily and his mother returned home smelling of starch from her long hours at the laundry. Gran's world had shrunk into Nott Street and the Llandeilo Café; tatws a pysgodyn served hot and greasy to the farmers from the mart auction, ordering double fish in their rough Welsh. By that time she had stopped the Sunday ritual of walking over to Ralph's grave in St. Mark's. Glyn often went with her, enjoying best the changing of the water for the flowers and the fierce pressure of the tap at the rear of the church. He would pick up handfuls of the white chippings, like crystals, so pure and dead, and trickle them through his hands like fossilised snow. They crunched and squeaked when you put your whole weight down on them and as his grandmother fussed and busied herself around the headstone and vase, the boy pressed his feet into the white surface, wary but defiant of the body beneath. One of his bad dreams was of the chippings erupting, forced upwards in a shower as the dead man lurched back out into the world.

Being there in the graveyard was never frightening though. There was a fir tree near to his grandfather's plot and he would collect the dropped cones for missiles. From this spot you could see too the backs of the houses in St. David's Street parallel to his own, and beyond, the hills stretching back inland to the remote farms. On windy days clouds would sweep quickly up the river from the bay and move the weather like a clock.

Glyn pulled across the line of traffic coming into town on the back road and drove through the wrought-iron gates, parking on the gravel of the V-shaped drive. The church looked smaller and nothing like as old as he'd remembered.

It must be twenty years since I bothered to look at this place, Just drove past every time as if it were nothing at all to do with my life.

He sat there in the car looking out to his right where the graveyard fell away to the back-yard walls of a row of terraced houses. There the graves were as old as the church itself, ornate Victorian angels, doves and floral crosses in stone for the comfortably pious dead. Most of the statues and markers had inclined with soil movement and the wind away from the true upright and the previous hot summer's drought had brought the grass up as high as the grandest angel's wings. They'd begun burning the stuff and it looked like stubble in a fired harvest field, as if Christ had come in blazing judgement and half done the job. Rain began to pattern the side window and he contorted himself behind the wheel to pull on a weather proof anorak over his jacket.

The driving seat and facia took a shower of water as he got out of the car. Slamming the car door behind him with one foot, without wasting time over fumbling with the keys, he walked quickly for the shelter of the church, hands in the zippered pouch of the anorak. He stood in the porch for a moment, shoulders bunching up and drawing his head down from the rain. There was no break in the downpour so he made his way around to the rear of the church, holding as close to the wall as he could. The blackened mass where they'd fired the long grass stopped short of the path and the plots at the rear of the church were still overgrown. There was the tap, its water-pipe loosened and bending away from the green lichen of the wall. The niche smelt of decay, the previous weekend's pile of dead flowers blackening in a wire bin alongside the top.

His grandfather's grave was close surely; forward to his left and just feet from the tap. But the sodden, matted grass seemed to blanket out all the graves' edgings and chippings. Only the grander headstones had any permanency -it seemed from the path that the earth had drawn into itself all trace of those whose relatives could not afford the hackneyed art of the monumental mason.

Jane Thomas   1862   18 years
Calm on the bosom of thy God, Fair spirit rest thee now
Ever while thy footsteps trod, His seal was on thy brow

and
Severed whilst in bloom

The rain stopped and the fir tree's soughing died with the wind. Glyn moved under the deep green of its lower branches and put his hand out to the trunk. The bark was hard and full like an exotic cork cut into vertical channels. He was aware of the town's traffic noise building up to the later afternoon.

This church is like a bad film set, he thought. The tree is wrong, it's not Wales, more a Japanese ceramic, though the houses surrounding the place are tight and comfortable in the way they hem in the graveyard. He remembered last summer's holiday on the Lleyn and visiting Aberdaron. R. S. Thomas' church, older than this one by centuries; small and simple, banked up from the sea and dominating the village's cottages and narrow, winding road. Linking by death the hills and the waves.

Here at this moment there are two points of focus; as surely as the traffic and the land's produce are drawn in towards the mart and market, so the neat townspeople who have built the town around that trade, are always moving in towards the graves at the end of their gardens and yards.

Two other churches: at Enbourne in Berkshire, a Norman squatness that had sunk lower into the earth over the centuries of its life, holding the dead generations of Pughs who had led to Ralph and John and Glyn's father and himself.

And the village church in Pembrokeshire which rose above Jobstone Farm, directly across the road from the farm's yard, that held the Barrah family and the Coles and Williamses and Vaughans who all formed Catherine and Rosie and the sisters and Matthew who'd taken a ship across the North Atlantic and disappeared in Canada.

The Church of England, The Church in Wales, the bell-ringing, the vestments and litany, the railway joining the two and letting the blood bypass the centuries of Welsh-speaking Wales, leaving him with a tongue outside the language yet stirred by the sense of being Welsh, of belonging here and nowhere else and wanting to understand his place, how Caer and west Wales had made him feel that way. A hybrid needing to draw diagrams of the twisted and confused roots that fed his life. He walked forward into the longer grass, feeling with his feet for the rise of graves, the hard edge of a stone kerb. There were two he located at the end of a row that must have extended beyond the tree. The first held James Davies and his wife Martha -1938 and 1945- *Cofio Rest Eternal* on a black marble book laid open with ridged pages frozen at the place. Next to it the rectangle he could trace under the matted grass with his foot.

There were the beginnings of brambles curling through the grass and he scratched his hands in pulling back the thick covering. The vase had slumped to its side into the dulled gravel and it shocked him to find the decay of remembrance so complete. How many years was it since Gran had tidied the grave of the man who was her husband? When had the Sunday ritual become redundant? Glyn could not remember her ever going to Church or Chapel. His memory of her refused to conform to the hat, gloves and Sunday Best of the proud, little women shuffling their way to heaven past their house and the green flecked gate he'd swung upon.

You learned to cope with death by developing a numbness, was that it? What am I doing here? he thought.

In loving memory of Dad
from Mam and the boys

What sense am I trying to make of all this, when Gran herself is lying in a bed two miles from here?

Why here? Why didn't I drive straight over to her? What sort of concern was that? Are the dead and our memories to hold sway over the living, the daily dying of ourselves?

Glyn picked up one of the grave's loose chippings. Trying his hand against its sharpened end, he threw it towards the fir tree and he walked back to the car. Here was the unifying image that could bring the generations to a point: this churchyard, the grave and its rain-polished chippings, this town with its pubs and chapels, and tired cinemas; this place, shaping all their lives like a funnel down which he fell. The novel he would start seeded and swelled like propagation in a speeded-up film as he joined the traffic and drove across town to the hospital.

107

Working with Cyril

I met him in 1968 in the summer vacation before the protests hit our campus. The Beatles in their prime, Mama Cass dead, and Luther King. Kennedy had become an airport.

Cyril was much the same as the other drivers—perhaps a bit younger, but basically in the same slicked-hair, cigarette in the lips style. They didn't like the work, but delivering Wright's Ice Cream meant a five-day week in the summer season and three out of season with £30-£35 a week, so they would all do it, and be content.

There were no chances to moonlight though, as the manager had boasted three weeks earlier when he'd taken me on for relief vacation work.

'It's too good a job for them to fiddle. These lads would have to work a damn sight harder than this for the same wage elsewhere, you know. And they don't exactly kill themselves in the winter!'

'But surely the odd ice-cream or something isn't missed is it?' I said, wanting to appear sharp and up to the ways of the world. 'Now at the bread factory...'

'Look here, lad. I'm a reasonable man, ask anyone. If these blokes want a block of vanilla for their tea, or a unit of fancy stuff for the kid's birthday party, then all they do is ask. A firm as big as this can stretch to that. Same goes for you, while you're here. Listen, I've worked all over for food firms, packing, delivery, the lot, and I'm telling you—you can't fiddle this one. Anyway, a clever college boy like you shouldn't be bothered with such things. What you've got to remember is that in the season the cream's running by the afternoon and you've got to be bloody sharp if you're to get it in the shops at the end of the list before it's trickling out of the back of the bloody van!'

He was right. Starting from the depot at Chester, just after 8 a.m., you had to shift to clear the load in time. Still, after living on a student grant, the money was good for me, and the previous year I'd had to work shifts in a bakery to make £20. Being out on the open road was a delight after the dust and sweat of that bread factory and the dislocating night shifts. For Wright's we covered the greater part of west and mid-Cheshire, so in between delivery points and invoice checks I could enjoy the wide landscapes of the plain and the mild, wooded hills of the southern part of the county with their wealthy wattle-and-daub gentlemen's farms.

Our delivery points were various: national supermarkets, mini-markets in the larger villages, small corner shops on the edges of towns. These last were small orders of twenty pounds or less. They had faded displays and glass sweet jars just like my father's village shop back in Pembrokeshire. I knew that they must be just as precariously balanced on the edge of the economy, small business, small returns.

These small orders provided the bulk of this particular day's deliveries from Cyril, with me as his 'mate', and the Friday Wirral run to Birkenhead. In its early section this had been a pleasant trip as we worked our way along the flat coastal villages on the east side. The change of scenery (and with it my mood) began at New Brighton. A mini-Blackpool just a ferry trip across the Mersey from Liverpool, it had now a mid-afternoon, numbed, eerie atmosphere with near-empty swings and amusements rocking, lights flashing, to themselves. What gift for a hungry, heady poet:

The Waltzer's blazing records drift
out to sea
as easily as paper trash and forgotten spades. A nun in blue
leads
four retarded, stumbling, aged children along the creaking boards,
the sea giggling beneath like ...

'Love letters?'
    'Eh? Sorry?'
    'Love letters—what you're writing.'
    'Er...no. Well it's...it...' My voice dried.

It wasn't a poem yet, a few lines that needed work, more polishing. I couldn't show an unfinished piece; and anyway I feared the scorn of Cyril. Or, perhaps more than that, I feared his pretended interest, his indulgence.

The paper burned a hole in my back-pocket as we rushed to finish off the handful of small 'drops' through the narrow streets that criss-crossed the slope to the Birkenhead waterfront.

The last of these deliveries was reached by a quarter past five, which we thought to be our best time so far for this run. Cyril humped the now weakening cartons of ice-cream into the corner-shop, leaving me to finish checking the cash and re-arranging the invoices in the cab of the truck. He was longer than he should have been, though, so I got out to help.

The shop was gloomy, its old, dusty windows in need of a clean. There was a scattering of the year's flies turning dry around the pyramids of tins. I thought of my father. You could dribble away your life in such a prison, eeking out some sort of living. The old man who ran this grim place was evidently pottering about looking for a pen, or his order or something, it wasn't clear, leaving Cyril drumming his fingers on the invoice and breathing heavily.

'All right? No problems are there?'

'Yes, yes,' then under his breath, 'stupid old git wants to get himself organised. The cream'll be running soon and then he won't bloody want it. You get back in the van and wait for me.'

I did so and five minutes later Cyril joined me, whipping off his cap and starting the engine. He whistled as we drove back down the road to Chester and passing Port Sunlight dipped his hand into his coat, bringing out the invoice and some crumpled pound notes

'Here's the slip.'

'OK. Don't you want me to clip the notes into the wallet?'

'Aha...not this time, mate. I shot him right up—the old scrooge—keeping me waiting over sod-all like that.'

Cyril slipped me a fist full of notes. Most were grubby, some torn. I unravelled them and counted. 'But there's fifteen here.'

Cyril smirked, 'I know it, mate. I gave him change for ten, ha, ha. Four quid for the kitty, boy!'

'You mean you diddled him?'

'Nah. Not really—it's his mistake.' Cyril tried to sound reasonable, offended at my suggestion. 'Look, if he's daft enough to...'

'Yeh, but...' I hesitated, Cyril was gripping the steering wheel with a clumsy strength. I didn't want an argument at fifty miles an hour. I said, 'I suppose he was awkward, quite disorganised; he was fiddling about checking and re-checking the cartons like they were gold ingots.'

'He was so bothered about the choc-ices cracking up soft that he didn't have any energy left for the money,' laughed Cyril.

'Won't he find out at the end of the day and ring Brian at the office, though?'

'What can he say? Can't prove nothing. His mistake. And you won't tell, will you?' Cyril's tone was that of offering rather than needing assurance. He was offering me part of the money. I grunted and turned my head away, pretending to watch a flow of factory girls from the soap works. I felt Cyril pushing my shoulder in a clumsy way.

'Anyway, they're all stinking with money, shopkeepers. The profits they make. If you can pick up a quid or two when you're on the road...well, it happens.'

'My old man isn't well off,' I said, bitterly. 'Do you think I want to do this instead of reading my set texts every summer?'

'Yeh, well...'

The cab went quiet and cold. I thought of my father's fourteen-hour days in what was no more than a tin shack with a freezer, shelves and a till. And I wished that the darkening sky would shower rain down upon us, washing and blurring the truck, the road, the journey. Nothing happened—the return trip was completed in a vacuum— my face turned away from him to take in the countryside,

111

with Cyril breaking into a monotonous whistling of 'Ferry Cross the Mersey'.

Later, back at my digs, I flung off the white coat with 'Wright's' across the breast in red writing, only to see a one pound note fall out. A quid to shut me up. It was then that I realised exactly what had happened, what sort of process had begun during our journey's strained ending. I didn't care.

Oh yes, I had been upset by the casual wantonness of Cyril's dealing, upset too by my weak objections at the time. I wanted to wash my hands of the petty theft; I wanted to escape the implication. But it was there—the £1 note. If I gave it back to the shop or handed it into the office his short dealing would be revealed. He'd lose his job.

No. Who was I fooling? It wasn't just that; that was surface detail. I wanted the money. I had not stolen it. It was put into my overall pocket. I needed cash, and so the toad work sat upon my shoulders. What was at stake anyway? The theft—call it a fiddle—had happened three hours before and was already trapped in the past tense .

My landlady, Mrs Ellis, called up to say tea was ready. I felt quite ravenous despite the prospect of her greasy chips with everything. The pound note got mixed up with my wages the next day and was spent.

The New Brighton poem was translated into ancient Egyptian as Mrs Ellis's washing machine paddled my trousers. I had not put any more work into it and knew that any attempt to re-write it from memory would be still-born.

For the remaining weeks of the vacation I tried to avoid being put on Cyril's runs. But later that year I did come up against him again, in a crowded Chester pub. He was wearing one of those lumber-jack bombers with a fake fur collar and a pair of black jeans with bottoms rolled up. He was on his way out with a peroxide plump, tipsy girl, younger than myself and obviously not his wife.

'See Everton today? Rubbish—worse than usual. Buy you a drink, me laddo—but I've got to go.' And turning to the girl: 'This lad were me mate, like, on the van. Bit educated he is—one of those revolting students. Ey, have

112

you written any more of those poems?' He stressed the work as you would something foreign.

'Well, I...'

'You stick to your studying, mate—writing things—be famous, yer little Shakespeare—you be sodding famous!' And he disappeared through the door, his arm pawing the girl's rump.

'When you're famous and on the tele I'll touch you for a drink!' I heard him call from the corridor.

As I turned quickly back to the bar to finish my solitary beer, my elbow sent a cluster of glasses shattering onto the floor and everyone turned to look at me.

Hedging your Bets

'Know thy enemy.'
Sun Tzu.

Chelsea away: that's going to be the end of it. The Jacks are down and out. Run ended. Out of the cup. No chance. A Russian billionaire's Chelsea plaything. Do you know what that team cost?. They'll run them off the park. Outclassed is not the word for it. I'll lose a couple of bob, but it will have been worth it.

I hate them. No, really, I hate them. I know it's not rational and that they are, in a sense, also Welsh, but it's Swansea, isn't it—the Swans, the Jacks; it's not us, City, the capital, the Blues, the Bluebirds.

A couple of seasons ago I worked out my system: it hurts so much when we lose, that on the big games if I place a bet on the opposition, then that mitigates things, softens the blow, turns it from being just a matter of the heart to being a matter also of the wallet. Lose –Win; Win-Win. Cardiff City winning is too important for me and so clouding it with a bet, money being involved, makes it less focussed, more complicated, less raw. When people at work or family friends bring it up in conversation I can deflect them, 'Won a few bob, though. Let me get them in; what are you having?'

No, this season for us really is all about promotion and to hell with cup runs. Been there: Wembley, done it, been there, lost. Move on. Move up. The Premiership, the golden heights, an international currency, global fame—being watched on the box in bars and huts all over the far East, Africa, even in America now—that is what this season is about for the City.

I'm sure that our boss threw in the towel in the first round of this cup: Northampton away. Helguson converts a penalty in the fourth minute, but it ends 2-1 to them. A crowd of two thousand, eight hundred and nineteen: I ask you. Sixfields Stadium. Badge has a lion, a griffon, a castle and a red rose. On a shield in front of the castle is a shoe. Northampton—'The Cobblers'. Strip: claret with a white stripe. Two—one. Ok, move on.

Back to the league and doing well. This is the season, I'm sure. Malky's the man—Manager of the Month twice already this season. But the Swans, as a Premier team, come in to the cup at the second round. Barnsley at The Vetch, no, make that The Liberty. Their new stadium is a shed, shared with the rugby team, built at the east of the town, well, east end of the city (promoted up to a city since '69 and the investiture of the new prince). It's a run of the mill-three-one. I put a tenner on them: little return.

Third round they draw Crawley Town; the Broadfield Stadium, League One. Badge has 'Red Devils' on it. Well, surely a piece of cake. Except that they were 2-all with fifteen minutes to go and an awkward return leg beckoned. That would have been useful, would have compromised their league plans as well. An injury-time winner from a corner got them off the hook; they squeaked through. Swansea's taking this seriously.

No problem: in the fourth round the big boys start to be drawn against each other and the real thing starts. Goodbye Swans; because they will put Premiership survival first and to hell with the cup. As teams like that do. Cups now are where the big four or five play their second best XI and their kids for experience and the others pick up the scraps. And Swansea are not really in the big boys' club, are they? Though they want to be.

In the fourth round they draw Liverpool—the Swans' former manager, the one that got them up two season back —Rodgers. 'Know thy enemy's enemies': Bill Shankly (probably). Good bloke, Rodgers: glad he left them. But then he leads Liverpool to beat us in last year's final. What goes around....

You'll never walk alone. Some of us are born into a town and a club; others are caught up in a moment—a cup run, Hillsborough, the Munich crash—and so we weld ourselves to a team. It can be a birthright, happenstance, a choice. Or one team that catches the essence of an era, your young imagination—Leeds in the seventies, Spurs doing the double in 60/61. A player even—Stanley Matthews, or John Charles, the Gentle Giant, who left the enemy for Leeds and Juventus. Bremner. Best. Shearer.

Wembley in front of ninety-one thousand: that was our early and abiding litany—Farquharson, Nelson, Watson, Keenor, Sloan, Hardy, Curtis, Irving, Ferguson, Davies, McLachlan—the 1927 FA Cup-winning team, immortal in Cardiff. Five years before I was born. In Cardiff and so it's *Bluebirds, Bluebirds born and bred—Cardiff Bluebirds 'till I'm dead.*

You'll never walk alone: I walk from my flat to the ground, always, rain or shine. Not through the part of the city where I grew up, but the ghosts of the port, the raison d'être—behind me is that narrow stretch across to England, the glint of the Channel, the water-front, then skirting Tiger Bay, past the warehouses they've turned into flats and gastro-pubs, over the Taff and west to the ground. Myself, then two or three, then dozens, tributaries into a river until all the roads around the stadium are a slow mass of fans. The traffic negotiates the crowds; all traffic lights are effectively suspended: friendly banter, the odd horn, which gets you no-where, my friend. Two point six miles: I allow an hour and a bit. Seven minutes to two for a three o'clock kick off.

Liverpool at Anfield: 3-1 to the Swans, de Guzman sealing it in the ninetieth minute. Explain that. The Shankly statue outside must have been shaking on its plinth. But my tenner's getting bigger and bigger, which mitigates the pain of seeing them seriously progressing. 'Relax, 'says my wife, 'They'll never do it.' West Ham, her team, beat them in the league last month. We went for dinner at Langham's

Brasserie. I come down to the flat in Cardiff on my own. It's better that way.

A quarter-final against Middlesbrough, a team only from our league: soft, really, and they do beat them at The Liberty, but only after an own goal near the end. Squeaky, but, damn it, my tenner's still growing.

Then a two-leg semi against Chelsea. Chelsea away and that's surely the end of it. Stamford Bridge, with those prawn sandwiches and vodka from the owner. I get long odds for my money: Swansea—no chance, not in the same class.

And we are still top of the Championship and maybe this is the season for us; we've got serious money. See, we've been bought by a Malaysian businessman. Do I care? Not if he's spending millions on the ground, the team and wiping out our debts. He wants to change the kit. We've always been the Bluebirds. In blue. But red is the lucky colour over there and he wants to build 'an Asian fan base'. Russian oil billionaires, Indian steel men, American baseball owners: everyone wants to own a piece of the greatest football league. Which we will be joining next season, won't we? It's the free market: and, lord knows, I've made enough over the years from the workings of the free market economy. No-one now follows those other teams—Lenin United, Trotsky Wanderers, Mao Zedong Orient—I don't think so, my friend.

Our supporters club are calling protest meetings and saying that the club's traditions are being sold down the river. Blue/red/blue/pink—I can take that: as long as the Malaysian puts the money in and we win.

In the first leg at Stamford Bridge one of the Chelsea defenders has a nightmare and Michu, the classy Spaniard they bought for a song, steals off him to score in the first half; you can recover from one. But then the same defender fails to clear and in the last minute they double their lead. Swansea with a two-goal lead going into the second round at home: this is serious. And the odds narrow.

A nil-nil draw at The Liberty sees them through to a Wembley final against—I don't believe this—Bradford City. When we won our cup in 1927 it was against Arsenal. Arsenal: Bradford City. It's all over. And to cap it all at The Liberty there's a bizarre incident in the semi late on when a ball-boy tries to slow down a Chelsea throw-in by shielding the ball from their winger, practically lying on top of it. The guy, understandably, is not amused, but in trying to kick the ball free from under this kid he lands one right in the pudgy boy's stomach: writhing like you've never seen before—makes an Italian centre-forward look like an Oscar winner. A red card and Chelsea down to nine men are done for. Kid turns out to be a son of one of their directors and had earlier tweeted #the king of ball boys needed for time wasting#. Need I say more?

Wembley is a foregone conclusion. It ends five-nil. Call that a match? Still, the Capital Cup (the League Cup) is not THE CUP, is it? 1927: that was the only time the Cup, any cup, left England, until now.

But you have to take your knocks and get up again. Unlike a Swansea ball-boy...

My tenner's grown to close on fifteen hundred: it's an accumulated and painful success. So I have decided to use it for the City. I'm contacting our community bloke and am offering to pay for seats, programmes, transport for disadvantaged kids—Ely, Gabalfa, Splott. They'll bring them to the ground for a match and get them on board, perhaps, plant the seeds of fandom. I'll be introduced at half-time and buy them drinks, hot dogs, whatever.

And looking on the bright side: if Swansea get tied up in Europe Cup-Winners stuff next season, it will surely stretch them and compromise them in the league. They'll go down as we go up.

'A matter of life and death.' As Bill Shankly said, 'I can assure you it is much, much more important than that.'

Look, take it from me: if you're on a train and some bloke says, 'Who do you support?' You don't say 'Nelson Mandela' or 'Fresh clean water for everyone in Africa' or 'A girl's right to an education in the developing world.' Do you? He doesn't want that answer; he wants Blank City or Blank United or Blank Wanderers. It's a conversation, not a philosophy. And if you're having a bad season he'll commiserate about the manager, the owner, that bent ref last week. And if you are riding high, you'll be magnanimous and say, 'It could last a bit longer this season.' It's a real and instant bonding; shallow, you'll say, but real.

Alright, it's a long way for me to come down from London for every match and that's why I keep the flat down in Cardiff Bay, my decompression chamber: I just can't go straight back. I leave the City to support my City. What I do in the City you might say has been dull and profitable—insurance, the markets, exchanges—I could have retired years back; three days a week I go in to the office. It's not the money: I like figures, graphs, economic analyses. The beauty of a spread-sheet, the rightness of mathematics, the ballet of the Stock Exchange. The market is aggressive—you win and someone loses; someone wins and you may lose. Know thy enemy: I need the Swans as the other guys, the not-City, the upstart Jacks who are not in the capital city. Did I mention that on my wedding day I got my carnation dyed blue?

Oh, and the name of that Chelsea player who hacked the Swans' ball-boy—Belgian international, Eden Hazard. Eden. Hazard. Sums up the human condition, doesn't it? We all fall from a state of grace into dangerous knowledge. My best chum sitting by us in the City season tickets seats is a published writer, prone to philosophising about football and the meaning of life, quite famous for his plays and novels, but you couldn't make that up, could you?

Throwing the Punch

If you want to know about a man, watch how he treats animals. Or promote him over his mates. Give a man power and he'll use it or abuse it according to his nature. In all my years underground I learned that. Put a man in the dark and put the squeeze on him then watch out for the bad blood to come up in a well.

Take the fight between McIntosh and Whistler on the night shift in Lady Margaret, oh, 30 years back or more it was, but as clear as day to me now. Mining was a protected industry, the war effort, Dig for Victory, coal against the Nazis. So we was working double hard. They drafted hundreds of lads into the mines at that time. Bevin boys. All in a line, balls in your hands, cough and then 'You-Army-You-Navy-You-RAF-you-the pit.' And so on. Lilly-whites most of them. Straight from school or their mam's apron. If they had two legs and a pair of lungs they was fit for digging. Only some of them wasn't suited to the pit. It's all right if you was born to it, father before you, accepting it as what the men in a certain village did, and that was that. But going down a pit is the nearest thing to hell for some. 'A daily grave,' I remember someone calling it.

Whistler was one of those Bevin boys. Only he wasn't called Whistler from the start. His name was Richards, I think, though it's so long since he was called that at work I couldn't be sure. Big enough for a lad—a pretty good shape on him really, so you couldn't have guessed there'd be trouble. But trouble there was—as soon as his turn come up at the top. As the cage clanked back up and the first men came out after their shift, Richards—Whistler—started to shake. Duw, the sweat came out of him—just like someone had turned on a tap. It was running down his face and neck soaking his shirt. You could hear his teeth, but he didn't say anything. I was next to him and gave Will Peters the other side a nod. We pressed him on both sides and managed to shuffle him into the cage. When the gate locked he seemed to let go and loosen against us. That's when the screaming started. All the way down we was deafened. They could hear us coming at the bottom like the bomb that's got your name.

He fell out of the cage, and Will Peters, having the room to swing now, laid such a bloody slap across his face. And that did it. Of course, there was no question of him going up to the face. A man like that would be too much of a liability at the coal-face. That's where the money's made, and those boys worked their stalls like little empires. No, the foreman got word and Whistler was put on the horses. That's how he got his name. The boy had a way with them, talking them calm (talking himself calm, I suppose, as well) and whistling the the whole time.

We must have had three hundred horses, maybe more, underground at that time in the Lady Margaret. Mining's always been a cruel industry. Back in the real old days they used to use children for hauling, and women, sometimes pregnant even, it didn't matter to the owners. They turned a blind eye to everything except the tally sheets. Keep the drams coming out steady and full, was all that mattered. Anyway, each of these horses had a name—Albion, Betty, Crusader, Dreadnought, right down the alphabet and back again. And they all had housing in stables underground. Once down there a horse would never see the light of day again. Better, more humane in a way, I suppose, because once they got used to the gloom of the pit their eyes would never have taken the full glare of the sun again. It's bad enough for a man coming up out of that hole after a shift and taking the strength of the daylight.

Whistler didn't have any horses in his background; I found out talking that he was just another Dai from Pontypridd whose old man had a corner shop. But he seemed happy with them. 'They're my real wages,' he'd say, 'I'm happy talking to them.'

He was so happy that after a week or so he'd almost bounce down in the cage. Mind you, he never went up to the face. Stuck to the horses and looking after them. He'd still be there today if it hadn't been for McIntosh.

Now, McIntosh was the son of a Scotsman who'd come into Wales back in the twenties to scab during the lock-out times. You know, everything changed after 1926. It were a good sense of comradeship you had in the mines until then. Afterwards the whole business went sour in the mouth. Debts and rumours and hatred and back-biting. Not so much of the Butties, but every man jack after his own slice, wasn't it? You could see it in the eyes narrowing, like everyone was looking for the next move from someone. Well, McIntosh followed his father into the pit and was always a big man for the money. I know what they say about the Scotch people, and a lot of rubbish it is to tar a whole country with the same brush I'm sure, but this McIntosh could have carried the whole blame on his shoulders. A real mean bastard he was, and doing anyone down that he could. He used to work times at the slaughterhouse in the next village, a big bugger with plenty of muscle in his arms, but a tyre of a beer belly pushing out against his buckle-belt too. 'Jock's the lad,' he'd shout in his bouts of bragging. He was a drunkard but a loner, for at work or after in the pub he'd set his temper on a short fuse.

If Whistler was considerate and caring for the pit ponies, then he was alone in that way of being attached to them. Men who'd never dream of kicking a dog in their back-lanes would kick out at a horse in anger underground. Coal-mining is a hard, frustrating business and with the pressure on you constantly to fill your drams and make your rate for wages, tempers can be spilled easier than coal. You daren't let fly at another collier though. The two things that are, absolutely taboo down below are matches and punches. One or the other gets you your marching orders, sharpish.

I'm not saying as this McIntosh was the only one, but he was renowned for his cruelty. Not in short blasts of temper, but slow, lingering, unnatural,like. I'd seen him take a rat and hold it with his boot against a rail so a truck would cut it living in half. 'Jock's the ratting lad,' he shouted in squeaky excitement. That business of calling himself by his own name, like he was doing something, but outside himself all the while,—all in all there was something peculiar about the man.

Well, this one night shift there was a sort of tension in the Lady Margaret. Two men had gone down under a fall during the day and one of them was near to death with a broken back it was said. The Penderyn District had come across bad workings and more gas than usual too. Sometimes when you cut into the seam it breathes and groans back at you. Some will tell you it can sing, or play like organ pipes—weird it is. Anyway, the feeling was that the sooner the end of the shift and the end of the week came the better.

McIntosh was handling a horse called Tudor, a tired lump of bones that poor beast was too, four tins of dog meat and a pint of glue as they say. Likely as not the horse was on the back-end of a double shift, for although the ponies were brought back to stables for cleaning down, feeding and watering after a shift, quite often it was that the tally wasn't held to and within minutes the poor animal was being drawn out again by a miner on the next shift. A man pushing to get his wages up to a living level isn't going to look too closely at the only horse he's offered. Sometimes a beast would work a double-header then, the second shift miner demanding as much from the animal as his first handler.

Tudor was pretty well done for, but there's nowhere to run to for a horse down there in the dark. He was craning his neck down to the feed-bag that was hung low down around him. That meant he was distracted from his job of pulling and McIntosh wasn't making the time with his drams that he wanted.

'Come on ya lazy bugger! Move ya carcass!' McIntosh punching the flank of the beast and lashing with his boot. And the horse leaning into the harness and struggling to take the Incline with a loaded dram. Well, it seems McIntosh called a halt and was bending down to wedge the wheels firm on the slope when the horse eased the weight and the back wheel came close to depriving the miner of his fingers. 'Jesus, I'll 'ave you this time!' and instead of

123

laying more kicks on the horse he goes cool-dangerous and takes loose the feed-bag from Tudor's neck. Uncoupling the iron shackles from an empty truck he adds them to the bag and replaces it around the horse's neck. Now those metal shackles must weigh a mighty bit; just think of that lumped onto an already tired horse. It brought the beast's head down to breaking point and the full dram to be taken up the incline too.

God knows how he made it, but he did, and the bulk of the rest of the shift as well. Then, when McIntosh has settled down for his food-break, tucking into his snap-tin like a pig, he leaves the weight on the horse and keeps him from the water too.

Now whether it was that Whistler happened that way or whether someone had dropped word of what McIntosh was up to, I don't know, but anyway, along he comes as if nothing was out of order.

'How's me Tudor then? Weary old boy, eh?' patting the horse along his flank and no doubt feeling the welts as he went. Then he goes to fasten up the feed-bag.

'Leave it be!' snarls McIntosh.

'Entitled to a feed like you or me,' reasons Whistler, and then, 'What's this, though? Where's his proper meal? There's a ton in this bag. What's your game, man?'

'What's it to you boy? Mind ya own!'

'Help me get this thing off, you cruel bastard!' said Whistler, struggling with the bag.

'Leave it bloody well on and see to your own business!' and McIntosh got up from this snap. 'e's my horse this shift and he'll work to my ways, the good-for-nothing knackered lump!'

Whistler had managed to loosen the strap on Tudor's bag and was removing the weight when the Scotsman's hand grabbed his shoulder. Whistler must have put everything into swinging round and planting his fist in McIntosh's face for the bigger man went down like an axed steer, blood spread from his nose and mouth and he coughed on it. Whistler's hand wasn't so good either after that blow and he completed the job of watering the horse mostly with his left hand. Welcome that water was for the beast too, but he hardly moved apart from his drinking head. It must have been all so much of a muchness to him after those years down the pit—the damp, the explosions, the curses, the constant low roofs paring down his back.

There was McIntosh in the dust, wiping his sleeve across his face and spitting out, 'Bastard horse! Bastard horse!,' over and over, low and bitter. Whistler had turned away to the horse again, and was unshackling the animal from the truck.

'There fella, there Tudor, boy.'

But at that moment along comes the overman. The thing about overmen is their noses. They can smell trouble from the other end of a pit working. 'Something up here, then?' he says. 'Bit of trouble?'

'Nothing, boss,' says the Scotsman, struggling back to his feet and trying to turn his head away from the light.

'Anything up for you, Whistler?'

'Old Tudor, here, be on his last legs. Looks to me like he's done a double shift. No point killing the horse for a bit more coal. He needs changing over.'

'Oh, I see. Well, that's all right then, isn't it?' says the overman, turning to go. And then, 'Caught a piece of rock have you, Jock?'

'Stupid bloody pit prop,' came the mumbled reply. It was hardly uttered with conviction, but Roberts the overman had more sense than to push it. Give a man a chance to spit out his grievance, and then let it be was the order of the day.

Word got round that shift and Jock gave his notice in that week. He left for the Jubilee pit over in the next valley but didn't stick it long. He moved over to slaughterman full-time. He had a real forte in that area, no doubt.

Whistler was one of the first of the Bevin boys we got in Lady Margaret in those war years. Most of them stuck it out, ham-fisted and grumbling. A couple threw worse fits than Whistler's—screams, kicking—you name it. One fainted as the cage began to drop and concussed himself on the gate, As the pace of production speeded up the manager began to throw the shaky ones back into the pool. Maybe some of them got landed in submarines or up icy crow's nests on the Russian convoys. We each gets his lot don't we?

Whistler was a quiet, good worker and I wouldn't mind betting he did some good with his influence over caring for the horses. Certainly, he had no call to bloody anyone's nose again that I heard of. But mining is no sort of vocation if you've got any sense and the price of a bus ticket, and Whistler was away as soon after V.E. Day as he could. I'd like to think of him going on with the horses, at a stables maybe, a brewery dray or settling into an old trade like blacksmithing. But that's just sentimental. He's probably on the buses in some city, or maybe worked up to clerking in an office and counting the days to retirement.

Sometimes we go all our lives pulling back from the thing we ought to do. But whatever happened in the long run, Whistler had his moment. You can't take that away— throwing the punch.

Film Night

In the second term of their film society Mary and Rees had high hopes of securing its future. They'd had a shaky start, but the reasons seemed obvious to them now. You couldn't expect the kids to leave a warm house and the cosy, mindless television to see films they hadn't heard of. *Alexander Nevsky* had flopped, even *Only Two Can Play* had drawn a small audience—the first was foreign and 'boring', the second lacked violence. Both were in black and white.

But with *Planet of the Apes* they felt they had a fighting chance. The poster and stills were bold and exciting. The facial make-up of the Apes themselves was totally convincing in a way that can be achieved only on the cinema screen. They had attracted steady interest and a buzz was building through the week. When Rees fixed up to show a trailer after school assemblies, success was assured.

By 6.45 that Thursday evening the hall was three-quarters full and a queue stretched down the stairs. The Film Soc. committee—Sinclair, Milborough and three girls from the fifth form—were furiously active. They fumbled excitedly with the change and filled coin bags one after the other. Milborough paraded up and down the centre aisle swinging Rees's new torch with a confident swagger.

'Retiring to the South of France after this one then Sir?'

'You just watch that torch, lad. You're not manager of the Top Rank yet.'

Milborough really would make a good manager, thought Rees, all those girls to be bitchy to, and the ice-cream money to total up. He's in his element.

By seven o'clock the hall was solid with bodies, the whole mass getting more and more agitated. Sinclair steamed his professorial glasses over with the excitement. He constantly adjusted the tension of the opening spool, checking the projector's fickle gates. Everything was primed and ready. Somehow they had the tail-end of the queue all seated by a couple of minutes past seven and Rees rose to give his introduction. He'd keep it short.

'... a classic Science Fiction film. I want you to think about the ending carefully, OK?'

Then he delivered the statutory, and more or less pointless, warning about noise and chewing gum and they were off into darkness. There was a pedestrian opening, six or seven minutes to establish the context of the space flight and the crash-landing, that moon-bare landscape, then the first terrifying appearance of the bully-Apes on horse-back, whipping and shooting the human Yahoos with a callousness that would have worried Dean Swift himself.

No words of admonition were needed; from the entry of the Apes the audience, mainly the first three years, but with an above average senior school contingent, was too gripped to be disruptive. Usually the Society's screenings were constantly interrupted by the audience's trips to and from the toilets, but this time far fewer bladders played up. No sweet paper pellets traced irritating flights through the fantastic beam the projector squirted the length of the hall. They were a captive audience. And when Charlton Heston staggered towards the Statue of Liberty, bizarrely angling out of the sand wastes of the 'forbidden zone', at that truly dramatic revelation—the *Planet of the Apes* was really a futuristic, mutated Earth—the credits rolled as a backdrop to a stunned silence. A heightened and quite affected audience of pupils made their way back out to Yorkshire and the world.

The committee girls set to the sweeping up, but there were no furtive cigarette butts or gum-stuck chairs. The film had clearly been a resounding success.

'We'll have to get the sequel booked, Sir,' suggested Milborough, wearing his managerial 'full-house' smile.

'Next year, next year,' said Rees, and he moved to the projector where Rawlings and Wilson were fussing over the re-winding like a couple of boffins setting up the first H-bomb. Their enthusiasm for the Film Society was strictly mechanical, but, Rees felt, that was preferable to the smug young executive pressure of Milborough at the budgeting and selection meetings. He would, no doubt, go far.

By 9.30 the hall had resumed its formal air of order and sterility—the screen rolled up, the chairs in straightened rows and the projector returned to the Geography cupboard. Rees was last to go, switching off the lights and leaving it like some great abstract event, a vacuum waiting to be filled by 200 reluctant worshippers the following morning. Mary was in the car huddled over the heater.

'Why are our film nights always freezing cold or soaking wet?' she asked.

'Or sweltering hot!' Rees said, settling into the seat, 'Anyway that's to test our dedication. '

The truth was that they both believed in the Society as a social, educative force in the depressing atmosphere of Bindthorpe School and the whole Bindthorpe valley; though each film evening seemed to leave one at best with a taste of uncertainty, if not plain disillusionment. If the film was a failure, then it was made clear—the kids would behave really badly—or they simply voted with their feet. Success meant good takings and the future bookings assured; but what did they get from the 007's and the Apes films? They raved over Easy Rider and Blow Up for the wrong reasons: they shunned *Alexander Nevsky* and *Last Year at Marienbad* for a host of reasons. Rees and Mary were, in a sense, re-living their college film society days and telling themselves it was missionary work in the West Riding.

As they walked to their car, Rees remembered those Wednesday nights in the Engineering lecture hall and Bunuel and Fellini and Renoir, the rare, coterie excitement of discovering foreign, arty films. He swung the car out of the school gates and grated the stick into a cold, clumsy second. But he made no further progress because the junction between Rotherham Lane and the main road was blocked by an ambulance; everything was lights and confusion.

'God, there's been an accident on that zebra! ' said Mary, 'What's happened... our kids..?'

'Hold on,' said Rees and he pulled into the kerb before the halt sign and cut the engine.

'You stay here, love,' he said, and slammed the door behind him.

A Morris 1000 van was bull-nosed up onto the pavement after the zebra, on the white zig-zag lines. It appeared to be unmarked, though on the pavement there was that residue of dislodged dirt that is spilled from wheel-arches near any car accident, indicating that some impact had occurred. A dozen or so children from the film audience were grouped near the front of the ambulance and they chattered in low, tense murmurs.

'What's happened, lad?' Rees asked Sparrow, one of the sixth formers he'd spotted in the crowd.

'Accident, Sir.'

'One of our kids?'

'Yes, don't know who though. It's bad, I think. '

'From which year?'

'Don't know, Sir—a boy that's all.'

The two ambulance men crouched over a vague, blanketed shape on the ground towards the rear of the ambulance, its position seeming quite unrelated to that of the Morris. Around the body was a magic circle no-one wanted to enter. A face, a name under the blanket: this dream-scene lit by the passing lights and the neon of the public house across the road was becoming too real.

Rees was rooted, his mouth dry as dust. He swallowed and called to one of the ambulance men, who was now standing, hands on hips.

'Is it serious?' There was no answer. 'I'm a teacher, is it a pupil?'

The man walked over to him and his face confirmed the worst. He said, 'It's a boy—looks like one of yours.'

'And...?'

'And it's bad, I'm afraid,' he replied, lowering his voice and moving closer to Rees's side.

'What happened, did anyone see?'

'You'd better have a word with the copper. He's with the girl—sitting in the back of the ambulance, they are.'

In the back of the ambulance a police constable was wrapping a coat around the shoulders of a girl. He seemed barely older than she was. He was trying to soothe her:

'Come on love. Take it easy, love,' he said in a practised, professional tone.

Rees stood on the ambulance's step, 'Did she see...? '

'Who are you?'

'Well, I'm from the school, a teacher, and I was wondering if the boy was one of ours. '

'Do you know this girl?'

Rees thought he had seen her, a thin faced wispy blonde in the sixth form block, but with over 300 sixth formers he could hardly place everybody.

'She's not saying a word. Shock. You can look at the lad himself, if they're not moving him. If you ask me, he was larking about, running over to the King's Head to get some ale before stop-tap. '

'Fucking copper,' thought Rees, closing the ambulance door to.

At the side of the road, the blanketed shape lay while the ambulance men fetched their stretcher. All this was too much of a shock, coming at the end of a hectic school day and busy evening. Rees felt the sense of responsibility, of involvement, ebbing away from him into the night.

He did approach the boy though; following the ambulance men back with the stretcher he broke the circle of watchers. The ambulance man who had first talked to Rees lifted the blanket to reveal the dull, pale face of a boy about seventeen. He was unmarked, save for a trickle of blood behind his right ear. It seemed to Rees as neat as make-up painted on. He gazed, with what must have appeared to be fascination, at that spot a full five seconds after the blanket had again been spread. Rees was a camera lens.

'Sir? We found a few pens and this in the gutter where he landed. Didn't stand a chance. Hit by the van, he was, and thrown clean over the top into the road.'

Rees accepted the pens and some papers from the boy. There was a film society membership card; it drifted into focus. He had supervised the printing of that card. His signature, and Mary's were inside: he knew without looking that they were inside. Where was Mary? With the card still closed in his hand, Rees returned to the car. Mary was talking to Sinclair and another boy, Rawlings, who helped with the society.

'Who was it, Sir?' asked Sinclair.

'I don't know him.'

'His name will be on the back of the card, Sir,' said Rawlings.

Turning over the card, Rees read: 'Member... M. Richardson.'

'Isn't he in the first year sixth? Came from Bishop's Sec. at the beginning of term, didn't he?' said Sinclair.

'Look, we'd better go up to the Head's house and tell him about this. You two better get to your bus-stop. There's nothing to be done here now, and your parents will worry about you if you're much later.'

'The ambulance is off,' pointed Rawlings. They followed its unsirened drive as it disappeared down the Rotherham road.

'Do you want me to drive? ' asked Mary, as Rees fumbled with the ignition key.

'Bloody hell, it's only up the back lane to Birdy's place?! I can handle this situation,' snapped Rees, who now welcomed the opportunity to drive up the road, to occupy himself with the detailed actions of the car and convince himself that he was coping in some tangible way.

Rees had never in his 27 years experienced Death with a large 'D'; Death as a personal fact, solid in his life. There was a life's young blood spilled and hardening back there on the road. He wanted to be detached, or at least controlled and professional, like the raw constable and the ambulance men. Rees wanted to cope, to prove himself by accepting and performing the acts necessary after the boy's death. The Head must know first and then God, the parents— someone should ring the parents.

Crowson, the Headmaster, lived close to his school. He was two years off retirement and had felt he'd earned it.

He'd seen the old Grammar School flourish, then become a Comprehensive almost over-night by the uprooting of a dividing hedge with the Secondary Modern and the building of glass-panelled corridors to join with the Grammar School.' Old names die hard.

Though they'd passed the place each day arriving to and from school, Mary and Rees, in common with most of the staff, had never been inside his house, a substantial late '50s detached. The door opened and there was Crowson's squat, solid form in dressing-gown and carpet slippers.

'Why, good evening to you both. Everything Ok at the film club? Come in.' His face darkened as Rees explained the reason for their call. 'Can't find any address, eh?'

'One of the girls thought he'd come from Denton—Bishop's Secondary,' offered Mary.

'We'd better check on the record cards down in the office,' said Crowson, ' Wait for me to put a coat on. A tragedy,' he muttered, and he turned to the stairs, looking now very much his age. The telephone in the hall rang then. It was the police, he said.

All the audience had gone by the time Crowson and Rees were let in the school. Outhwaite the caretaker shrugged his shoulders and fiddled with the bunch of keys; 'Terrible,' he muttered. As each record card snapped past Crowson's thumb, Rees, looking over his shoulder, felt a sort of numb tension building up. He was glad that the job of telling the parents would fall to someone else—Crowson, the Police? Someone else, anyway. It seemed so arbitrary, the event was already distant. Playing God. It was so final. Out of the office window, the street lights glowed a pale yellow and the traffic rolled down the road to Rotherham.

Their drive home was fifteen miles across country, out of the valley and into the flatness of the growing fields and the gouged sand-quarries. It was a slow and measured journey for Mary; a blur of the familiar motions for Rees. In his head swam the turning blue lights, a doorbell, a half-eaten sandwich, a thick milky skin settling across a cup of coffee; and over everything stars like splinters of glass in the sky. That night in bed, his dream drifted beyond his body, the snugness of her arm around his chest, drifted down growing heavy into darkness.

In his morning registration the class was particularly excited. Bindthorpe was a tight, closed village of terraced miners' houses and cramped post-war council estates.

'Most of the kids know more about last night than I do,' thought Rees. Hearsay and rumour—that's what the school ran on, fuelling its collective imagination.

But Mossley, a usually quiet boy who seemed to withdraw behind his long, end-cropped hair, came up to his desk as the rest were leaving for house assembly.

'As you walk along, Sir, you can see the blood on the road where it happened,' he said, and without waiting for a response he walked on after the others.

Rees totalled the marks and entered the number.

Through the house assembly hymn, Crowson's platitudes about loss and road safety and then the games results, blurred into a bizarre confusion for Rees. With the pupils still snaking their way out of the hall, he squeezed out of the side-door. The morning hit him with a blaze of sun, a sharpness of late autumn air. Blood still staining the road-grit?! Christ, something should be done... he could phone someone. Who? The police? The Council? There must be someone responsible. Some people must have to do those things.

He walked towards the staff-room, but stopped outside the main office and pretended to read the day's notices. A typewriter rapped pertly into action: a hustle of bodies from the hall swelled the corridor traffic. Rees felt the pressure to act closing upon him. Without consciously arguing any decision, he walked along to the staff room door and very strangely (like a robot, as one of his sixth formers later reported) turned sharply left into the cleaner's broom cupboard.

There in the pale naked light, the stale air heavy with polish and the abrasive stench of cleaning bottles, Rees's hand closed around a mop handle.

Bill Rowse

At my second school I learned an important lesson about teaching: it isn't the headmaster who runs a school. No, the man with the power is the man who holds the accounts in his hand. Now, he may be variously termed Bursar, Registrar, or some other grand title, but whatever the sign on his door reads you may take it that he's the man to be in with.

Bill Rowse was the bursar at Bindthorpe School. He occupied a huge desk at one end of the general office and at first I wondered why he hadn't insisted on a room of his own. It soon became clear though that it suited Bill to be right in the thick of the daily trials and disputes that the running of a two thousand pupil comprehensive throws up. Bill was somewhere in his fifties and a striking man because of his uncanny resemblance to W.H. Auden. He wore grubby shirts with a constant striped association-of-something tie and the same crumpled suit. His face was almost as gnarled as the poet's, like a long-shot of the moon's surface. There was the constant cigarette and the same sunken eyes. Bill's eyes quizzed you over the top of his reading glasses. Mention money and they would move like two startled apricots in brandy. I'd seen him on the top corridor and in the staff toilet at various times during the first week. He'd be standing at the urinal, his head in a smoke-haze, wheezing like an old steam pump. But I encountered the man in his element on the second Monday of that first Autumn term.

Jimmy Oldham had been voted monitor by 1A, my form for the year. Jimmy's duties included the delivery of the dinner money to the general office. I'd supervise the whole thing the first time, showing him right up to the office counter, but on the second occasion, with Jimmy flying solo, a note had come back querying the amount collected. I went up to investigate the matter during the school assembly. Bill was blunt.

'What a choice for monitor, lad! The Oldhams are as near as damn it the Borgias of Bindthorpe. Notorious they are. A bloody living legend!'

'But we had a vote in class and he won easily,' I said.

'That's hardly surprising. So did Hitler. The little tyke had probably been around twisting locks of hair beforehand.'

'Well, they're only a first form. Quite a nice group, really,' I added.

'Listen, lad,' he leaned further over the cluttered desk, breathing thinly through his wobbling cigarette, 'you're new here. The first thing you've got to realise is that these kids are tough as old boots. Basic rule is to assume that they're fiddling, then that they're lying, especially kids like the Oldhams. All that little Jimmy has to do is mention his brother Dicky and he can name his price around here. Notorious, like I said. Put a copper's eye out and got away with it, did Dicky. Was here a couple of years back. Like the Mafiosi. A proper little bastard, he was.'

Bill's language was, like his constant cigarette, quite detatched from the school atmosphere in which he worked. He smoked and swore with the same breath and it soon became clear to me that this man had a very special position in the place.

In the second half-term I began a school film society and had to formally open an account with Bill for the payment of the lending fees and receipt of the takings. Money was his fascination: counting it, touching it. The man was happy with the stuff in his hands. Coloured change-bags from the bank blossomed on his desk at such times and Bill fussed over them like a flower-arrangement.

'Keep things straight, boy. Nothing worse than shaky books. Good clean columns is the secret.'

And though he spilt ash constantly down his shabby suit, and wore only two different shirts, one white, one green, in my time at the school, the books had a neatness and were handled with the reverence due to a family Bible.

The third film evening we had was Steve McQueen in *Bullitt*, with that archetypal car chase; it was our first big success. The head had finally agreed to my idea of doing a trailer in the lower school assembly, between the day's notices and the house football results. The evening was a rainy one but Steve McQueen and the exploding gas station had packed them in. We were weighed down with sticky loose change and as I could see that the office light was still on I took the money over and knocked the door. Bill was doubled over the desk but his head came up as I entered. His face looked awful—'Like a devil's sick of sin,' flashed through my mind, but it didn't fit the man. Bill's worries, whatever they were, fell short of the cosmic.

'What's the matter, lovely boy?' he slurred, his eyes taking the colour of a nearly-emptied bottle of Scotch that stood next to the phone on the desk.

'I've brought the film money—we've done really well with this one—see!' I chinked the bags of change in both hands. 'Could I leave it with you now ? Save messing about in the morning.'

'Have a drink, young Rees,' he offered. It was obvious that I'd better humour him, so I poured a small measure of Scotch into the second glass.

'Always drink with two glasses, see,' he said, crypticallly, 'shows you believe in life.'

He asked me if I realised how long he'd been in the school and I said no.

'Fourteen years in the navy, Merchant Navy, you know—none of that Royal Navy bull's milk and moonshine. Running this place is like a ship—that's the point about the boss. I'm Crowson's right-hand man, officer in charge. Eight years. Since the war that creature hasn't really lived. You know, it was like that for a lot of chaps. How could you settle into civvy street after living for three or four years with your guts in your mouth and a system of common-sense rules ? That's the trouble with these kids, little sods like Oldham, all of them—no system. Whip their bottoms raw!'

I realised for the first time that people like Bill worked themselves into special positions. Being rude and hectoring would become associated with doing the job efficiently. The institution was getting a bonus. Bill kept a tight fist on the books, and added colour to a grey place. It might upset the more sensitive members of staff and pupils, but Crowson evidently saw his bursar as his adjutant. With Bill around, the war's values lived on.

'Anything we want—Bill can get it,' Crowson had boasted when introducing him after I'd been told that the job was mine.. This was substantiated by staffroom stories, not to mention the fruit and vegetable business which he ran regularly, every Friday, under the school stage. The staff left for the weekend, their briefcases bulging with Bill's provisions at prices lower than Doncaster market the following day. Certainly, as I came more and more into contact with him through the workings of the film society, his various and dubious interests became more apparent.

'Just had this bloke on the line,' he said, one morning, exhaling smoke, 'offering me thirty-three stone of cod-heads.'

'Codheads?' I said, expecting a joke.

'From Hull,' Bill added significantly, a worried look in his eyes. 'I asked the daft sod, what would I be wanting with fish-heads in a bloody school?'

'Soup?' I suggested, looking for a smile, 'Or cats?'

Bill's eyes cleared instantly. 'Bloody catfood—that's it!' he exclaimed, bringing his fist down onto the desk and knocking a cup of tea over a pile of invoices.

Bill warmed to me in a sort of dirty uncle way, as the success of the film society grew. But as our film shows became more of a regular thing I realised that Bill's drinking in the office after school hours was an established and frequent habit. One night when I went to take the money in, he turned on me. 'You're a bloody nuisance with your loose change and grubby coins and phone calls. And I bet you're not even taking a slice for yourself, are you ? Grow up, my dear boy. Who checks this stuff ?' And he scattered the contents of a silver bag over the desk and onto the floor. 'These snotty kids who run your films for you wouldn't miss a quid, would they? Put it in your tank for the travelling. No-one gives you owt, as they say in this dump, for nowt in this life. You and me—we're a rarer breed than these Yorkies, eh?' I left him very drunk and morose that evening.

In the second term two incidents involved Bill. The troubles in Ireland had made depressingly frequent features on television and the first bombings over here on the mainland had made everybody jumpy. One Monday we had an alarm in the third period. The kids went wild, spilling out of their classrooms and going like crazed ants in all directions. Harvey and Harlow and Miss Paddock eventually succeeded in briefing the equally confused staff, and some semblance of a drill was achieved in the top tennis courts. The day was a disaster though, with no-one settling back to order or work and the kids were as high as kites. What made us all really angry was the fact that it had been a hoax call. Bill burst into the staffroom at afternoon break with a face fit to explode.

'Bloody hoax—and Mrs Travis panicked in the office!'

The Head addressed the school the following morning and words such as 'appalling', 'hooligan', 'fibre', 'coward' and 'disintegrate' were emphasised by his right fist on the lectern. 'Rather like Chaplin as Hitler,' someone remarked.

However, later that day the alarm was again raised. This time it was Harlow who had taken the call. The school poured out of its cells and frolicked onto the playing fields.

'I could see n-no ch-choice,' he said afterwards, 'the voice sounded f-foreign to me.'

It was obvious to everyone that the whole business would quickly break what semblance of discipline we clung to at Bindthorpe. Every kid with a grievance, everyone afraid of having no homework to hand in had an escape route. Telephone lines to the school would melt under the strain.

Bill had his own way of doing things, though. On the following Monday a call came through which he picked up. He listened. The eyes narrowed and pulled back into that relief-map of a face. Then he uttered slowly into the phone what Mrs Travis would later refer to as 'an expletive of the worst kind, believe me.'

There were no more bomb calls.

Bill had that special position: placed firmly on the top corridor where the decisions were made or botched up, but acting beyond the conventions of office. You couldn't hold a man to account if he owned nothing and owed no-one.

The second incident that Spring Term was indisputably Crowson's fault. His love of the armed services meant that the school was lumbered with every military band, Alsatian handler and motor-cycle display team doing the rounds. Lesson plans gave way and anyone who was not on a G.C.E. syllabus was drafted in as potential cannon-fodder.

What a god-send was Albert Wright to such a man. Albert turned up one Monday morning and presented himself rigidly to Crowson's door and its traffic lights. The Old Man's elbow brushed over his desk button, his green light flashed and in Albert marched.

'Morning to you, sah! Wright,sah. I was a pupil at the school a couple of years back. Left early. Joined the army. Home on leave and thought I'd pop in and look the old school over. Offer me services. Bit of extra duties, sah. Gym. Anything to help, like.'

Crowson was hooked instantly. Here was a non-academic type; thick perhaps,but solid as a rock, who'd fitted perfectly into the military system. A corridor slouch transformed by discipline into a Regular. 'Yes, Wright. Yes. Of course, welcome back.'

Kennedy the games man, being a bit of a fascist bastard himself (cold showers and towel-slapped backsides a speciality) and further, needing to humour the Old Man to get a new strip for the soccer team, accepted Albert as a helper. By the end of the week Kennedy was feet-up in his room having a crafty smoke and the morning paper whilst Albert barked press-ups at his classes in the gym.

By Wednesday, Albert was seen in the staff-room pouring tea. There were serious rumblings from all sides, but as no-one could actually remember his being in school as a pupil, nothing firm could be levelled against him. The crunch came when Dolly Adams Needlework barged in through Crowson's red light, making him spill his mid-morning tea over a batch of letters to the governors. Dolly had a serious complaint concerning Vernon Waincote from her 3E . Vernon was an obese lad who chewed constantly and picked his nose.He was excused games with a doctor's note for asthma. Albert had taunted the boy and had made him hang from the beam, attempting an impossible three chins. Vernon had rolled out of the gym blubbering and holding his heart.

'Vernon Waincote is an emotional fatty and there will be repercussions, mark my words,' pronounced Dolly Adams in the staffroom. The boy's mother was up to school in a fury the following morning.

'Who's the naffing comic been messing about wi' me Vernon?' she screeched down the top corridor. Crowson's light flashed red.

Mrs Waincote was a shop-steward at the local elastics factory and was more than a match for Crowson. She was on to the whole business like a shot. Albert, it turned out, was not in the army. He'd never even blown a bugle in the cadets. The boy was unemployed and taken to periods of delusion. His social worker had a file on him that read like a novel—son of Walter Mitty. Old Crowson hadn't checked on him at all.

That day, when the mother eventually emerged from the head's room, Bill waylaid her and practically pushed her through into the general office, clearing Mrs Travis and the girls out and locking the door. No-one knew precisely what happened in there during that fifteen minutes, but the Waincote woman came out hard-faced and quietly left the premises. Some people thought that money must have changed hands; certainly, Vernon was persona grata at Bill's break-time tuck window for the rest of that year. No queuing, and generous helpings of everything. His weight problem was, after all, emotional.

Others said that it was bound to be something to do with Bill's mysterious friend, Joseph.He was a strange pop-eyed man who often drove Bill home the worse for wear after his late evening sessions of drinking in the office. He worked as an overseeer at Grainger's Plastics and could, presumably, put the finger on Vera Waincote.

Crowson was visibly shaken by the incident and stayed in his room for weeks—like Howard Hughes—without the money.

The end for Bill came just after I'd left Yorkshire. He'd been going downhill fast all the previous term. He would appear at film evenings, barging in and glaring through watery eyes at the screen. He began to push the kids about in the corridors and one night almost fell through the doors of the big hall and into the projector-stand, sending the Bell & Howell crashing to the floor and narrowly missing Millbrough's toes. Joseph was more often in evidence too, beginning to turn up mid-afternoons to hang about at the main entrance until the end of school rush had subsided, and then waltzing up to the office to Bill. He'd apparently given up his job at Grainger's and now he and Bill were said to share a flat in the village, though no-one knew exactly where.

I felt that I was well out of the place, in a new school back in Wales. Just before I left though a break-in was discovered in the general office. A largish sum of money had apparently been taken, including Bill's tuck-shop takings for the week, and the money from the cigarettes, tights and biscuits he sold to the staff. A detective arrived with two lumbering coppers and generally disrupted the block for the rest of that morning. They dusted the area with dainty powder-puff brushes, but the whole school must have left its mark there. Without a lead, nothing came of the incident. But before the end of term it had happened again—the hatch through which registers and dinner monies were handed each morning was left in splinters, and in addition the lock on the main office door had been crudely forced. It was a strangely bungled job, and reeked of professionally-feigned clumsiness.

Joseph began to appear at the school gates in a new sheepskin coat which fitted superbly, if incongruously, over his baggy trousers and worn, black shoes.

One evening a month or two later the police called at their flat and found Bill and Joseph literally with their trousers down. Unfortunately for the two of them, young Jimmy Oldham was in a similar predicament on the sofa. Jimmy was one of life's survivors and when questioned talked like a budgie. Jimmy's break-in was forgotten in the face of the sodomy charge and apparently a tidied-up version made the inside pages of some of the Sundays. Bill, it emerged was an old-time queen from his navy days, procuring for Joseph and himself, and given his business drive, possibly others. At one point in the proceedings there was even a whisper rippling against Crowson, but the Old Man was a magistrate of some years standing and whether there was any truth in it or not the suggestion was quickly washed away.

A colleague sent me the Leeds newspaper cutting. Bill got four years and Joseph five. Shed no tears, I thought, justice has been done. But it wouldn't surprise me if within weeks Bill was getting the prison governor cut-price stationery and sorting out the kitchen supplies. In his prime, I picture him, with his constant, cremated cigarette, taking mouth-washes of Scotch, at his desk like a captain on the bridge of his ship, navigating his way through moral icebergs and legal squalls. But the way he dispatched that bomb hoaxer. The word for that is 'style'.

Into August

I'm flying over the Saranac mountains, flying into August.
The big, curly-haired guy asks if there's anyone else from
Lake Placid.

*I'm a Conroy, Nick and Robert and me—Richard Conroy—
three boys—our father just died in the hospital. Lung cancer. And the
way it works out it was fine—we were all with him for a reunion last
week. And now this week I'm flying back for the funeral. Lived in
Lake Placid all my life. Willard and 4th. Lake Placid High. What
is your name, ma'am?*

Conroy, sitting in the front, has been turning round
since we levelled out from Syracuse airport, with loud jokes
about the twenty-seater and the two blurred propellors. He
claims the co-pilot read a magazine at take-off. I dislike him
for his clumsy humour, his irritations. Then his stream of
words finds a level. He is, after all, flying to his father's
funeral and is sharing the pain with us, sending it back
down the length of the small plane until the engines and air
whistle it into nonsense.

I guess he was slowing down for the last two years.

Gil and Deborah back in Binghamton have given me some
books and an etching of a reclining nude. It was a good
visit. And now I am reading Ron Kovic's book about their
war. He's in a Vets hospital in the Bronx, lying in his own
shit, dead from the chest down. He has won the Purple
Heart. Soon he will decide to write this book, about
Vietnam and after. All the time, whether he sleeps or cries
or writes, the bag strapped to his leg fills with waste. The
writing is his other tube out to the world. His future
streams back in to him, pressured through it.

Far below, pines cover the Saranac hills like wiry fur on
an animal. It is July and boats make bird shapes in the
clustered lakes. On the first of August I promised myself I
would get drunk. It is a year since my father died, right to

144

the day. He was slumped on the toilet seat and my mother half-carried him to the bed. His last breath—the ceiling, the wardrobe, the tiny window. Five hours gone from us by the time I had driven down to Pembrokeshire.

How quickly the flesh falls away from the living. His lips shrinking back from the swollen gums, the eyes closed, a streak of shit on his pyjamas.

On my third day in Vermont, I wanted to drink down that pity. It was gesture meaningless to anyone else. The party got rained out. Past one in the morning I calculated the time-difference, how it must be at home, and in my body's time. The last dribblings of the year since he died. That concern with accuracy and commemoration is a sort of defence; the way we pick our cuticles to occupy our hands. How we need to keep score and map the events of days and weeks.

It's a long walk. Between the lights the pathway back to the dormitory sinks away into the night. I navigate by touch, hands stretched out from my sides. Fronds with the wetness still on them, thistle, Queen Anne's lace, Goldenrod, my shoes steadily holding to the packed earth and gravel. Though my body pulls taut in the blackness, I keep to the same pace. Proving myself against old fears. A bat crosses low in front of me. The crickets sing like machines. I hold to the same pace, moving from light to light.

There were nights he kept us waiting up after the tv had finished, with me straining to read a book under the tired, yellow lights. My mother would boil milk for another last nightcap, neither of us saying anything.

His headlamps flooding the room, then swinging by the side of the house: a car door, fumbling to get in quietly through the kitchen. Then some nights—nothing. We'd go out to find him hunched over the wheel as in thought, or slumped back in the seat, his head loose on his shoulders, the veins in his eyes filled with blood, his lips slack and wet.

In the morning he'd act as if nothing had happened, tickling and teasing her, asking about the lessons I had that day, or about a rugby game.

He'd say—*I can drive better drunk than most men do sober.*

Always he came home. There was never a mark on the car.

On Lake Champlain the yachts flowered like Queen Anne's lace, from such a height, so delicate, so perfectly white.

I could have answered Conroy, joined him in his words, in another place—a train perhaps, the rhythm of the rails, trees and telegraph poles opening up our talk. We would tell, by turns, of their unfinished lives, the faults, the drinking, the mean, cutting disappointments of the two fathers. How for us it would be different; how the death of one's father clarified everything. Their own ambitions and their ambitions for us in the world resolving into something bigger, something to do with making sense of the whole mess. We would say *fucking mess* and shake our heads and clench a fist.

But the plane was too small, too noisy and one of us too close to home. I drew back into Kovic's book, leaving Conroy to talk out the ache in his guts. Doing it among those upstate people—business men, an aunt and her niece in new-bought clothes, a baby in the back seat, nursed, but crying.

The photograph I carry with me is a transparency from January last year. It is a room in Morriston hospital and my father sits forward in an armchair, my son held between his knees. Gareth is wearing the red football kit he's had for Christmas, his face wrinkled as it Dad had tickled his ribs. It is a good shot—clear. Holding the slide up before my desk-lamp I can see the overgrown grass through the hospital window. A wet January, as it always is in Wales, the grass sodden and bent over. My father's face is clinging to its skull. Under the paisley pyjamas he wears a huge dressing over the wound. There is a crescent from chest to back where they rolled the skin up in a flap to dig at the rotten lung. Imagine being unhorsed by the clumsy arc of a peasant's scythe.

I brought the photograph with me to start my writing. I came here wanting to write about these things. I know that now.

The trees shake their snow
like a dog at your window.

The world is plant and animal –
it melts, it dies, it falls.

So we make of it art.
Those dry brown grasses in the snow:

The summer's Queen Anne's lace,
old women laying their bones against white sheets.

That gust of wind, the hand
lifts snow dust from the pines.

It powders across the field, turns to
breath in the air. Something to do

with letting go.

At Syracuse airport again Deborah and Gil come out to photograph the plane as I leave. I lean forward in the seat to smile, stomach tight against the belt, my head framed perfectly in the round glass of the porthole.

The engines start up. Gil waves. He silently shouts— *Look out—on your left—Lake Champlain.* Deborah's mouth says, *I promise to send you a copy.*

Canada Dry

'Why Edward, this is beautiful. Just beautiful.' Ruth stood out in the entrance hall and narrowed her eyes towards a picture which neither Martin nor Sally could see from the living room.

'It's Dearnley trying to be Hopper,' she said with certainty, 'the shadows, the cafe windows. Those Thirties New York streets.'

'It's Wallace, Raymond Wallace. Middle years,' said her host. 'Ruth, I love that dress; turquoise is your colour and it flows around you.'

'Yes, derivative Hopper,' mused Ruth, as she moved on down the hall, 'and thank you, Edward. Our host is dapper as always.'

'I bought it, if I recall, at a group show in Montreal in the Sixties,' said Edward, pouring a second brandy into Martin's glass.

'You've got a beautiful house,' said Sally, 'some lovely things.'

'Thank you. Some brandy?'

Sally declined, saying she's had enough. As if to test that, she rose from the Chesterfield and moved over to the fireplace where the spring-cleaned grate held an ornate brass poker and tongs set.

'This is a fine brandy,' said Martin, taking a large sip and closing his eyes on the warmth filling his throat, 'the same vintage as that superb Citroen of yours, Edward?'

'I doubt that,' said Edward.

'Oh, my word! This must be a Garner—that slash of orange—it's Hugh Garner.'

'Which are you looking at, Ruth? The one next to the mirror?'

'Yes, did I tell you I met him—at a reception Jack and I went to in the I of T gallery a year before Jack died.'

'If it's the one to the left of the mirror, a Mexican scene, then it's Jacques Blaise. He gave me that when we were in

148

California.' Edward smiled and poured himself another brandy.

'Come and look at these,' said Sally, who had picked up one of a group of small carvings on the mantelpiece. 'Come on, Martin,' she said.

The smooth stone seal felt cool and alive in her hand. She wanted to share the feeling, to draw Martin off the Chesterfield where he seemed to be sinking with his brandy.

'Oh, may I touch these?'

'Of course. They exist to be touched, not merely to be looked at. Please, enjoy my house.'

'Who did them? Are they Canadian?' asked Martin

'Very Canadian. They're Inuit carvings. The stone is soapstone—soft and easily worked. But easily broken as a result. The others are not ivory but caribou antler or fossilised whale bones. See how they use the line of the bone, and the coral effect of the decaying bone.'

Martin ran his fingers along the back of a bird. He picked it up and, yes, it was deceptive, the weight he'd seen wasn't there in the touch. The wings were smoothed and feathery. He could believe that they flew. A bird, a seal, a woman, a hunter. Two Eskimos lifting a seal: the bulk of the dead seal hung over their linked arms—food, light and clothing cradled between them. Their squat, muscular bodies tense and lifting, caught at the precise moment when they had the body of the seal equally between them.

'This is wonderful,' said Sally, replacing the seal.

'I could steal this one,' said Martin, smiling at Edward, and he held out his glass to take more brandy.

'This harlequin,' called Ruth, 'the lithograph?'

'Where?'

'Here in the dining room. Edward, why can't you show me properly around your place?'

'I wouldn't dream of doing that,' he said. And then turning to Martin and Sally, 'Ruth is taking so much pleasure from her visit—like an old woman in a candy store.' He raised his voice to tell Ruth, 'It's a Mark Allen etching.'

'Ruth's not really old. Is she Martin? She's coped really well with this awkward husband of mine.'

'She has,' agreed Martin, turning to Edward, 'but I'm not awkward. I've given way to all her whims, her desires, her imaginings. It's her home and we want to be as little trouble as possible. I've even moved to sit in the back seat of her bloody car because she says I make her nervous. I make her nervous!'

'Ssh!' cautioned Sally.

'Well, it's difficult having two sensitive artists under one roof,' said Martin.

'I'm sure your wife is just the perfect referee for a tough game,' said Edward.

'Splintering sticks and hissing ice, in one of those end of the season play-offs,' said Martin, performing. He took in the last of the brandy in his glass and returned to the Chesterfield.

Edward was glad Ruth had brought her guests. Maybe he'd had too few people around through the winter. The girl was bright and fresh, an English rose gracing her thorny husband. Though her slacks didn't quite go with the green blouse and her flats did nothing for her posture, he noted. The British: when they were informal they seemed to lose their way, dress-wise.

Ruth had phoned that morning—it would be their last whole day with her in Toronto and so she'd booked a table at the Vernay Clam House. Did he remember they'd been there a year back with that painter... Tilson was it, or Wilson?—anyway, this English writer she'd exchanged with was quite a rising star—two stories in the *Hudson Review* and one coming up in *The New Yorker* and his wife was a real lady.

Edward hadn't seen Ruth for months, not seen her properly to talk to since Passover at the Weider's in mid-winter. He'd worked with her husband Jack in the History Department at McMaster and then renewed the acquaintance several years later when they moved into the city. Jack had been completing his doctorate on the 1812 War with the USA, whilst Ruth had just published her edition of Singer's stories. The book had slipped out of print before he won the Nobel, the year everyone wanted to read Isaac Bashevis Singer. Ruth had raised hell with her short-sighted publishers, Jack got dragged in and, who knows, that could have brought on his heart failure.

The son, Jeff, had held his mother's arm at the funeral. Edward was at the other elbow. He'd taken a sabbatical at the end of that semester and gone to Europe. Fifty-two years old then. So why should he suddenly need a wife?

'Edward, I love your house. You have such good things,' said Ruth from the doorway, standing there, sweeping a gaze around the walls.

'We were just admiring the Eskimo, sorry, Inuit, pieces,' said Sally.

'Why, that would be the thing for you to take back to England,' suggested Ruth enthusiastically. 'Real Canada. I have a couple of small, but very good pieces of Inuit art on that high shelf next to the door. Didn't I show them to you? I thought I did. Anyway, I can phone the MacDonald Gallery in the morning and John MacDonald, who's an old flame, can show you something suitable. Genuine Inuit, and not too high a price. John is such a sweet man. Just take the subway to Spadina and it's two blocks south. Perfect.'

'Lovely,' said Sally, smiling.

'We may, my darling, be skint,' soured Martin, 'anyway, what do those carvings cost?'

'Oh, I paid thirty or forty,' said Ruth.

'But Ruth,' said Edward, 'you've had those years.'

'I bought them when we moved back to Toronto and Jack went to an auction. It was before the galleries arranged for fair distribution of royalties to the artists in the communities. Well, maybe you're right about the price, Edward.'

'You should get something for under a hundred—maybe one-twenty,' he said.

'That's settled, then' said Ruth, sitting down in the arm chair next to the coffee table and picking up a magazine.

'So you fly out tomorrow night. Are you sorry to leave Canada?' Edward settled back in his chair.

'Sally's missed the kids. Well, we both have, of course,' said Martin. 'It's been too short a trip to really see the country, and yet I think we are both ready to go back. It's been a fascinating introduction. A taster.'

'It's been a nice break though for some of us,' Sally said, pointedly at Martin,' a well-earned break too.'

'I've worked just as hard as you over the last few months, let me tell you, lady. My wife, Edward, suffers under the illusion that typewriters work by themselves. They're degenerate playthings for those with pretentious visions of themselves and their surroundings. Whereas you will know that we bleed from our foreheads with the strain.'

'Try 4F on a Friday afternoon—then you'd need a holiday!'

'Just because I escaped that school grind. I dug an escape tunnel. And now it's really your choice to work full time, Sally.'

'And who'd keep you in squash racquets and records if I didn't?'

'Are you saying I'm a kept man? Martin pushed his free arm around Sally and tickled her. She yelled and slopped her drink over the arm of the Chesterfield.

'Stupid! That was silly. Can't you take a joke? Shall I get a cloth from the kitchen, Edward?' Their host insisted that it was nothing and fetched a cloth himself.

'A joke. It was a joke.' Martin fielded the look Sally gave him and moved to the end of the seat. He smiled to himself and finished his drink. 'I'm sorry, Edward, that was silly. Perhaps we're a bit high with leaving and everything.'

Ruth, still flicking pages and remaining above it all, said, 'Edward, have you seen this interview/feature thing on Rachler in *Canadian Book News*? Where is it? Here, last month's issue—no, it's February. Well, how could I have missed that? Anyway, it's that woman Bennett from Buffalo scurrying across the border again to pick up extra bucks and credits. Well, in any case, how often do we need to peck at the gullet of a writer? Baring the innards like that.'

'He's a wonderful writer through and people want to pin down the secret of making it big like that. They want to learn about it. OK, maybe Rachler was ploughing the same ground rather too often; all that sensitive boy stuff of his. Growing up in the ghetto and launching out into the unsuspecting world.' Edward turned to Sally and Martin, 'Is Rachler big in England too?'

'But look, Edward, she makes that point with some smart-arsed quote from someone, Homberger or someone, yes Honberger,' Ruth persisted, 'Listen—'Rachler's work has a real quality. I buy his book everytime he writes it.' It is smart-arsed isn't it? You have to admit that, Edward.'

'Ruth, I'm not arguing. It's smart-arsed. And I've read that article—it's on my coffee-table and I've read it.'

'But listen to this, Edward. 'In an age when minority is majority, when WASP is definitely un-chic, Rachler was in first with a colourful, engaging Jewish minority of mythic, if dubious, properties in Montreal.' That's terrible. That's just so bitchy. You don't have to like him to see what he was doing in those early stories was worthwhile.'

'I didn't read it as being that aggressive; anyway it's a hackish sort of piece with quotes and gossip from all over, bunched in with an interview. Probably done over the phone.'

'She called collect, I bet,' said Ruth clutching the magazine.

'What does it matter? There are books—so there have to be articles, reviews. My novel...ah, who cares?'

'I didn't know you'd written a novel, Edward?' said Martin, and straightened up.

'It was nothing much. I needed to work some things out and writing another essay on the Canadian Pacific or a paper on early provincial government wasn't quite the way for me to do it at that stage.'

'But novels—those are the real thing. The real writing. The big canvas,' said Martin.

'I would burn every copy of mine to have written Chekhov's 'The Grasshopper' or John Cheever's 'The Swimmer'. Little jewels'

'Edward, your book is fine. Don't listen to him, Martin. It was a pretty good book,—and the reviews were good, pretty good all round, I remember.'

It seemed to Martin that Ruth spoke with genuine concern.

'Pretty good is what I mean. Precisely,' said Edward, pouring another drink for himself.

Martin wasn't convinced. A novel. That was it. The wide canvas with room to move your characters around and paint the world in sweeps. He sulked inwardly as Ruth started up again with other extracts from the magazine. He'd never do it, that ambitious sweep of narrative. His pieces were short fictions—some closely observed details from life experience, some filched from reading. He could do the sensitive growing boy trick—the sexual embarrassment, the grubby innocence, but his patch wasn't particularly ethnic or poetic. He'd swap the Home Counties for the East End or the Falls Road any day. It all fell short of Rachler's ready myths. Imagination. His dynamo had barely turned over. Close observation and misty-edged memory was no more than first-cousin to journalism. A hack with pretensions. He put his glass down on the carpet: the brandy was doing more harm than good.

Ruth let out a long sigh, 'Would you look at this. Edward, have you seen this notice of Grace Packer's poems? "The strongest voice since Adrienne Rich and Sylvia Plath".' 'I ask you, what is that supposed to mean?'

'Well, someone likes her, evidently.'

'I don't understand it. She's just riding in on the women's wave. I mean, how many ladies of persuasion do we need? They've got their freedom and now they're crowing for a higher status than the rest of us.'

'But a lot of those things had to be won, didn't they, Ruth?' said Sally. 'We had ground to make up.'

'My dear, I'm not denying that. Lord knows, I've seen things get better in the sixty years of my life. Of course we need to win an equal share. But you'd see if you were over for longer, or had to work here, how so many things have turned sour—against men (well, you'd expect that) against marriage, against straights. If you aren't a minority here now, you're a minority.'

'Dykes' Rights,' mumbled Martin.

'Now Martin, I don't like that sort of word. It's offensive. When I began a college career women were only just emerging from tweeds and a nun's vocation. That wasn't right. Male teachers were expected to marry, while the women were supposed to shrivel like prunes. That was stupid and had to be swept away once and for all.'

'But you have your Chair now, Ruth,' said Sally.

'It's not a 'chair' exactly. This isn't Cambridge, but yes, I have tenure and a full professorship at Grant Rogers. I don't say it can't be done and I'm not being personal, but will you listen to this:

I wake with your
hair in
my mouth. Love
we have been
womanly we
have been
sisters we
fuck politically.

That's just climbing on the bandwagon.'

'And on your sisters,' said Martin, not quite under his breath.

Edward sighed and said, 'It isn't great poetry. And didn't Auden go beyond sexism with that Thirties lyric?'

Martin got to his feet and crossed to the fireplace. ''Lay your sleeping head, my love, Faithless on my human arm, Time and something...' isn't it strange how you can forget even the most wonderful lines? They all slide away.'

'Like people, ' said Sally. 'You didn't go on to tell us about your novel, Edward. Please do.'

'Edward will give you a copy. Won't you, Edward?' Ruth said.

'I certainly will not,' said Edward, quietly, but firmly. 'Being given someone's novel is the worst thing. If they are

155

close friends then you have to offer some sort of commentary within two weeks, or you avoid them; you dread a phone call. And even if you're far from home and unlikely to meet the writer again, there's always that nagging guilt about the thing. No, if Sally or Martin want to dig out *Channels of Regret* then that's fine. I'm not going to chain it around their necks before they leave, though.'

'Martin has plans to buy up dozens of the New Yorker issue with his story in and send signed copies to friends and influential contacts. Aren't you dear?'

'Rubbish!' retorted Martin, who reddened and glared across at his traitorous wife. 'Who is this?' he asked, diverting the conversation by picking up a silver gilt framed photograph. 'Is it you as a younger man, Edward?'

'Do you think so?' Edward smiled, 'It's my father.'

'Who was it—Ginsberg or Updike—who said that the only really valuable copies of his book were those that were unsigned?' ventured Ruth.

'Rare,' said Martin.

'Rare, that's it,' beamed Ruth, ''The only rare copies of my books are those that are unsigned.' Isn't that witty?'

'That's my father, but there he's in his early fifties.'

'Remarkable. Look Sally, isn't it a remarkable likeness? It could be you, Edward.'

Sally took hold of the frame. 'It is it really is you to a T, Edward. I only hope my husband looks as fine and distinguished at that age.'

'I could sing the beauties of Lauren Bacall,' countered Martin. 'The thinking man's wank!' said Sally.

'Now there's a woman who had style,' Martin accounted. 'So rare— style.'

'Oh, Edward used to do a marvellous Humphrey Bogart. Go on—do Bogart for us,' pleaded Ruth.

'I've never in my life impersonated Bogart. In fact, I don't remember doing anyone else either. What are you thinking of, Ruth?'

'Well I must be mistaken then,' Ruth was a little ruffled.

'Martin used to be good at people, didn't you?' said Sally.

156

'What do you mean? Don't women get some funny ideas, Edward?'

Sally's face hardened. 'There's nothing too funny about most of the ideas men have got, is there, Ruth? You take my brilliant, not-so-young husband there, poised as he is on the edge of greatness and the New Yorker. When we met at college he did good impressions—the Goons. You know the Goons. The radio programme. Much loved by the Prince of Wales. Martin did Eccles, Neddie and Bloodnok. All the bloody time he did those characters. He had two voices: he was either the concerned, intelligent student of Literature, or he was a bloody Goon character. I was wooed, if that's what it was, by a Goon.'

There was silence. Sally felt as if she'd gone too far. She stood up, and finished her drink in one swallow.

'I don't think we ever had that radio show here,' said Ruth.

Sally asked directions to the lavatory, then clumped up the stairs.

Martin said, 'I'm sorry. The trip's been a strain for her. She's not as used to flying and I'm sure she's beginning to miss the kids badly. I don't suppose you've even heard of the Goons. Right through our school-days, they were the show everybody listened to,' he smiled to himself. 'Radio programme I mean—zany, strange characters. Stupid voices —a sort of Theatre of the Absurd without pretensions. What's called Classic British Humour now. Everybody, well, lads of my age, did these voices. It was a nervous thing. Really, a voice is always that, isn't it? Something to hide behind.'

'Why don't you do one for us?' asked Ruth.

Martin coloured. 'I couldn't. Not after all that from Sally.'

'Go on,' persisted Ruth, 'while she's at the bathroom.'

Martin hesitated, then screwed up his lips. 'Phew—I can't,' he blew out.

'I understand,' said Ruth.

'I once roomed with a guy who could do a marvellous Jimmy Stewart,' said Edward.

Ruth's face relaxed into a victorious smile. 'Ah, that's it,' she said, obscurely it seemed to Martin.

'OK. Here goes,' said Martin. He took a deep breath and launched into the high, zany Spike Milligan voice. 'Hey-ho Bloodnok and Moriarty approach! They must not see me. Mm, Min, Mm, Mm—Neddie!'

Neither Edward nor Ruth knew what to say. Martin sat down again, sullen.

'It's really quite incomprehensible unless you know the original. You see, there wasn't much point in my doing it,' he said.

'Good humour, like a good wine, doesn't travel very well,' ventured Edward. 'I expect all that classic TV comedy —Burns and Allen, Sergeant Bilko—I suppose none of that stuff would cross the Atlantic too well.'

Martin pointed out, 'On the contrary, I was weaned on Phil Silvers, Sergeant Bilko and Private Doberman. The Bilko Show was unmissable. Every Saturday night. My dad and I used to fall about.'

Ruth said, 'I always think humour is so difficult.'

'You mention that Burns and Allen Show, Edward,' said Martin, ignoring Ruth. 'Now there was a real problem. We didn't have shows like that made in Britain and I remember having problems with the whole concept of the thing. I mean, part of that show would be front of the stage curtain and the rest a sort of sit-com with George Burns and Gracie Allen at home. And do you remember the coloured servant, the black guy what was his name?'

'Rochester.'

'Yes, that's right, Rochester. He was years ahead of Civil Rights. Well, what confused me were the switches from the sitcom parts to the stand-up jokes when Burns used to come out of the set and tell gags. He'd walk right out of the sitting room, towards the camera. The curtains would close behind him and he'd start into a monologue about Gracie and the whole time he'd be sucking his cigar. Not that I understood the jokes, but the audience would roll about. It would have been a real audience in those days too and no canned laughter. I don't know what Sally's bitching about—everyone did those voices.'

Edward rose and left for the kitchen saying he'd make some coffee. Ruth sighed and finally gave up on the Rachler article. 'May I borrow this issue of Canadian Books?' she called through to the kitchen.

'Please, take it. I read little in it anyway.'

'He's a nice man,' offered Martin, 'I'm glad you suggested the meal this evening.'

'Oh, I'm very fond of Edward,' said Ruth. 'I should see him more often, but things get so hectic at the university. Anyway, he's retired now and is always on a plane somewhere, or up in his cabin. Everyone said he should publish a second novel, but it's never happened. It's like he's written one and that was it. Enough. Wish satisfied.' She walked over to look at the bureau with a fine roll top. Then she moved to the fireplace. She picked up the photograph and looked at it long and hard.

'Was this taken in Toronto, Edward?' But her question was lost somewhere in the hallway for Edward had started up the coffee grinder.

Sally held on to the edge of the wash-basin. A wave of lightness swept across her head, then passed, and she focussed into the mirror. Thirty-two. Middle of the way. Too much brandy. Or not enough.

They'd both needed this break and the writers' exchange had been a way of getting out of the country. She couldn't understand now the bouts of guilt she'd had before leaving the children with her mother. They all needed a change. Returning to teaching had pushed her back into the world. Richard and Beth were in their own school worlds too now. Now it seemed that they were four individuals again, having individual lives in addition to their collective one as a family.

Over the last ten days she had felt herself growing back closer to Martin. At home, stuck in the round of meals, ferrying the kids, baby sitters and the strain of work, they had grown in parallel, like plants sharing a pot. It was a strong growth, but firm, rubbery, crudely groping for support. 'At home with the creepers.' So in a sense, these days in Canada had frightened her. Wide days of freedom, leisurely browsing through stores and galleries. Talking into the early hours; making love in the mornings when Ruth had left the house. Long, slow breakfasts of coffee and fresh orange juice with maple toast. The new shape of each day pointed up the dull sameness that life at home had become. With the restricting, shaping force of family life temporarily removed, she had felt at times a light-headedness. Things could be loose, independent, and dangerous.

Two days before they'd visited Niagara. It was so commercial, really, a gross self-parody—but the Falls themselves were magnificent, taking your breath away. They'd posed, leaning back against the railings above the Horseshoe Falls while an elderly American man had used their camera. 'Throw her over!' he'd shouted, waving his arms. And Martin had picked her up without warning and lifted her precariously on to the guard-rail. She screamed, but he'd held her there, doing a Tarzan grunt, while the delighted old man had shot off the reminder of their roll of film. By the time he had put her back down on her feet they'd attracted the attention of most of the visitors on that cold clear Easter day. She laughed with relief, but felt uncertain about the act. That night in the motel bed she'd turned away from his overtures. Then, submitting to their mutual need, had taken control of their love-making, racing ahead of him, scratching his shoulder as she came.

The memories ran out and she re-focussed herself in the mirror, catching herself unawares—an intense, rather romantic look, she thought. She ran the water.

'Now I remember, Edward, you always used to add cinnamon when you served coffee. This is fine. Tell me, when was that photograph taken? It was in Toronto, North Street, wasn't it?'

'Ruth, dear, the photograph dates from the end of the war. I was scrubbed and fresh out of the navy and Dad wanted all of us to have our photos done. I'd brought back this classy camera from the Pacific and said I'd do everyone in turn. So that's what we did. I posed the whole family one by one and Dad took me to complete the set. And that was in Ottawa.'

'Well, there it is then. And I was sure you'd told me about that one before and it was North Street.' Ruth had got herself ruffled again and slid her coffee away across the low table. She took up another magazine from the rack. Things never did seem to go quite right when she was with Edward. All those years back at McMaster there had been moments when she had been strongly drawn to him. With Jack buried in his research and Liza and Isaac at kindergarten the days stretched lazy and empty. She'd encounter him in the parking lot; their paths would cross at the library or the supermarket. He was a late thirties bachelor stacking cans neatly into his trolley, absurdly concerned with prices and brand-names. She was performing a dull chore, throwing the stuff into her rattling chariot, distressed and at one point collapsing a mountain of sugar bags and walking away from the avalanche.

Then Jack had acted as Chairman of the department for a period and they'd entertained with dinner parties every couple of weeks. Edward had been a regular guest at that time, paired off with each spare female visitor the necessities of college hosting would cast up. She could see now that, in a looser decade they would steadily, inevitably have become lovers. What different paths their lives would have taken then. No, no—that was too facile.

She dismissed the idea and concerned herself with the magazine as Edward was drawn by Martin into recounting some of his naval experiences in the Pacific. It was all so proper and clean-cut. He still affected the neatly trimmed hair-cut of those years. On a younger man these days in mid-town Toronto it would have been a gay proclamation, that short hair. Had Edward ever gotten involved with women? There was that McClerran woman—just a jokey think Jack used to tease Edward with. But anything serious? She'd heard nothing, but then they'd hardly been in touch for long periods since Jack's death. Edward was always so cool and assured. She couldn't imagine his being ruffled by a lover of either sex. In all those years he'd never so much as hinted a pass at her. She couldn't be certain, but there must surely have been times when she'd given indications of her willingness? Anyway, it was all too late. Now she'd never know. Edward gave away little of a really intimate nature, and she'd be sure to make a clumsy fool of herself if she pushed those sort of questions at him.

'I'm afraid we'd better be going after coffee, Edward,' said Ruth. 'I'm getting a headache, and these young people have a flight to prepare for tomorrow.'

'Oh, I could stay here with his charming gentleman all night,' laughed Sally returning through the door, deliberately annoying Ruth.

Martin was glad she'd at least snapped out of her previous mood. Almost a bitchiness directed him.

'Yes, this is such an interesting house, isn't it, love? But perhaps we'd better not make it too late an evening before our trip home. And there's Ruth's headache,' he added, rather lamely.

'But I haven't viewed all of Edward's pictures yet. Have you?' Sally countered.

'Well, I suppose I haven't seen them all but...'

'Then I'll do the gallery walk while you finish your coffee,' she said, and she walked through into the dining-room.

Martin sensed that there was something different about her. Sally's moments of firmness were less—well, firm, in that public sort of way. The evening had run its course as far as he was concerned. He'd enjoyed the meal, drunk brandy, seen Edward's art and retained a polite deference towards Ruth. Edward's casual attitude to his published novel had disturbed him though. Could it be that all such things lost value when you had them in your hands? Or was it just Edward's manner to play the book down? No criticism of him and his own eagerness to publish had been intended, he realised that. Still, he felt boyish, tied up in his own game-system of success. No, he didn't want to read Edward's book. No matter what it proved to be like, at this stage of his life he'd settle for the achievement of being in those hard covers. That clear refusal to land him with a copy anyway, that showed the real class of this gent. He could learn from Edward. So cool and calm, very much his own man.

'So it's back to the sceptred isle is it? And are you glad to be living in England now? Can these things we hear be true? Is she the tarnished jewel of the North Sea?' Edward had fetched in their coats from the hall's cloak-cupboard.

'We've certainly been impressed with Toronto,' said Martin, trying not to sound condescending. 'Back home it's all a bit dull, as jewels go. Rather pasty. We're a tired nation, or rather four nations tied up in a bunch of islands. The only real energy seems to be generated by the need to break apart. Being English is confusing. Unlike the Irish and the others we've no great national grievance to focus our frustrations on. Anything we've got landed with is undeniably our own fault. We're an uncertain butterfly trying to squirm out of a great bulky misshapen cocoon of empire. Trouble is, we have that uncomfortable feeling that, once out completely, we may only have a brief day to fly our way.'

'Beautifully put!' said Sally from the doorway. 'Martin's a natural talker, but, you know, I'm beginning to see the beauty of words. I wouldn't be surprised to find myself writing something in the future. Edward, I love that water-colour in the dining-room. The one of exotic flowers. Must be the pull of empire from deep shared memory.'

Martin had not intended his speech for Sally.

Outside the sky was full of stars. April—the final cold edge of the uncertain Canadian spring, an unreal season holding off for a few brief weeks the hot sweat of summer. The Main Street bank had flashed a temperature of one degree centigrade as they'd left the Vernay Clam House earlier that evening and Martin found himself shivering the moment he walked out of Edward's screen door. It might have been the Arctic wastes as far as he was concerned. Then before Edward could unlock the car Sally said she'd left her purse in the house and Edward had to open the front door again for her, while he and Ruth withdrew into their coats and snorted icy breath into the night.

'Nice one, Sally,' he complained.

'Tha's nesh, lad,' she said in her best Lawrencian Woman, 'thee's likely nut used to th'cowld where tha war brung up.'

'I do the funny voices, remember,' said Martin.

'That's not a funny voice. It's a dialect,' she countered.

'Anyway,' she added as she slid across the back seat of the Citroen, 'He do the Police in Difference Voices.'

'Jesus. Don't get cryptic with me, love. It's too cold,' said Martin, pulling the car door shut.

'Let's get you good folks home,' said Edward. He started the engine and the car's suspension pumped them up to its driving height.

'Edward, I think this beautiful car is your central work of art, your piece de resistance. Doesn't Roland Barthes give an essay devoted to this model? "The Semiotics of the Citroen D" or something?' inquired Martin.

'It is sort of special. I've had her ten years. Goes smoothly, fast enough for my needs, and has the sort of detailed finishing that Detroit never considered. She gets her spring and winter preparations and hasn't let me down yet.'

'I hardly know one car from another, except the size,' said Ruth.

There speaks a rabbit who drives a VW Rabbit, thought Martin. But he felt tired and said nothing. He pulled down the arm-rest and sank back in the cushioned rear of the Citroen. It was all grist to the mill. He considered: I find a way into a character's mind by seeing a face that fits the part. Or a place. Take Niagara Falls. There's this retired US businessman who is anxious to bump off his secretary. He's been having her in the sack, but the Inland Revenue are on his back. She's memorised the accounts, so there's some horseplay above the Falls and she takes a dive. Tragic accident. All seen from inside the guy's head. 5,000—6,000 words. A story. Or a novel.

The lights of the traffic and downtown buildings swirled and flashed around them.

'Hey, Martin—it's 'faithless',' said Edward, without turning round.

'What?' said Martin, coming out of his plot.

'Your quote, back in the house. It's been worrying me. It didn't sound right.'

'The Auden quote. Yes, I remember now,' said Martin, feigning interest.

'It's "faithless arm",' began Edward.

'Lay your sleeping head, my love Human on my faithless arm.

Time and...'

Martin finished the line: 'Time and fevers burn away...'

'That's right, Edward. I had a feeling it was wrong.'

'Act by your feelings,' said Sally, as if it too were a quote. Though no-one took it up.

'Isn't that where they're building the new Crombie and Macey's deli?' asked Ruth as they passed the flashing red lights of a construction site. Edward thought not, that the deli was over in Trent.

Martin felt tired. Too tired to talk or think out his story. He moved closer to Sally, leaning into her. His hand rested in Sally's bare arm, cool and smooth like the flank of a carved seal. He closed his eyes, heavy with the brandy, and saw his children back in England running towards him. He longed to play with them, to see then tear open the presents they'd been bought. He saw them jump on him, punching and pummelling his stomach and chest until it hurt wonderfully. He held to that image which excited him in a way that was realised quite suddenly when Sally's lips, open and warm and needy, kissed his.

His hand moved up to her arm to stroke her neck. Her free hand unclenched, dropping an exquisitely carved

Eskimo woman, without a sound, onto the Citroen's thick carpet.

Switching lanes, Edward caught the kiss in his driving mirror. 'Two lovers in a car,' he said quietly, to no-one in particular.

'So why not?' said Ruth, smiling at him for the first time that night.

The Robinsons' Court

The one positive thing to come from the demise of the Robinsons' marriage was the way their friends moved closer together, as if witnessing the failure of someone else's marriage sent a shiver through one's own and left the two of you clinging on to each other. It was as though folks formed a ring around the death-bed.

And there were lots of friends; or at least good acquaintances, for the Robinsons had a social energy that swept up other people. In the six years since they'd moved to town their parties had pulled together a variety of people —young professionals, play-group mothers, John's squash club opponents, colleagues from the Tech., babysitters and their boyfriends, a potter, five visiting Americans through Rotaract, a professional rugby player from Hull, a landscape gardener whose wife was in a therapy unit and so on and so forth. The marvellous thing about a Robinson party was the unpredictability of the assembled crew. The blonde sitting at the foot of the stairs might be a model or a dentist; the paunchy man with the banker's glasses and the greasy hair could be in insurance—or was that the German with the Colonel Sanders franchise for Stuttgart? Each year there were four parties at least: Christmas, of course, Easter Monday, Mid-Summer's Day and Halloween. Traditional rites preserved, Christian and pagan.

Right from the start the Robinsons were different, certainly unlike the other people we knew. But there was more to it than that: they were, in a sense, unlike themselves, or what you'd expect them to be. I mean, how did a man who taught Liberal Studies at the local Tech. get to know all those people? And that life-style—the large parties—was made possible only through the house. Though perhaps one could explain the house. Of course, John couldn't possibly have afforded that Edwardian seat on the Searise Road without help from the dead, or a wrist-slashing mortgage. But people do leave acres or shares or shop fronts in their wills. No doubt he was the little-seen and sentimentally-favoured nephew of someone somewhere with civic largess: he had been at Oxford.

Or perhaps she'd been remembered by a distant uncle as a sweet child of three in curls and a pink bonnet framed in a bright summer doorway. And then remembered in his will.

Guests rarely turned down a Robinson invitation. Leaving their kids with docile babysitters in front of the video, they drove out of the estates of semis and turned their backs on that banal security. Couples would enter Cape House through the large, stained-glass porch like the portals of a castle. Their eyes widened, they salivated and their sense of self-satisfaction shrank. The Robinsons' hi-fi was always loud, music flowing in a continuous arrangement—Sixties pop, Beatles, Tamla, Stones, with spaces of baroque selections and then classy finales of Billy Holliday or Ella Fitzgerald when the early hours yawned in. Whatever good fortune had marked the Robinsons' card, they were prepared to share it around. Certainly, Laura and I enjoyed being invited.

Cape House had the confident solidarity of a three-master. Built by a sea captain before the Great War, its three storeys sided into the westerlies that cut up the Channel; and on some particularly foul night each winter raised slates along the terraced side-streets and clattered down the dividing creosoted fences of the new estates across town. The stained-glass panels of the porch doors seemed left-over from the old man's travels. A buxom Polynesian girl with a frozen-sly smile offered fruit over the inscription "Bounty" in one frame, while the other had a full-sailed clipper above 'Discovery'.

The gardens, too, were impressive—a large lawn at the front with a monkey-puzzle tree at the drive gates. At the back of the house there was a patio with slate designs, some fruit trees and then a lawn tennis court. The grass had been laid expertly back in the twenties but frequently neglected since. There was a dry-wall each side of the court and a privet hedge back from the baseline. The net was patched but the supports were pretty upright and the winder worked like an oiled mincer. There was a marker of some age that ground out the whiting like a reluctant snail. It was John's toy. He always made a great show out of pegging and marking the court at the beginning of each season. He pushed the line marker, before him like some convinced water-diviner. A tennis-court, that was the clincher. A lawn tennis court with privet as sight screen spoke of old money, class rooted way back, in the Empire.

Shortly after they'd moved in Barbara had found a bundle of old shipping notices stuffed at the back of a bedroom cupboard and John had framed the best of them to line the staircase. The old sea-dog had, evidently, circled the globe year after year—tea from India, railway equipment to Buenos Aires and the Cape Horn runs.

The Robinsons didn't sail but were always being offered trips across the Channel crewing for friends. There's no doubt they could have opted into the Yacht Club circle if they'd wished. In any case, they'd appropriated the sea-going credentials of their house. Like some second generation *enfants terribles* they chose not to put to sea, yet had the worldly confidence of the travelled. John and Barbara had, of course, travelled before the kids came—hitching over Europe in the middle sixties before the riots closed things up and then across the States in the early, heady days of Skytrain. It seemed that John had driven an M.G.B.—the Mighty Grumpy Beantin he called it—in his Oxford days and had dated a future BBC Newscaster for a time. They'd smoked grass there with the son of a cabinet minister. Barbara, on a secretarial course, had bumped into him outside the Bodleian.

There was nothing showy about these stories. The Robinsons held audience by virtue of the unfinished, that which remained unsaid. They were deep. You kept wanting more. Did the P.M. pull strings after his nephew pissed in the port at high table? Where had John first met Mandy Rice-Davies? What had brought them to this tired little port on the Bristol Channel? After fingering the zip-flies of fame, why had this pair drifted and snagged themselves in our rough backwater?

169

'John has it in his mind to write a book,' Barbara announced to the Young Professional Women's group at her first meeting, though nothing seemed to come of that. Summer friends who called for tennis would find John in his study, or scratching notes in the pages of a ring-file when slumped in a deck-chair in the shade of the privet. I would guess that he spent more time on tending and contemplating the court than writing. The Robinsons always had a decorator in to keep the interior spruced, (God knows, that was a hefty task) and an old boy cycled across town to maintain the garden, but John himself managed the court. He'd spent three seasons reclaiming it from the weedy neglect it had suffered under Miss Williams, the aged niece of the sea-captain. He'd pretty well tamed the grass, doctored, fed and rolled it back to fitness. He'd cut and shaped the high privet hedges and raised the walls at each side. Though the court had its idiosyncracies: a heavily sliced serve would beat the wall and have to be retrieved from the flower-beds, and an over-vigorous smash at the net might clear the hedge, threatening panes in the old greenhouse at the foot of the gardens, John's court had a feel about it of *l'entre-deux guerres* leisure. A luxury, but serving a practical purpose too, so that it had rather more grace than absurdity. The Robinsons themselves were casual players —mixed doubles, social tennis with Barbara's sandwich teas and John serving drinks. In any case during the second season of play on the Cape House court Barbara was pregnant with Toby and then the following summer she was carrying Teresa.

Children bring a new perspective to every marriage; for some they signal the end. Living in a house, even a large house, with three other human beings is ten times more complex than life with one. 'It is people who constitute our extremes of heaven and hell,' John proclaimed once in the hazy, early hours of one New Year's Eve party. 'We imagine that we buttress ourselves against life's cold neglects by reproducing our like. The truth is that we bind our arms around responsibility, we cast hostages to fortune, we stretch our feelings to snapping lengths.'

Toby and Teresa were lovely kids but, looking back, it's clear that cracks began to appear from that point. John was, of course, a sharing, enlightened father, involved from the first bloody, wonderful birth, playing his part in all the chores. Barbara, naturally, fought the indifference of the local maternity ward and breast-fed Toby, then Teresa. John, for his part, encouraged her to keep up with her Women's Group meetings and then to try out pottery at an evening class. He'd mind the children and suffer a share of the teething nights. About that time Laura was brushing up her conversational French and she'd met Barbara in The Gallant Cavalier after classes. They seemed to get on quite well and we began to be drawn into the Robinson's circle.

One hot early August day Barbara rang—Toby and Teresa were with their grandmother for a couple of days, so we were invited over for 'Court, Cocktails Balls 'n' Booze,' Laura said, but she was nevertheless glad to be asked. Laura's never been much of a sports person. On a tennis court she has no control on her backhand and she has a soft, ballooning serve. I played a bit at school and what I lack in height I compensate for in aggression. I've always been a bit of a jock and hate to lose in a fair match.

Barbara was short and firmly-built. Though she'd become hippy after the childbirths, she moved quite fast and could deal out an effective volley at the net in support of John's squiffy serve. She was a more natural ball-player than he was and had clearly been practising.

John was one of nature's odd servers. A lefty, he'd contort his face and shoulder into a bizarre parody of effort, biting his lower lip and slicing the ball diagonally over the net. If he managed to time one right, the ball would squirt over at you and skid sharply away off the grass. You're left feeling that something unsporting has been perpetrated.

That August day was a hot, heavy one with the moan of a foghorn out in the Channel. An afternoon when the long iced glasses were to be taken more seriously than the tennis. Anyway, we went through the motions of three or four games, none of which Laura and I looked close to winning.

I did scrape a game then on my service, but they finished off the set when Laura skyed one over the bottom hedge. 'Game and first set to the champs of Searise!' John proclaimed. 'First set?' queried Laura. The Robinsons were obviously taking their tennis more seriously this year.

I did the gallant thing and went to retrieve the ball from a tangle of rhododendron bushes beyond the collapsing greenhouse. When I rejoined the others on the patio there was an atmosphere; for some reason the mood had changed and John was sounding off.

'I'd have thought most women would be relieved to lose their hostages to fortune for a week. But Babs here has to play the grieving Mother Goose.'

''I don't want to talk about it. All I said was...'

'What d'you think, Laura? I bet Laura would, wouldn't you?'

'Well I can see...' Laura looked uneasy in her role as marital tennis ball.

'Laura doesn't have any children, John.'

'I still think the point holds, Babs. Sorry Laura.'

I went to Laura's aid: 'I hope there's plenty of vodka in that lemon thing, love, I need to fuel my elbow. I know you're not supposed to beat your hosts but we might manage a couple of games—if they insist on another set.'

'It's too hot, really,' said Barbara, flapping the front of her shirt. We'd been to a couple of their parties by then, I suppose, but that flushed, irritated moment in the garden was the first time I realised how desirable Babs was. She'd been the organised, prim hostess at those events. The guests got wild, fresh, high or sick while the Robinsons kept the spirit circulating- That afternoon the sun and the set of tennis had left her flushed with colour and panting. Exertion drew out her looks

It was clear that she'd slipped her cool, but whether it was some confusion of feelings about the children or in-law trouble or just a banal squabble wasn't so clear. John pulled her back onto the court for a second set and she lolloped through several games with barely-disguised disinterest. We held our own, though it was a hollow success in the circumstances. John scampered around more and more furiously to cover the gaps his partner was leaving. Even so, he soon found himself serving at 4-5 and 30-40 to save the dying set. He corkscrewed his arm into a vicious serve that caught Barbara full in the back. She yelled and straightened up. Then pulling away from his attempts to console, she stomped off to the house.

Barbara did not re-appear and we left shortly after the incident. I'd had one too many of the vodka spikes so Laura drove.

'There's something quietly falling apart at chez Robinson,' she said, looking round at the big house as we rolled back down into town. And not so quietly,' she added.

I turned to look up Sea-rise and found myself focussing on Laura's neck. There, behind her left ear, on the edge of the hairline she has a beauty-spot, a mole. And at that moment the sight of that imperfection annoyed me more profoundly than I'd previously admitted.

We were invited that year to Halloween at Cape House. It was a strange mix from the beginning. A few of the guests went as witches and wizards and the rest remained painfully terrestrial. John welcomed everyone in the hall. He wore a flowing Merlin gown that looked every inch a professional costume, down to the chain-locked tome of spells wedged under his arm. However, the large lounge was disco-lit, as it usually was at their parties, and there were no bats or broomsticks hung from the ceiling, no apples to be bobbed; just the usual party trick-or-treats drink flowing and the fog of marijuana in the air. Barbara didn't appear until past ten. She wore a strapless, starched gown—a lovely pastiche of a fifties graduation-ball number at the J. Edgar Hoover High in some movie. That was the year transatlantic nostalgia was imported. The dress was trendy and expensive.

Laura had got herself tied up with the man who'd taught her French evening-class. He was slipping in and out of conversation practices whilst working her into a dim, bookcase corner. I moved away and got talking to Barbara.

'I bet that dress is the same size you'd have worn at your sixth form ball.'

'That's not true. What's so important about seventeen, anyway?'

'At seventeen I could play five sets of tennis without breaking sweat,' I said.

'At seventeen,' she turned and drained a large measure of red wine, 'At sweet seventeen I was head girl—I'd grown out of hockey and tennis and was no longer a virgin.'

Lacking my own stories of precocious adolescence, I've always felt threatened when other people parade their superiority in that area.'Oh, really? Back of Chuck's Chevy at the drive-in?" I tried my best American accent, a sort of squeaky Dustin Hoffman in The Graduate.

'Don't you like the dress? It cost a packet.'

'The dress is marvellous. Honest—it's a great party-dress. Dazzling, witty. But shouldn't John be in a white tuxedo...with a football helmet or baseball bat or something?'

She poured more wine and, without asking, filled my glass, carelessly slopping some across my shirt sleeve. 'It's fucking Hallow'een. John's a prick. He's Merlin the prick. Except there's no magic.' She laughed. "Oh, Christ, this is awful. Come on,' she said, taking my free, dry hand, "Come and see my etchings." And then at the foot of the stairs, 'It wasn't a Chevy. It was a Morris Oxford. Lay-byes, lanes, and in yards. After Gilbert & Sullivan rehearsals. It was the Art master.'

There was only one more party—at New Year's Eve. I tried to pull us out of it, but Laura insisted. Early in November she'd discovered she was pregnant. It wasn't exactly planned, but it was no tragedy either. I was in line for a new department and a rise and for Laura her desk at County Hall had lost its charm. Our bank balance could handle the strain, without question. I just hoped that our marriage proved as solvent. It wasn't just the thing with Barbara, I could handle that. An adult marriage collapses only if its bases have been eroded over the years. Our session in her guest room that Hallowe'en night had been one of those rare animal moments—flouncing petticoats falling to the floor and natural timing. Our handful of snatched and shady encounters over the following weeks never repeated the intense pleasure of that heady midnight hour.

After Laura's annunciation I felt I needed Barbara more, but, at the same time, felt a growing sense of guilt. Our small-won affair slid away before it had become a habit. We let it go. Nothing was said: we just loosened our hold on the thing. It has been all down hill after the Debbie Reynolds hump in the big house. That was bold, dangerous, leg-over the coach's daughter stuff. The stolen evenings in my car or her old Escort were an awkward silliness after that. If doing a thing causes as much pain as doing without, then it's best to return to base.

The New Year's Eve party was fine—the usual crowd: the fat German was over, several painters from the Arts Co-op, and when we arrived there was some guy in a kilt hogging the punch-bowl and getting very drunk. He began to perform awful impressions of Kenneth McKellar, but in a thick Geordie accent before leaving the room through the French windows, shouting that he wanted to piss over the tennis net. We didn't see him again. He missed the linking of arms at the twelfth and final stroke of 1980. He also missed the fight.

In a sense it had been brewing up all that evening. Babs had been with a man called Williams, Neville Williams; when Laura and I arrived I'd determined to avoid Barbara and was relieved to see this pair tied up for the evening. Laura had insisted we go to the party and I felt that a faked headache would be quite out of character and might have her sniffing all sorts of dead rats. I needn't have worried. Barbara hardly seemed aware of us, or of any other guests. Williams was clearly unencumbered: I remembered that I'd seen him before. He ran a camera shop in town and I'd bought a second-hand Leica off him about a year back.

John had been cosseted on the settee with the fat German, a bottle of schnapps passing from one to the other during the last hour of the year. They entered into the body of the party only at midnight. Babs and the man were noticeably absent from the singing cluster of instant camaraderie that linked arms and swayed uncertainly into 1981.

It was about 12.30, and we were considering it a decent time to leave, when Barbara re-appeared. She always did have a fine sense of timing. There was no sign of Williams, but John went for her right away. She was a tart, a cock-happy bitch, no mother, and a disgrace.

'Why don't you take off on your own for this year? Start as you mean to go on? Just fuck-off!' He was drunk and tired. He had no chance of dodging the slops as she threw the punch-bowl over his back. The funny thing was that he didn't turn around again, it was as if throwing the punch was what he'd expected. We beat a retreat from the melee while he was still looking out of the French windows, a smear of fruit down his shirt. As we fumbled for the car keys in the hall, Babs brushed past on her way upstairs.

On our drive home Laura began to work out the various scenarios that might explain the remarkable events of the party. I played dumb and bit back on all the things I knew. What puzzled me was John standing at those windows. Was he frozen there in shock or anger? What could he see of the night outside Cape House? Perhaps only himself looking in at his life there.

When Laura had become pregnant our lives changed for ever. We saw nothing of the Robinsons for months and heard nothing of significance, but early that summer Barbara rang me at the office. Could I get away that afternoon? She needed a favour, something to do with the kids. For old times' sake. And I was pretty well my own boss, wasn't I, so could get away—would I? Please?

She met me in the porch and, red-eyed pecked me on the cheek. Toby dive-bombed into my knees as we entered the lounge.

'Has school finished already?' I asked.

'No, that's the problem. That's what you can do for me." She poured me a coffee and lit a cigarette before sitting down next to me on the settee.

176

'I'm leaving John," she said.

I said, 'Oh,' and wanted to ask what on earth that might have to do with me especially, adding, 'I didn't know you smoked.'

'Only when I really need to,' she said, 'I've given up.'

'What will you do?'

'It's Neville—do you know Neville?'

'He was at the party. You danced with him all night. I was totally furious, I can say.'

'I knew you'd help,' she said, splintering the cigarette into a large glass ashtray. 'You see, I need to tell John and it's bound to be a rough-house so I don't want to involve the kids in that sort of scene. I don't want to complicate things with their grandmother, so if you and Laura...'

'You want us to have them for a few days?'

'A few days, yes, while we sort things out. John can be awkward. You've no idea. And there's a lot of things we have to talk about. I've got a lot to tell him. It's best to clear up everything at once.'

'You don't mean...?'

'No, not that thing with us, you're safe. Other stuff.'

She walked over to the French windows and opened them. A sharp breath of air came past her carrying the voices of Toby and Teresa playing on the tree-swing.

'I pulled them out of school for the afternoon and then thought of you. They're going to be the most difficult part of all this.'

I said that I could well imagine that and she went on to tell me more of the details.

She had met Williams two years ago, through John. John had some spare capital and was interested in a scheme to set up a video outlet in town. He'd met Neville Williams at the Squash Club and it seemed for a time that their photography and video interests might link up. John was finding the job at the Tech. tedious and felt that one astute investment could carve him an escape from the second oldest profession. Williams was more cautious and finally decided that the video boom would burn a lot of fingers and prove riskier than a specialist camera shop. After a lot of talking, they'd amicably gone their separate ways, but Barbara had fallen for the guy. He had a flat above the shop so they enjoyed early closing afternoons, the kids at their grandmothers; and sessions in evening class time. It had been as messy as these things usually proved to be. I said I understood.

'And me? Where did I come in?'

She'd broken free of Neville and resolved to clear up her life. Still, it was Halloween and old habits died...well, those needs were slow to cool. And, besides, she'd always liked me.

'It was fine, what you and I had. It was fun. There was no harm in it. was there?' she said. She walked over and touched my knee. What could I say?

I went outside to play with the kids while she slipped a small suitcase into the back of my car. Yes, they'd love to spend the night with Auntie Laura. Could they take our dog for walks? Would our baby be coming out of Auntie Laura tonight?

On our way across town I stopped at a phone-box on the promenade and let them out of the car while I called Laura's office. I kept back the details but convinced her that this was something we should agree to do. She was intrigued and promised to cut home early that afternoon.

Toby and Teresa were at the stone-wall overlooking the beach. He was lifting her up to the swivel telescope. I fed in coins for them and they tried to focus on shapes out in the Channel.

'We can't see ships at all,' they chorused, 'It won't work.'

I took a turn. The focusing screw was worn and kept slipping but just before the shutter closed the view out, I picked up a ship, a dismal little coaster. There was not a lot of romance in that tub, but she was shining where the sea hit her and was heading confidently for port.

As we went back to the car Toby and Teresa walked on either side of me, each holding tightly to a hand.

The children stayed for just one night on that occasion —Barbara phoned the next day to say that she had handled the situation and could cope. She came over to pick them up and said that she and John were working towards a compromise—'the 49th parallel' she called it.

Cape House was big enough for both their lives, so they planned to split it in half. John would have the upstairs as a flat. He could enter and leave quite independently by the old fire-escape which a builder friend would strengthen. Barbara and the children would be based on the ground floor. It seemed a liberal, almost fashionable arrangement that avoided the trauma of an immediate breakdown and separation, but over the following weeks we and other friends were called on more and more to look after Toby and Teresa.

The children couldn't adjust to the '49th parallel',' the concept of two distinct territories divided by an imaginary frontier was beyond them. Eventually John had the stairs blocked off by a partition. It seemed radical, but necessary, like the amputation of a limb. Then John had a fire. A pan of chips went up on the gas-bottle stove he was using. A curtain had caught and he'd been hard put to contain and douse the flames. The children had screamed hysterically at the foot of the fire-escape.

More shattering than all that though was Williams's decision to move in with Barbara. Though when it had come to the crunch he'd pulled back, got cold feet. It seemed that his previous marriage was still open. In the beginning of June he put the shop up for sale and began plans to return to the West Country. On Mid-summers Day, in the late evening, Barbara swallowed a bottle of headache pills. She turned up the hi-fi—Mahler's Second it was said—very loudly, before passing out so John raced down from his rooms to complain and was in time to save her. If she'd held hopes of that sort of drama bringing them together then the scheme misfired. He went into her hospital room the next day and announced to a pumped-out, washed-out Barbara his demand that the house be sold. He hadn't even taken her flowers.

There was at least one more overdose and several pitched battles that involved other sets of friends, but our baby came in late July and we dropped out of the

179

Robinsons' lives. By all accounts it had developed into a full-scale soap-opera. September saw Cape House empty and sporting two different estate agents' signs at the end of the drive.

One October Sunday we packed Jonathan's carry-cot into the back seat and went for a drive. The beach looked uninviting, the sea was slate-grey and a wind that promised winter blew up the Channel. Neither of us mentioned the place but I turned the wheel at the end of the promenade and we climbed the hill to Searise.

'We might as well drive on past Cape House,' I said casually.

'If you like,' said Laura, 'but I'm sure there's nothing to see.'

The drive gates were closed, but the chain hadn't been locked. I pulled up and reversed.

'Only a quick look,' I said, 'there's no harm.'

Laura thought it too cold for baby Jonathan, who, in any case, was fast asleep, and so I got out of the car alone. I walked up the drive to the front door. The porch was gathering free papers and catalogue prize offers. I went around the side of the house to the French windows. Curtains were still hanging, but they hadn't been drawn and I could see the length of the lounge. It seemed stark without its furniture, denuded, cold and hollow. I shivered and regretted not wearing a coat.

The corners of the patio held the first fallen leaves and I thought, 'If they're not swept away there'll be moss'. The privet hedges had already grown high; they were bushy and unkempt and between them the tennis court itself was sorely in need of attention. The grass was three or four inches higher than its best autumn length and leaves were beginning to clot at the net and behind the baselines. The net itself was wound up taut as if a game had been interrupted by sudden inclement weather and the players had never returned.

I walked towards the centre and almost turned an ankle over a discarded ball. Then I noticed other balls—three, five, six—they were this season's, still yellow and apparently unworn. They looked as if they'd not seen a game, so why were they scattered in the grass, and who'd left the court like this? Had some well-meaning estate agents clerk come to take an inventory and wound up the net in ignorance? Or had John and Barbara played one last game there before turning their backs on a host of bad memories? 'No, that would be stupid,' I said out loud. That really would have been soap-opera.

I bent down to pick up one of the balls. It was heavy and soft, the rain had soaked into it and made it quite useless. I turned it over in my fingers and brushed against a small slug on the wet underside, then ran the ball along the net-cord to scrape the thing off. I walked back up to the house and from the patio turned to throw the ball hard into the sky. It rose and looped to land with two dull bounces the other side of the net.

Terminates at Newport

It's a simple but real satisfaction to have a reserved seat on the 125 when it's packed with end of the day business travellers. And even better when you can actually get to that seat and claim it. The 5.35 from Paddington on that Friday was pretty well jammed, but the Evanses settled in their places, Owen by the window and Jane on the aisle, his best suit and her new outfit, suitcase stashed away and the *Times*, the *Guardian* and the *Independent* to pass the time. Although it was early June and the journey back to Wales would have plenty of those green stretches of Berkshire and Wiltshire through the window to set off pieces by Vaughan Williams or Howells in the mind, and it promised to be a pleasant two hours.

Owen was not particularly patriotic or sentimental, but passing through such a landscape, he was always happy to opt into that English part of himself: his family, farm labourers, blacksmiths, herders, had for generations worked that lush and rolling land before wars and jobs on the GWR had shaken up the mix and brought his grandfather down the line, an earlier line than this high-speed one that cuts almost straight across middle England to the Bristol Channel and a tunnel to Wales. God's Wonderful Railway engineered by Isambard Kingdom Brunel, that fierce little man in his stove pipe hat and fat cigar of achievement. In any case, following the afternoon at the Palace, a sense of being British, English even, had washed over them.

By Reading the aisles were clear of the standing commuters and Owen left his window seat to fetch coffees while Jane got on with the Guardian crossword. The buffet car was a few yards away in the next carriage and he timed his run when things seemed quiet. Buffet cars when they are occupied at all seem to attract the lost and lonely, people who talk to the long-suffering steward, students and young people who hunch up on the floor of the concertinaed linking passageway, as if claiming a seat would somehow enrol them into middle-age or the middles-class they were not yet ready to join. This one had a man in a tired jacket who looked as if he travelled on the knocker for Betterware, a woman in her thirties with blonded hair, wearing a crumpled suit, obviously squiffy, who was pouring with some difficulty two miniatures of vodka into a plastic cup of orange juice and two big guys, unshaven, cropped hair, with tattoos on bicep-bulging arms that were straining inside their Ts as they tilted their cans. The predictable crew.

Owen had forgotten to slide those corrugated cardboard holders around the cups, so was glad to make the twenty paces back to their table without negotiating other passengers and scalding himself.

'What's the capital of Botswana?' asked Jane, 'Six down —I've got two Os and a G.'

'Hang on, love, let me get these scalding cups safely down, I forgot the cardboard thingies.'

'And what's 'a court case gone wrong for a cricketer' five across?'

'I'm not even sure where Botswana is. Wonder if one of those flowery national costumes in the Commonwealth procession was Botswana? It could have been as all the former colonies are represented at garden parties, I'd think. It certainly seemed like it.'

Jane didn't look up from the newspaper and Owen felt that was a bit churlish. She'd been so negative about the invitation—'Well, you can count me out. Go on your own if you're so keen. I thought that you didn't give a toss for the Royals.' But she had relented, though only when in their next phone call to their daughter Rhian had said she'd happily come as her dad's escort as it would be 'interesting'. In truth, Owen wasn't sure that he did give a toss about the Royals, but besides being 'interesting' he felt that this pair of Buckingham Place garden party tickets was owed to him.

Six months before he had been taken ill. Very ill. It had begun a week or so following a trip to Bologna for the firm. These conferences or fairs or follow-up visits after orders had always been seen as a perk at Fallow's and he had been given precious few jaunts in the fifteen years he'd been with them: a two day trip to Brussels, that boring capital of a boring country, and a wet weekend in Leeds were high points. Bologna had been different: a fine Italian city with classy buildings, fine food and a buyer who had excellent English and dressed in that considered elegance which seemed to be a natural quality in the Italian business men and women he'd encountered.

A couple of good restaurants, an afternoon in the National Picture Gallery and the Museum of Archaeology followed the promise of new orders once he'd explained their development plans. A dip in the hotel pool—was that where he'd caught something? Or that crammed journey in the commuter train? The plane's dodgy air-con? An old school chum of his had become an airline pilot and confirmed that most firms, especially the budget carriers, instructed their pilots to fly with as little air-con fuel used as possible. Whichever, or none of the above: Owen had come down with something that presented as an early summer flu which had clung on and become something much more serious; not flu at all but something rare and life-threatening. So much so that he collapsed and ended up in the University Hospital in Cardiff. After three weeks of tests and lumbar punctures and drugs he'd rallied sufficiently to talk his way out. He'd lost track of time in that way you can with an illness and with being in an institution: Rhian's birthday had passed, though she and her boyfriend at the time had visited several times, apparently; Wimbledon fortnight had passed; and an eclipse of the sun had occurred, rare and dream-like, without warning for him, though he did remember being helped to the window of the ward, wearing sun-glasses to see this once-in-a-lifetime, especially in the state he was in, experience.

Something had got into Owen's brain; some infection or bug had unhinged the works so that it took months for him to recover. Many months; though he'd returned to work after six months to draw his salary, it had been too soon and he was clearly not functioning properly. Gerwyn, his sector manager, had realised this and he and colleagues had covered for Owen's problems and lack of focus. The firm had been a player in rejuvenating the Rhondda and Rhymney valleys in trying to lift people out of its post-mining slough of despond, so for a number of years they'd had an allocation of a pair of garden party tickets from the Welsh Office or someone for those efforts. Usually it was one of the Board who'd gone, but this time Gerwyn had sent them his way; compensation for brushing the dry, cracked lips of Death; or for 'soldiering on above and beyond,' as he'd put it.

When Rhian said that she'd take up the offer if her mum maintained her republican stance, or 'chickened out', Jane had agreed to come, got the time off school, and went shopping for a summer outfit and a hat, though she usually hated wearing a hat. They'd had the night before at a decent hotel in Bloomsbury and seen a play at the National by someone she'd done at university. Brecht: very loud and quite long, Owen thought. Still, those additional treats had got her to the Palace.

He'd known that the event would be interesting, but not that it would be quite so stodgy between the interesting bits. All sense of privilege evaporates when you see that there are thousands of people in the grounds, from beautiful people straight out of the fashion pages to scout leaders, the armed services and many many-splendoured national costumes, and at one point before the Queen and Duke arrived a column of foreign dignitaries, their staff and their families who were ushered into what seemed to be an exclusive compound with marquees and laid tables. It was all tightly choreographed. At one point a flunky in a suit sidled up to the couple they'd been standing next to and asked whether they would be 'interested in meeting Prince Andrew?'

'Andrew was impressively tall,' Owen said, 'And the Palace gardens were impressive.'

'Not as impressive as what's through that window, the countryside we're speeding through now.'

'Ah, nature. The poetry of nature. This green and pleasant.'

'No, seriously, you could hardly see the gardens for the mass of bodies. Though I did get a souvenir.' Jane reached into her shoulder bag and pulled out a fistful of tissues in a small plastic freezer bag with some leaved poking out of the side.

'What? You didn't.'

'Well, Anne Biology said that garden party guests do it all the time—a crafty cutting, the quick snip of a shoot. A cunning pull from the bushes as you bend down to see to your shoelace. A little bit of Buckingham Palace will forever be 35, Heol y Parc. Could you pop to the WC and sprinkle some more water on these, to dampen the roots?'

Owen could see that the toilet light was indicating free but before he could get past Jane to the aisle it turned to "Engaged" and he sat down again. 'OK. And I'll get rid of the empties. Above average BR coffee, I'd say.'

The Thames, the Kennet, the Avon: rivers and woods and hills; the English countryside rolling, then flattened, then rolling again. South Gloucestershire, Bristol Parkway, then under the Severn estuary at some point halfway through the darkness the land becoming Wales. But now there were immobile cattle, a tractor coughing smoke, crops ripening, small Norman churches adrift down lanes that had once been roads of some importance.

'Somewhere showers becoming arrows out of sight... Someone bowling... an appeal you'll never know...'

'Have you got that clue?' Jane asked.

'No, it's that poem you helped Rhian with for her A Level. Philip Larkin. Wedding parties he sees on a long train journey. How railway journeys sort of punctuate our lives. Or used to punctuate our lives before we all had cars.'

'And then Rhian said that she was deprived of real insights because we drove her everywhere and she'd hardly been on a train. Look, the toilet's free for that watering.'

But just as he got up the squiffy woman and one of the big T-shirts appeared in the corridor. She was distinctly wobbly, her hair more of a mess, and he helped or was it pushed her into the loo and the 'Engaged' light came on again.

Owen sat down again just as they entered the tunnel. 'Oh, great timing.' But then his irritation was tempered by intrigue. Two people in a train toilet? And when he looked again the second big T-shirt guy was outside as if queuing up. When a young man made his way down past their seats and tried to make for the toilet or the buffet car, the big guy blocked his way and said something that made him turn back.

'I don't like this, Jane. There's something not right. I don't like it and...'

'Don't get involved, love. Whatever you think, stay and wait your turn.'

'He's not queuing up, that one, he's standing guard. This is all wrong, I tell you. I should...'

'What? What are you saying? They're probably drunk.'

'He's not drunk, he's shifty and scanning the carriages in both directions without appearing to. I should do something.'

But Owen wasn't sure what to do and then the light went to green as the first T-shirt came out. His view was blocked by the second man, so he couldn't see clearly, but the woman seemed to be stumbling out; and then both men moved out of sight.

'I'm telling you, that could well have been a serious assault, a rape, anything.'

'But there's two of them and they are huge, brutes, Neanderthals. You can't be sure. And you need to look after yourself. It's not like we can pull the communication cord— even if there were such a thing now. Don't you have to smash the glass or something. Forget the water, love; stay put.'

Trains, planes—once you were seated you were in somebody else's hands, their judgement, their determination. Owen was a natural car driver: his seat, his heater, his music. He looked into the darkness of the tunnel and saw himself dimly mirrored, now almost back to normal, but still a bit drawn and thin after his illness, though it had been months now. It was as if he had stared into a tunnel of blackness, muffled noises, half recognised voices and things not connecting. At this point the guard appeared and walked past them quickly down to the buffet car. He had his cap on and looked very official; but then shortly after a voice announced, 'We regret to inform you that this train will now terminate at Newport. Newport, the next stop.'

'But we always stop at Newport, for those unfortunate enough to live in the place,' said Jane.

'Not 'stop', terminates, he said, as if we are not being taken further. There's a problem. It's all connected, I know it.'

There now appeared to be a number of people in the buffet car. The train slowed and then pulled into Newport station. But no-one seemed to be getting out and for a long moment there was a strained quiet, a few murmurs and then they began to see police men and women on both the platforms and walking across the railway lines. There was an electric click. The train was surrounded and they were locked in. 'It's like a spy film where they're stopped at the border and the Stazi search the train,' said Jane.

Two or three policemen opened the door of the buffet car and the two T-shirts, swearing and putting up a struggle, were manhandled out and along the platform. 'I knew it,' Owen said.

An announcement informed them that the service from London Paddington to Swansea was terminating at Newport and that, when instructed, passengers should take their luggage and vacate the train. For those passengers proceeding beyond Newport other travel arrangements would be provided. There had been an incident and the police would like to speak to anyone in the vicinity of the buffet car who could assist them. Jane and Owen got their coats and the suitcase and joined the queue to get out of the carriage. As they neared the buffet car they could hear the sound of crying and then some swearing: Owen paused to look around the door into the buffet car and saw that the toilet woman was on the floor propped against the wall with two police woman kneeling down by her. Her jacket was crumpled up and acting as a pillow for her head; her legs were splayed out.

They joined the people who were offering information and were directed into a waiting room where they sat, more numbed than shocked. Owen said, 'I had a very bad feeling about this. It was so obvious.'

'Well, only now that we know something has happened,' said Jane, 'It wasn't that easy to see clearly. We should try and compose ourselves and agree on what we think we saw. So that we can be focussed and helpful. Which one pushed her into the toilet?'

A policeman shortly arrived and took notes; he had a clip-board and a pen and wore a proper coal scuttle helmet. Owen almost expected him to lick the tip of his pencil and say 'Evening all, folks.' Dixon of Dock Green, Newport, Gwent. They'd worked out which of the T-shirts had pushed and which had stood guard by remembering the tattoos, but despite the fact that all this had happened less than an hour before, Owen was disturbed by the fuzziness of his remembering: what bag had the woman carried, how old was she, what had she been drinking in the bar? Was that his problem, or did that happen with all witnesses? They both agreed that the woman, the victim, seemed drunk, 'Or it could have been that date rape drug Rohypnol,' suggested Jane, but the policeman did not write that down. Then he read their account back to them in a stumbling way and Jane insisted on seeing the statement for themselves before they signed it. 'It's 'aisle' not 'isle',' she said, 'Not Wight or Man or Caldey.'

They were fortunate that an Arriva local train pulled in shortly after they'd finished and they made the fifteen minutes or so into Cardiff Central smoothly and with the last of the sun a glowing background to the out of town estates and outlets and then the high office blocks of the city. They said nothing to each other until the train slowed for platform six.

'Dismissal,' Owen said, 'a court case gone wrong for a cricketer—it's a dismissal.'

On that evening's television news there was a brief item reporting that a packed London train had been halted at Newport owing to 'an incident on board'. Early the following week they were phoned by the police and then sent a form to indicate their availability for a court appearance if called to give witness. Then there was nothing. A week, a month, two months passed. They told their friends and colleagues and the narrative became a bit of a party piece. One of Jane's colleagues said that she'd heard that some Valleys hookers were working the trains to London. Rhian told her parents that her young professional girl friends, lawyers and social workers, were reluctant to use the toilets on trains as the doors hinged inwards and it was the simplest of things to nudge someone inside and join them. 'It's a received wisdom,' she said.

Owen had figured it out: what he should have done was to approach the lookout man outside the toilet and offer assistance for the woman who appeared to be unwell. 'I couldn't help but notice that your lady friend was ill. I'm Doctor Evans, and might be able to help.' His was a Ph.D in polymer instability at extreme temperatures from Bath, but 'Dr Evans' would have been convincing, wouldn't it? It's easy to be wise after the event and, as Jane pointed out, it might not have worked and he could have been attacked, though he like to think that if he'd stayed cool and confident and feigned a professional innocence, then he could have defused the situation.

Eventually they stopped talking about it, but it still lodged in their minds and he pursued the matter further, getting through to the transport police and then being phoned back from Bristol to be told that they would not after all be required to give evidence as the case had been dropped. 'The CPS have decided not to proceed, and I'm afraid that I am not able to comment further.' But Owen pressed him, saying how Jane and he were still disturbed by what had happened and that, in a sense, something had happened to them too. 'I understand that; it's a natural reaction. Look,' the officer said, 'I can say *off the record* that the CPS decided that the woman's character would not hold up in court. I'm sorry.'

So that was that. Now Owen and Jane are both part-time and sliding towards retirement; they usually travel up to London three of four times a year to a play or a concert or for the Royal Academy's Summer Exhibition madness—Pimm's and paintings—but nothing dramatic has ever happened again. Two brothers from Thomastown in Swansea were the following year charged with the rape of a student in Mumbles, but it was impossible to make a clear connection. When Owen told the guys in the office, Gerwyn said, 'What do you call a man from Thomastown wearing a suit?—The accused.'

And whatever happened to the woman, sadly drunk, or a working girl? What might her life be like? Both Owen and Jane, on a train journey or in dreams, re-compose the story: she's almost forty; the suit is grey; black shoes with heels; there's a salmon-pink blouse, rather low-cut; one man wore blue jeans, the other black ; they had duffle bags; one an ear-ring, the other a Harley-Davidson belt-buckle.

Rhian's been promoted and travels in First Class now for board meetings or for cases at the Court of Appeal. But Owen still has that Doctor Evans ploy in reserve: he got back to full fitness in body and brain within a year but he still feels in some way culpable and is determined to be more positive if anything happened again. When you have a gut feeling and did not act, when you could have made a difference but miss the chance, things move on, but the moment doesn't return, does it? All we have is the clicking clacking of the rails and points:: Reading, Swindon, Bristol Parkway, Newport, Cardiff Central, Bridgend, Port Talbot Parkway, Neath, Swansea: Malin, Fastnet, Sole, Humber, Finistere, Dogger,Viking—the rhythms and litanies that guide us, that stay with us over the years and remind us of where we've been, and where we still have to go.

A Night with Nina

Sleeping like a baby...

Who is this lad, really, I wonder? Curled up like a big baby in my bed.

'Where am I going to sleep tonight?'said Bullocky Bill the Sailor.

Out like a light... when all the lights are out on another bloody black-out night. Another bomber raid.

The lad's uniform would fit me... and a fine jolly tar, I'd make... on a dark night.

Going my way, Ducks? Going to get 'em down in Chat'em.

These dark air-raid nights are kindest thing to a lady of my—how shall we say?—maturity.

Where am I going to sleep...

And let's see—his papers in the top pocket:

'Able Seaman William Amos Scourfield.'

Able... Seaman... Willy...

Able... Spunky... Semen...Amos...

A...s...was...

'You may sleep within my bed, Sir,...' out in the cold, the fucking deathly cold Atlantic. Out over the Galway horizon, 'No room for two in a bed.'

'I'm a Tenby Scourfield,' says he. 'Serving under Captain John, that's Caspar John the son of the famous painter, they say.'

One of Gus's legitimate brood—there's dozens in London that were made outside the sheets, I'll bet.

What a funny old business this war is, eh?

Able seaman...able, spunky, semen. Go safely back to your ship with Augustus's son. Sail on through. Amen.

'And I'm from Tenby too,' says meself. Tenby born and Tenby fecked-off-as-soon-as-I-can from the place. Frosty, fusty, farty place.

'Worked the boats—mackerel and trips to the island—father and boy,' he said.

'Watched the boats from Gran's in Lexden Terrrace scuttle over to Caldey Island away from the brass band and the donkeys plodding and shitting their way across the South Beach,' says I. Little Willy's father at the wheel and tipping his cap, no doubt. Bored in the sunshine and feckedoffassoonas he could, m'deah.

Chelsea, Brangwyn's, the Royal Arsehole School of Art. Augustus and Jacob. I trod the boards—the Aldwych, you know—they all wanted me—Roger Fry, Anthony Powell. The best tits in London town, darling. Just needs someone to lift them out of tiredness. Walter Sickert did me nude on numerous occasions.

Me bust's in the V&A, don't you know—me bust with half a bust—perfect, but the left tit's knocked off. Passports to Russia, Paris and the Cafe Royal, these tits. Artistic baggage.

Dear Henri the French sculptor and me classic torso. He did me proud and immortalised me tits. It was like this. You see, this poverty-stricken genius was over from France to learn the King's lingo. He was in from Cardiff and Bristol as a clerk for a shipping firm. Then he washes up in the Fulham Road with his chisel and mallet. Lovely hands. Don't them Frenchies turn it, eh? It's that accent of theirs. 'I'm very poor, so would you model for me?' And I took off my clothes and posed for him. And then he took off his clothes and I drew him. And then we 'took tea'. Later, he wants to do me beautiful body. No marble. No money, so no sculpture for me immortality. Henri Gaudier Brzeska—a waterfall of a name.

So one night I shinned him over the stonemason's wall and we half-inched this classy piece of marble from the *Sadly Missed* and *Dearly Beloved Husband of*. Then back to his place and hours, days of me holding a pose. Which I can still do. I've modelled for the best of them. Henri and me, chip, chip, kiss, kiss. And that's me Torso in the V&A.! My stolen likeness. Stolen from death.

Not that his 'sister' Sophie could stand it. His mother more like, she was, with her fussing him and giving me the witch's eye. He could hardly move without her in tow. I knew all along they weren't Jack and Jill up the hill. Sister Sophie was his moll. Kiss, kiss, Siss, Siss. I stayed with her in Gloucestershire after the war, after Henri. What a strange bird! Always making jam—enough to feed a whole village. That was all that kept the locals from reporting her as a German spy. And the moon—how she'd never face the moon, always walked with her back to it, 'Don't look at it,' she'd cry, 'it will capture your soul.'

She was becoming madder and madder; and who could blame her after losing Henri? We both lost Henri.

He had a lovely wildness in the eyes, Henri, and his hands—the hands of a god. Last time I saw him was in Richmond Park drawing the deer, some of 'em ever so tame they came up to kiss his fingers. All blown away in France in the War. Fingers...all of him. That other war.

Poor little Amos there in my bed. And what's to become of you, young man, eh?

Wars where we fuck 'em and fend for 'em. And weep for 'em.

Another fire engine screaming away down a burning street- Ring! Ring! Ring! Ring! Ring!

Where am I going to sleep, tonight? Said Nautical William.

When the Hun got too close to Paris that first time we all fecked off... Oh, the Dome, the Boeuf, the Rotonde, the Cafe Parnasse, the gay times in Montparnasse... Modigliani pestering us with his handful of three franc drawings, Pablo and Chagall, Soutine, Zadkine the Ruskie carver and Pascin who painted me. Poulenc who played as I sang—one bomb would have turned the clock back on art and music and everything. Absinthe and Pernod Susies and oysters, and the smart set and the negro jazzy boys blowing the smoky night away. All on one night. Just one of those Big Berthas' big bangs would have put paid to us all—BOOM! Just like those poor buggers that night last year at the Café de Paris —Snakehips Johnson and his swinging west Indians, blown to smithereens by a Luftwaffe bomb in the middle of The Sheik of Araby. BOOM!

Still asleep, little Amos…what do you know of such things?

Oh, yes, I'm in our usual corner and Marc Chagall is making wings with his arms and laughing. Then a little man comes in. He has a bowler hat, always a bowler hat, and, whatever the weather, a rolled umbrella. A little man, a Charlie Chaplin man who was a piano magician, a traveller on music that carried you out of this world. All of it out of the head, from beneath the bowler hat; all of it out of this world which frightened him so that he carried a hammer under his coat against the dangers of the Montparnasse night. '*Allez, allez!*' He'd see them off, fierce little Eric.

'Monsieur Satie, Monsieur Satie! Who do you think will rob you? And what will they rob you of, what? You think the shadows will bite at your willy, lift your coat and bugger you? Eric, scuttle off back to your little *apartement* and tickle from the ivories your teasing little tunes.'

One night Modigliani chased me down the avenue and I shinned it up a street-lamp to give him the slip. I was up there half an hour as Montparnasse lit up the sky for me. Horse cabs, the good time girls. A Rolls Royce passed. And then soft rain.

Paris, Paris, Paris the centre of the whole world turning. And me dancing naked on the tables, the Coco Chanel number falling like a veil. I dressed to kill, in the best… hand-me-downs… from the very, the very best of society.

And then the bloody Hun came to wreck the party.

But I haven't lost my voice: *Oh, we don't want to lose you, but we think you ought to go…* poor, darling Henri. I see him face down in a trench…sometimes hung on the wire like a piece of sculpture. Did me torso. This torso.

Oh, we don't want to lose you, but we think you ought to go…

So, discretion being the better part of what was available, we all called it a night. I took the rollicky, bollicky ferry back to old Blighty. Didn't go back much after that.

Aw.. 'I have a pin that'll just fit in,' said Nautical William.

Left in the middle of doing the roofs of Paris, drawings, an oil. The roofs there, free out of any window and stiller than any model. I loved the roofs. And under those roofs Modigliani worked and died. His room, freezing and bare and rat-shitten, so that he had the frights. After he died— cold, starved, who knows? Afterwards Zawado showed me his death-mask. There was no dignity. And no noise to cover that there was no dignity—his mouth loose as an old fanny. It was nothing like the man. I lost his drawings, his three franc drawings. But that was later, years later, after the war. After the Omega Workshops with Roger Fry—who laid me out like a jazzy design on his bed. The Kaiser buggered. Henri dead. Fucked in Flanders. And my husband, my brief husband, Edgar the Norwegian god, had piddled off, to jail, to Belgium. After the baby. Who came before its time and did not last.

Crash! Another bomb. Not too far away this time. Little As Was sound as was a baby. Dead to the world. Nautical Amos from Tenby. BOOM again—though this time they're louder, and there's dozens—black wasps, not like the Kaiser's big, fat sky sausages.

Bombed last night, and bombed the night before.

Goin' to get bombed every night and...

*And...*and fucked the night before.

Need a drink. Amos has had enough, but Nina needs a drink.

Wally Sickert could have painted this place. It's brown and dark enough. I could play the tart, pouting in a dingy light, the right light. Spread-eagle on the bed, legs open. 'Open all hours—come bombs and Huns—we never close!' Wars, or dreary peace.

'You stick with your Uncle Walter, my girl,' he'd say.

'I never stick with any of 'em, Walter m'deah,' says I.

And none of them sticks with me.

This tunic smells of more than Amos...

But this time the Yanks have come—'The Yanks are coming, the Yanks are coming, the Yanks are coming... especially there'— there to me little pussy. It brightens up the old place with chewing gum and noise. And the good booze, juice of Scotland, quality stuff. The bony farm boys from the prairies. The sharp city Jews and Italians. Same names, some of 'em, as the Huns they're fighting.

Lots of moolah, spondoolicks with the Yanks. They'll pay for everything, and anything. Cheers, my boys, my Yankee boys.

And then there's my special Yank, my dearie Jay, the captain of the air. Picked me up in the Dog and Duck. He buys my work—no, my *work*—drawings, oils. Says I keep him sane with my 'crazy pals'. While he packs them off, his air force lads—the farmer's sons and the big city back street weasels, the drapers and the down and outs, all of 'em rising out of the flat fields into the blue. And the black and blue. And the bleeding and the burned, those of them that come back. And lots of them don't.

Jay says he wants beauty. 'Booty'. Doesn't talk much about the dead boys, the boys when they've gone missing over Munich, buggered over Berlin. Jay waves 'em off and wishes 'em back. And prays, I bet.

He loves London. 'Touching base,' he calls it. 'New York's old lady'. And me the Queen ... of all I survey... the Kingdom of Fitzrovia. And Lord Augustus of Fitzrovia.

More fire engines—clang, clang and fading away. A bad one somewhere else tonight. Though these blacked-out nights are made for mystery and malarkey—the click-clack of heels round the next corner are full of promise—they are our morse-code of naughtiness.

But still tonight's boy sleeps sound. Sail on in your dreams my Tenby lad—Caldey Island and the mackerel and those summer girls with their mums and dads you couldn't take your eyes off.

And here you are, little Amos the boatman beached, wet and glistening on old Nina. Dry old Nina. What a most pec-u-li-ar Tenby coincidence.

You laid your greatcoat at the feet of a London lady... the Queen of Fitzrovia. A cloak at the foot of the Queen, so's she can't see the shit on the street.

Amos and Jay... A to J and back again. Amos's little pin. Lynch pin. And Jay's tins—pineapples, beef. The Yanks are coming—loud and full of it. But Ma'am, they sure do bring colour. Rainbow Corner buzzes like flies on meat. The Colonels taking their pick of the whores and the pretty boys—like a Cairo bazaar. Cunny for a pack of Camels. Cock for candy. Bum for bully beef and chewing gum.

But my *Lew-tenant*, my Jay wants more than that. I'm his guide—Fitzrovia, the Café Royal. Jay wants 'booty' and I'm his queen. He's been introduced to the whole of society—Lucky Lucian Freud, Roos and the two queer Roberts, Violet and Gus. He's seen the whole parade round here. The Fitzroy fellowship.

Gus lording it as always:

John! John!
How he's got on!
He owes it, he knows it, to me!
Brass earrings I wear,
And I don't do my hair,
When I walk down the street,
All the people I meet
They stare at the things I have on!
When Battersea-Parking
You'll hear folk remarking:
There goes an Augustus John.

Gus is the Emperor and I'm the Queen. He's more famous than the rest of 'em put together. Always good to me, Augustus—Paris to London, we Tenby folk stick together. Whatever floozy's on his arm, he still comes across to see me, and stands me a gin. 'My Welsh beauty—famous from St Florence to the Fitzroy,' says he.

'Oh, Lord of the brushes, Prince of the palette,' says I, 'Mine's a very big gin, m'deah.' Buys my pictures too—now there's a man of taste.

But that funny sister of his from Tenby, Gwen, ended up in France. Quiet little soul, with a cat wrapped round her all the time. Rodin's model, they say she was, and his whore, no doubt. Rodin's little pussy. Though she'd dried up by the time I got to Paris. Shrunk and skinny, ditched and alone, but then she got a rich yank to buy her work. I could have done with that.

A good man is hard to find and harder to hold. Good men—Jay and Gus—and this boy Amos for all I know. They go, the young men, all of 'em. To death. Or respectability.

Augustus's son Henry, the one who found religion and then 'love' and then him going off a cliff into the sea. Probably jumped, pushed over by love unrequited. Henri and Georges and Cocteau's pretty boy Chrissy Wood who saw no future, or saw the future all too clearly and threw himself under a train. Came back to England and went under the three-thirty.

At Salisbury, for God's sake! Keep off the opium, m'deah. Christopher Wood, the boy could paint too. Strange in the head. Queer business, you might say.

I sometimes wish when I am tight
That I were an hermaphrodite
And then, united to a black
Deep-bosomed nymphomaniac
We'd be wafted up to heaven
In position forty-seven.

Here's one more drink for all the boys—the Yanks, the toffs, the trumpet players and the Taffs.

*

199

The most famous Taff's Young Dylan who's got himself a cosy number in the war films business: 'I'm the Welsh secret weapon against Adolf.'—hush, hush—says he'll try and get me a part. 'I'm a museum piece,' says I. 'I'll dust you off,' says he, 'And make an exhibition of you.'

There's words...

Need a wee-wee.

Piddle's like a mountain stream...oh, that's better... that boy could sleep through a Tenby downpour... and Nina's piss is a fine vintage.

Champagne, m'deah? The sort of champagne Alistair drank—Chateau de Pissoire. I've known them all—Crowley the black wizard thought he'd have me for libel in court, but I had 'im! More wanker than wizard, was Alistair. But he did for that lovely Oxford boy, did for poor old Raoul Loveday. The Oxford lad knew nothing, was young and daft as only those as goes to Oxford can be. He died after that nonsense at the Abbey at Sicily, where Crowley held his black court. Crowley. The things he made them do—drink goat's blood, cat's blood. The chanting and get-ups. Living in shit, eating shit, they say.

Is that what he was so fascinated by and frightened of, the Loveday boy? With that mumbo-jumbo nonsense and danger. You'd think he'd have known better. All of them. All of them watching Scarlet Leah fucked by a goat and Crowley cutting its throat at the climax. More than the little death, that one!

Abracadabra—wallah, wallah, wallah!

Crazy, crazy Crowley—the man who served the best cocktail in Paris—one of his Kubla Khan's No 2, and my deah, you was transported, with no need of the Devil's ticket and that satanic mumbo-jumbo.

And then the miserable shit sued me in court—for the truth I told in my *Laughing Torso*. Libel, my arse! And the truth came out. And I took him for a pretty shilling! Took him for his shirt! Kept me in gin and furs for a while.

Dropped your shirt little sailor Amos. Let's tuck you up nice an' warm.

She was poor, but she was honest....

'Where am I going to sleep tonight?' said Bollocky Bill the Sailor.

'You may sleep within my bed, Sir,' said the fair young lady.

'There's no room for two in a bed,' said Bollicky Bill the Sailor.

'You may sleep within my thighs, Sir,' said the fair young lady.

'What shall I find between your thighs?' said Bollicky Bill the Sailor.

'You shall find a nice pincushion,' said the fair young lady.

'I have a pin that'll just fit in,' said Bollicky Bill the Sailor.

A pin, a pin. Nothing but a pin. Their pins are the pricks of this world we hide for them. Make them safe.

'Where am I going to sleep tonight?'

Here, little Amos from Tenby. With Nina from Tenby, who has seen things you can't dream of. So dream that those bombs are the lifeboat's call out. And the Blitz's fires streets away are a warm breeze off the ocean. The red glow from the East End is the last flare of a summer sun falling over Giltar Point.

Here comes Nina again to warm you up. 'Cos the cold, cold ocean waits for you.

You'll need sleep nowhere else tonight. No where. Else. But here.

A Cuckoo in the Nest

Sally

I cried. On many occasions I cried. In a matter of weeks she'd lost so much weight, her skin was pale, her colour gone. When I helped her shower, near the end of it all, clumps of her auburn hair came out and Mike had to clear the drain. Once when she tried to move up from her bed I heard her ribs crack. That would have been the wasting, I thought.

Until her illness Jane was undistinguished; I mean, in the sense that she was another one of my students, another in the arbitrarily assigned tutor group each of us picked up every September. Average height, mousey hair; just average in a cohort that had a range of tattoos, piercings, racial and religious indicators, including one niqab and one lad with a hearing aid loop system and a mic for the lecturer. She had said little in the first seminar group on Sylvia Plath and her essay had been as competently plodding as the rest. But I'd seen her later that day on a bench on campus looking a bit forlorn and had sat down beside her and asked how she was settling in to university life. She was from Lincoln, a long way from home, and had been made to go through Clearing. We were not any of her university choices and she'd had trouble getting digs as a late entrant. Rentals were at a premium as the two new call centres –insurance and loans—had brought more young people into the town. Both her parents were now dead and she'd been brought up mainly by an aunt. Recent deaths were implied and so I guessed that her A Level grades had slipped and her offer from Bristol had turned into the new and barely-formed University of Stroud and Women's Writing 101 with me. I'd been on the point of inviting her for a coffee, but the hearing loop lad had come to sit on the bench with us and then Jane had gone off to the library. That term went without her really making another blip on my radar and it wasn't until the beginning of the January term that I'd learned of her illness.

Mike

Of course, Sally's commitment to the girl and her predicament became ours to share. I wasn't at all sure about the sense of having her to live with us, but Sally had got really involved with her situation and it was, clearly, the Christian thing to do, what with her parents being gone and the severity of her illness. We couldn't let her live in shared digs and fall back on the sympathy or otherwise of rudely assembled undergrads in their first and wild year.

As soon as I mentioned it at work young Lewis from IT support went all concerned and before you could say three hail Marys he'd taken it on himself to raise some funding; sponsorship for the Bristol half-marathon, proceeds of the office New Year raffle with prizes including a week's stay at the manager's cottage in Brittany, and a balloon trip in Bath. All this after just the one visit to Sally's study, which had become Jane's sick room. Why bother, I thought? When you are that seriously ill the NHS has everything covered, don't they. And we were not yet at the stage of needing Macmillan nurses. In any case, Sally was practically full-time caring between her teaching commitments, and the bits of cooking she was still doing for us. Research on the Feminist Novel in Scottish literature had gone out of the window.

Then, after the half-marathon raised several hundred quid Lewis announced that it would be Lourdes; that he'd always meant it to take Jane to Lourdes. He pinned up a total-raised graph on the notice board by the coffee machine with a photo of Bernadette's Grotto. Lourdes! Ye gods, what on earth could that possibly mean? Organising the travel, with a wheelchair probably; how does one get insurance? How uplifting can it be to join the procession of the hopeless faithful, the desperate doomed, the last-chance saloon-bound and their pushers? A desperate grab for some kind of immortality. Lewis, the lapsed former altar-boy, was transformed by Jane's predicament into a startlingly unexpected lay enthusiast. One half-expected him to leave the firm and take up holy orders.

It's an ill wind..... as they say.

Jenny

At least I still had my room at home; they kept that clear. My Adele posters were on the far wall, the framed print of the V&A Bowie exhibition above the door; and my bookshelves were intact with complete sets of Harry Potter, Jacqueline Wilson and Roald Dahl, in chronological order. Mum gave up her study in mid-January and Dad had pushed her desk into one corner and assembled the single bed in there. Talk of a specialist final days bed with all the gismos never came to pass, or goodness knows how they would have managed. When I went home briefly at Easter I saw that Mum had taken to marking essays on the kitchen table. I saw little of the patient: she needed peace and quiet and I was focussed on revision and my final year project until the June; when it was all over anyway. They'd pencilled me in for the Lourdes trip as a helper, but, of course, it never came to that. To be honest, brutally honest, I never bought into the whole Samaritan thing: I swung between guilt and irritation. Mainly irritation. She was almost the same age as me, but I found it difficult to relate to her or the illness. My then boyfriend Marcus began giving off critical vibes: 'You can be so cool, so detached.' But he didn't have to witness the destruction of his family, he wasn't the one who felt more and more peripheral in the family home. Anyway, Marcus and I moved apart, geographically and emotionally after graduation: I never bothered to share with him the whole story. When we learned the whole story.

Sally

It would be crass to put it down to empty nest syndrome. I mean, Jenny had been at Durham for two years and though it was too far for us to pop up to for visits on mid-term weekends she was coming home in the vacations and probably welcomed her freedom. I overheard her describe me at a summer barbecue as her helicopter mother. That may have been the garden party punch and Mike's carefree splashing into it of gin and something lethal we'd had left over from a Greece trip years before. Later, he threw the punch dregs on the border and I feared for my roses.

Jane seemed so bereft—losing her parents, dropping grades, then cancer, that I did what seemed natural at the time, what any mother would have done; though that may have been impulsive in retrospect. I should say that it was my idea. She didn't push for the room or our hospitality, though her alarming weight-loss and those sunken eyes were compellingly sad and moving. What if it had been Jenny, I thought.

'What if Jenny needed help and didn't have us? Miles away in some strange place?' I said to Mike.

'It's just Durham, not Darfur,' he said, 'and there are regular trains; besides, the motorway takes us a fair way up when we drive.' And then, 'It's not like Jane's related to us.'

In truth, I'd been settling into a middling life at Stroud: manageable mediocre teaching, the odd conference paper and my dusty Scottish feminism PhD from ten years before barely brought back to life. Like blowing into one of those ambulance practice dummies.

Either Mike or I drove her to her appointments at the General but, of course, it was not our place to go in with her for the consultations, the tests, or to discuss her prognosis or possible treatments. I'd wait in the car and put on Classic FM while doing some marking. On one of his turns Mike nearly completed the Telegraph Cryptic one afternoon, but for one clue: 'In labour, seeking the PM'. I could never match that. The year before, on our break in

Lanzarote, the Torygraph was the only non red top we could buy and I found that crossword impenetrable even when checking the answers the following day. Sometimes answers are so obliquely related to their questions that the route's not worth straining for. And sometimes it's so obvious that you create your own fog of incomprehension.

Cryptic: pertaining to a place where the dead are put to rest.

Mike

If I am being selfish about it then so be it; because having someone else in the house just as we had got used to having the place to ourselves for most of the time was not what I had expected or welcomed. When your child goes to university and grows away from you it is, initially, a cold chill of absence that you have to deal with. They have physically changed and, lord knows, have they been through the teenage mill. As have you. But it is still a body blow to lose them to another city, another set of relationships and mentors and to face completely losing control over their development—character, intellect, life decisions. They've flown the nest and you wait for those witty texts or the Facebook asides; if you're lucky, a photo from WhatsApp. And then it goes quiet and you realise that they've switched to different media for the real stuff that's going on for them. The stuff that has nothing to do with you and is no longer your business. Though missing them becomes a less constant ache. You know they'll be alright, won't they?

Not to mention the freedom: a sense of loss segues into a realisation that you two have the place to yourself for the first time in almost two decades. Evenings, weekends are yours. You rediscover your sex life; could well re-invent it if those Sunday life style magazine columns are to be believed.

Well, thanks to Jane, all that's fucked.

I accept that Sally did most of the hands-on stuff. And at least Jane could get to the spare bathroom from Sally's study. I'd offered to go up and read to her in the evenings, but she'd not been able to engage with that. Once I'd got to the second chapter of the new Rankin, then tried pieces from the Guardian Weekend, then ventured into McEwan's *Saturday* but she'd drifted off and I gave up. My fault perhaps, but I'd felt awkward from the beginning. If I'd stuck to it and tried to properly engage with her perhaps things would have been clearer earlier.

Sally

I can see that Mike would need to keep some distance from her: one of us had to. I know he'd occasionally take up her tray; and there was his offer of reading to her; which was sweet, though that didn't last long. He didn't seem to engage with who Jane was. I suppose he left that to me, or perhaps I didn't leave room for anyone else. In any case, everything I learned about her I shared with him, whether he wanted to know or not.

After three or four visits to the hospital she seemed resigned to things and kept herself to my study, her room. She didn't want to sit with us in the lounge. She had my old PC on the desk so could watch TV and play music. I introduced her to Brahms and Mozart, but kept her clear of late Beethoven and the heavy, dark stuff. We sat together through Vaughan Williams's 'Pastoral' a couple of times; though I didn't say that it was the music that I'd chosen for my funeral. She wasn't much interested in the newspapers, young people seem to be able to exist without them anyway; she slept more and more, which was to be expected. That time when she stayed in the General overnight for treatment she again insisted on being left and collected in the main entrance hall. So we respected her privacy and her determination to see things through using her own resources. Her parents and other family memories were out of bounds, though she did speak affectionately about a collie dog they'd had for ten years or so, Jess. And trips to an uncle in Norfolk when she'd been at junior school. Concerning the demise of her parents, she spoke not at all: 'It's still very raw.' Both had been office workers of some sort, we gathered. We assumed that she'd lived with an aunt or someone before coming to uni. When I checked in the college records the home address was in Stoke-on Trent, but had been crossed out.

Jenny

I was happy to lend her my boxed set of 'Girls', the first two series. Though neither mum nor dad actually asked me before offering them to her. Nothing about death, but plenty of body issues with Lena Dunham. And there's always that channel which shows every episode of 'Friends' on a continuous loop anyway: day into night and back into day. Saviours of the sick and house-bound. The week or so I spent at home in the Easter vac before going to stay with Marcus in Edgbaston was when I should have realised. I had looked in when the door was ajar and although she was invalided under the covers I could see the light of her mobile and hear the text going off. Also, I had a suspicion that she'd been at my bottle of Beyonce *Rise* 'The spirit of *Rise* encourages women to be all that we are.' Because there was an aura around her which wasn't entirely what sickness should be. Classic death-bed scenes in art and novels are always about the light and feelings, not the smell; though serious illness, I thought, would give off more than student bed fragrance mixed with Beyonce. The *Rising* of Lazarus, I thought. And then immediately felt guilty. I suppose I had had enough of her death-scene in my house, my home, and I was looking to lift the lid on whatever was going on. Sympathy fatigue setting in early. Every night Mum would fetch Jane's phone down to where we all charged ours in the kitchen; I once took a look when unplugging it: lots of texts and emails, most to the same two numbers and addresses, which I took to be her aunt. But weeks later, near the end, when Mum had the phone in her hand walking back up the stairs to return it to her it rang; it was Jane's dead father who was on the line.

Sally

He sounded normal enough. He had been moved around with his work and they had been in all those places Jane had mentioned, except it wasn't the army. Of course it wasn't. Doug, 'Call me, Doug, I've never been Douglas.' He'd been something between counter and back-room in Barclays and had been chasing promotions, moving from branch to branch. Her mother had left them around the time of the Leicester move and had never made it to Lincoln. He'd assumed that Jane had stayed up at university to settle in and study: they'd never been much for family gatherings and since the split often had Christmas and birthdays apart. He'd assumed she was with college friends.

As for his wife, 'the mother' he called her, they were not in touch and hadn't had anything to do with each other since the divorce. 'Might as well be dead,' he added. Indeed.

I told him that Jane's case had been before the faculty board and that in everyone's interest it had been felt best if she took a sabbatical to gather herself together and sort things out. She had moved out from our house and not left her forwarding address with the university registry. What surprised me most was that he did not blow up, protest, query or in any other way react to what I assumed must be both disturbing and annoying. What if our Jenny had pulled the same trick on one of her tutors at Durham? We would have been distraught. We turned out to have been the victims of the inverted proxy in Munchausen's by Proxy Syndrome. Or whatever. The clumps of hair she'd cut to take to the shower. The anorexic throwing up after meals. As Jenny said, 'The Oscar for Best Supported Actress.'

There's nowt so queer as folk. Or gullible, it seems.

Really, it was my anger, embarrassment, confusion of feelings which I was projecting on to this man Doug. Doug the bank clerk. Did banks even have clerks anymore? Was he the smiling face at the counter? Or the bloke they sit you with in a nondescript room when you want to change your car, or get a loan to put your daughter up in her university town? Did this guy actually make decisions which affected people's lives? Computer—it say Whatever...

He didn't call me back and I thought, let him sodding well sort out the mess of his own marriage and his family.

We've moved on. Jenny's on her gap year in Stockport: Children Reading for Freedom has their head office there and she may get to visit Swaziland after Christmas. They say.

I've bought a new rug for my study and Mike's re-decorated. It's what the TV property programmes call a 'make over'.

Mike's busy with his golf lessons and re-roofing the shed, which he hammers at constantly. He reads less and doesn't seem to be able to stick with a book. The new Sebastian Faulks I bought him for his birthday has the bookmark stuck between pages 97 and 98. I've been checking. When I challenged him he said something weak about trying to edge one for his century. Which I knew was cricket, but pretended to be perplexed. Which I am.

The whole thing is perplexing and unresolved and I want to move on. Or back to working on Mitchison's *Cloud Cuckoo Land*, A. L Kennedy's *So I am Glad* , Ali Smith's *Hotel World*, Val McDermid's *Clean Break*. And, of course, Miss Jean Brodie. Because I'm in my prime, aren't I?

Jane

There's a dream I have. It's at the seaside and I'm on a promenade or a pier, some walkway alongside the sea. And it's like I've been moved out, evicted from where I live, with stuff from my home laid out as if it were some boot sale, or something. Wherever I was moving to either I'm not there yet, or maybe that's not where I'm going anymore. Gulls dive, gawp and squawk. That old-fashioned front room lamp we had in every place before we moved to Lincoln is there, and a sideboard and the upright piano I had lessons on in Leicester and in Salisbury, is floating out to sea. Upright. *La Mer.* Debussy, or something. There's a box of odds and ends—lamps, china, books, that wooden duck my mother took with her when she left. And the cane backed, striped cushioned conservatory chair, though we never had a conservatory at any of the places we lived. With dad being in the army we moved around an awful lot.

I am walking up and down, pacing really. What is it I am waiting for? Who is it?

The weather is not good, not seaside weather. I am wearing that shiny blue mac I had in the sixth-form. And a scarf. It flies in the wind off the sea like a flag, like that dancer whose scarf caught in the wheels of the sports car and killed her. Isadora Duncan.

I am turning my head as if looking for someone, or as if someone had called my name. But there's no-one there.

H.M.S. Cassandra

I picked him up from his bus-stop this side of Cardiff. He hadn't shaved and carried a battered suitcase tied up with string. It was like some debris from a refugee camp, but had a fresh Lufthansa sticker on the side. He had been given the trip to the Berlin Poetry International the previous winter. Opening the door of my car was like letting in the muggy waft of a public bar.

'That's the first bloody sky-lark those buggers at the Arts Council have thrown me in years,' he said, 'Probably because no-one else wanted to go.'

I asked him what it had been like. 'So fucking cold it was, boy—a cold city Berlin. If you're sober. Not that many of us were. Full of heavy-jowled, be-suited official poets from behind the big curtain.' I hadn't known it was East Berlin.

'Oh, yes, boy, it was the wrong side of the Wall. Or the right, depending on your flag. The commies—Russians, Yugoslavs, Czechs—they're always having these arty jamborees to prove they have real writers. You come away knowing nothing more about actual life over there. And caring even less. The stuff sounds like a badly dubbed film from the war over the translation headphones—all tractors, freedom and uncovered Nazi atrocities. Half their lives are spent in profound contemplation on a snowed-in railway station somewhere.'

'You didn't enjoy the trip, then?'

'What ? Course I did. No complaints. I cut away from the forums and hit the beer-cellars with this Pole—Eric, I called him—couldn't understand a bloody word. A slice of life though—all grist to the mill.'

All this was in the late seventies and Griffiths would have been in his early fifties; that time when there was a late flowering of the work—those dark bitter poems. Life slurred through broken-down teeth. It was year or two before that collection *With a Long Spoon* came out; the one that went into paperback and won an award in London. He hadn't made it that big at the time I'm talking of—a couple of books from the Welsh publishers—the odd half-hour spot on t.v. from Cardiff. He was the poet they'd wheel out if there was a nit-picking issue about Wales and culture they thought would fill a token half-hour slot. The state of Anglo-Welsh Literature, that mouldy chestnut of the English language being allowed at the Eisteddfod—you know the sort of thing. Sometimes I think that arguing about Welshness is the only thing that makes us Welsh. Anyway, he'd liked some of my stuff in the magazines and we'd exchanged letters and phone-calls. We had never met, though he lived just a twenty-minute drive across the city. He'd been invited to do the Dyfed Music Festival, a couple of readings with music. Well, I hadn't a clue, but a student of mine put me on to a singer who lived down in west Wales and was cheap. The three of us were to do an afternoon in Glanmor and another in the grounds of an hotel between St. David's and Fishguard. Two sets of poems, with the singer coming in between to give some relief from the words.

He talked incessantly on the drive down to Pembrokeshire. It was July and the traffic was heavy. I had imagined he'd be cold, keeping his distance, but he talked and talked, mainly about other writers, gossip with a sharpened edge. He couldn't stand Margot Evans, 'that Queen of the salons,' he called her. And then he'd deepen the conversation and come out with something heavy like, 'I write in order to slow the whole thing down—I want to catch death by the balls.' All the time his left hand clutched the passenger door handle as if he thought I was going to turn us over in a package of windscreen glass and blood. I move along a bit, but I've never been that bad a driver.

I think the trouble for him might just have been machines, any machines. There's that poem in *The Collected Poems*—'the grunts and slobber of cogs and oil '—something like that. He'd got by over the years with train tickets, and the Tube when he was on the staff of a paper in London, but he didn't seem at ease with things as personally controlled as a car, or tape recorders, or cameras. 'The tedious inevitability of human error.' Perhaps that's why he was so aggressive on the box; sometimes he'd snarl past the camera as if it were some voyeur who had no business eavesdropping on him. At other times he'd glare directly into the lens like a blood-and-brimstone preacher, right into the hearts and guilt of the pews beneath him. Of course, at other times he could be what Margot called, 'a pussy cat'.

At the St. Clears traffic lights I had to brake hard behind a cattle-truck with no tail-lamps and his knuckles went white. He pulled a hip-flask from the inside pocket of his jacket, took a mouthful which he rinsed around his mouth and between his teeth before swallowing. He offered me one, which struck me as odd, but I refused of course, which is why he'd offered, no doubt.

When we reached Glanmor I parked the car in the new multi-storey and then called Ralph Dawkins from a phone-box on the main street. Dawkins was our contact for the reading there and I had a paper from the Arts Council with his details. Griffiths paced outside the phone-box like a chained, moth-eaten tiger, smoking and picking at the stone-work of the old town walls at each turn. Dawkins told us to call at his restaurant before going up to the venue on top of the West Cliff. He warned us against bringing the car; it was a narrow and awkward track, he said, and the weather was for walking, wasn't it? He had a high, whiney voice with an accent that was Lord Cut-Glass, confident, born to lead. Everything that Griffiths hated, in fact, and I feared there would be trouble.

He wheezed and moaned as we walked slowly out of the old walled town and started along the West Cliff road. 'Bloody English settlers. Why can't this Dawkins bloke drag himself away from his money-making to pick up the poets, then? What is he—some sort of sodding English leech?'

I tried to steer him off the subject. 'The Emerald Hotel over there,' I said, 'My old aunt used to wash up in their kitchens every summer. Came in from her rotten little cottage back down the Swansea road. Probably the only time her hands got washed too. She must have ruined a few holidays with what she brought in under her nails.' I began to remember more details of Aunt Annie and would have run through the stories of her wart charming powers and other witch-like behaviour, but we found ourselves outside Long John's, which was Dawkins's place. It was on the first floor of one of the large, eighteenth century townhouses looking back towards the West Beach and the harbour. A man greeted us from behind the till by the door:

'Ah, our poets—so good to see you. And right on time. Welcome to you both. I'm so looking forward to our first poetry reading.'

He was a lanky man with a stiff bearing and a firm handshake that altered the impression which I had formed of him from my phone call. He was a few years older than I, in his late thirties, and I had expected an older man. He sat us at one of the tables with a view and offered white wine from a carafe. We both said we'd eaten before leaving Cardiff, though Griffiths took a round of prawn sandwiches with his wine. Dawkins explained that the cliff-top house had been in his family for years, coming to him three years back when his great-uncle had died.

'I mentioned the Temple on the phone, didn't I? The old boy had it built back in the early Twenties—the last of the Welsh follies, sort of. There 's a story about Isadora Duncan dancing there. Isadora or one of her followers. He'd certainly bring a string quartet up for parties in the garden. I've been looking for an opportunity to put the thing to use ever since the place came to me. There's a tremendous view from that point. So, finish your wine, gentlemen, and come up and see it for yourselves.' He took off his apron and gave instructions to a waiter. We were due to start at 4.30. and I was getting worried about the singer, who'd not been mentioned. Griffiths wasn't bothered about anything by then. He'd smiled and nodded at Dawkins's story of the Temple, while finishing off the carafe of wine. The last two glasses even encouraged him to muse a little: he began to extol the beauty of the sand, the bay and the old town.

'Imagine what it must have been like before the Great War, before that waste of young guts in the mud, eh ? Under Edward—horse-drawn, tea and tiffin under the parasols, ankles sexy in the waves. Cigars and walking-cane. And then a slow train creaking its way back up the line to Carmarthen. I sometimes think I was born too late.'

I was about to remind him of the stream of broad socialism and dissent that had coloured his writing, but he was mellowing there in the sun that began to shine strongly through the bay window, and I let it go.

The climb up to the West Cliff was a trial. I was pretty well in trim in those days with regular tennis and two young kids to chase after, but the sun had strengthened through the cloud cover and Griffiths had slowed down to a crawl. After three or four minutes he stopped and sank sideways into the hedge, saying he'd had it and why hadn't I used the bloody car? Dawkins apologised, but said that he always walked to the restaurant, as exercise; he also pointed out the pot-holes, which were certainly a problem for cars. He promised to return us to the car-park in his Land Rover. 'I'll be done for by then,' protested Griffiths, rubbing at his chest. But, after a long mouthful from his hip-flask, he got back to his feet and we continued. We made another hundred yards or so then cut through a hedge into a large, landscaped garden laid around a low, white house. There were neat shrubs and an ornamental fish pond into which Griffiths hawked loudly and spat. He was looking as flushed as a wino by then, but as we followed the path around the house and down the steps to the Temple he almost broke into a run.

At first I was disappointed. The temple was a mini-theatre along Greek lines, with a semi-circle of stone slabs banked into four rows of seats. The performing area was four or five yards across with a couple of broken doric pillars framing the view across the bay. It was this view which made the place. Over the edge of a wall between the pillars was a sheer drop to the rocks creaming the sea, over a hundred feet below. The curve of the cliff opened up a fine view of the old town. You could see the line of the medieval walls, the harbour and the old fort on the hill. The sky was clear now with just a fleck of cloud remaining to the east.

'Just like postcard, boy. What a place for a reading, eh ? Worth that bloody climb.'

Griffiths seemed fully recovered and was raring to go. And indeed an audience had materialised behind us. There were five people: three elderly women who seemed quite happy to be out in the air and talking to each other, a studious, self-contained boy of about seventeen who wore heavy glasses, and a man in his late thirties who had a distinguished air. He was casually dressed in cords and a pullover, but everything about him looked quality tailored, leisure made-to-measure. Ralph was returning from the house carrying a tray with glasses, a bottle of mineral water and a carafe of white wine. He smiled at the audience and introduced the man to us as his brother, Jeremy, who was visiting. 'Do call me Jeremy,' the man said.

'Where's the bloody musician?' grumbled Griffiths, breathing smoke and wine breath into my face. I apologised and began to explain the tenuous nature of the contact, but he lost interest and turned back to the view.

He was in the middle of his third poem when the singer noisily turned up. He finished the verse, paused to glare at the lad, who'd flicked open the catches of his guitar case, then completed his first set of poems. The audience had swollen by this time with arrival of two more elderly women, and then a family of Brummies who'd obviously taken the wrong turn off the cliff path and were too bewildered to leave. Jason, the singer, had brought along four friends, which, at least, made the whole performance seem more credible as an event. Still, I couldn't dispel the feeling of disappointment which the reading was giving me. I read reasonably well, mainly to impress Griffiths, but he, after the rather turgid, committed ballads of Jason's interlude, put everything into his second set of poems. He ended with 'Cold Blessing', which he introduced as a new poem. I thought it was stunning, and one of the women clapped. This was indeed a real poet. The man who'd written that could be forgiven for anything, I thought. Then he sat down and the rest of the audience, myself included, clapped. The Brummy father came up and said it wasn't really their line of country, but thank you.

Griffiths signed a copy of one of his books for the women who'd clapped, then Dawkins pointed us up to the house. We were to have refreshments which his wife had prepared. I was thinking it would have better if she had come to swell the audience, but when she entered to serve us coffee all was forgiven. Audrey was an attractive woman, late thirties, slim with expensively cut hair and a Laura Ashley summer dress. I felt high after the reading and warmed by the sight of her. I couldn't stop myself staring at the wisp of hair at her neck as she moved around us with the tray. There was a brushing of soft hair under her arms and her face, without make-up was strawberries and cream in the way only Englishwomen can be.

'We were so pleased to be able to put the Temple to good use,' she said. She thought perhaps they might interest the local drama group, and there was the possibility through the Arts Council of a string trio from Aberystwyth.

Jeremy came in with the singer. He said he had liked Jason's stuff, bland, folksy pathos and concern, and was inviting him to play on his ship at Fishguard.

'Got a yacht, have you?' interrupted Griffiths, mouth full, spraying biscuit.

Dawkins explained that Jeremy, his half-brother, and he had both joined the Royal Navy from school. 'I resigned my commission five years ago, but old Jeremy here has gone from strength to strength,' he said, matter of factly.

Jeremy said to Jason, 'The chaps with me in *Cassandra* would love to have some live entertainment, music on the bill this evening—we can't pay you, but I can say with confidence that a good time will be enjoyed by all. The Royal Navy knows how to entertain, believe me. Well, what do you say? Are you game?'

'The Queen's Navy never spared the bottle or the grog, as I recall,' said Griffiths, 'Those navy boys were a riot in London in the war.'

Jeremy was shaken. The sailor's eyes flickered twice, quickly and his mouth poised around a show of teeth. But he rode the blow with professional grace, saying, almost without hesitation, that, of course, we were included in the invitation. In fact, some of his chaps were keen readers and that a couple of poems might make an interesting interlude in the evening's musical entertainment.

Later, as I drove north towards Fishguard, I said to Griffiths, 'What the hell have we let ourselves into?'

'Take a chance, boy,' he said, 'We've got to be in Fishguard for tomorrow anyway, so why not accept the hospitality of Her Majesty's Navy?'

'No matter how grudging that may be,' I said, 'I mean, do you really think he wants us, too? He asked the singer.'

But he was off on one of his long speeches about the role of the poet, the eyes of the blind, a prophet unsung in his own land. How, in Wales, the poet was the natural successor and antidote to the ranting priest. 'You've got to shout. take the bastards on. Otherwise they'll grind you down with their indifference. Because they care only about their cars, and their double-glazing, and their wives's sagging tits. You've got to be outside it all—take it from me. Look to the chances. They're few enough in the grunting banality of this world. And, hey, that Ralph's Audrey was a bobby-dazzler, wasn't she? A jolly roger raiser. A high class filly, that one.'

We reached Fishguard around tea-time and I drove down to the harbour to check on the place where the *Cassandra*'s launch was supposed to pick us up. We had two hours to kill and found a cafe. Griffiths didn't want to be bothered with inspecting the B&B place we'd been booked into, but I phoned them from the cafe anyway. Then we walked up and back through the small town with its gift shops and docks smell. Griffiths grumbled at every gift shop—the rock, the plastic beach stuff and cheap mementoes. I remember buying one of those flying disc frisbee things for my kids. Back in the car park I tried to show Griffiths how to throw it. He was quite hopeless and quickly used up all his breath. I was starving, but he said to wait, as the British Navy would be sure to feed us like kings. So, I drove back down to the harbour and parked the car in the grounds of the Hotel Westward, which gave a good view of the quay we needed.

In the bar Griffiths began on pints, several pints. 'They live like kings, those British tars. Last of the Empire. You mark my words, boy, there'll be good grub and a stream of booze.'

I drank a Campari and soda, a literary drink, I thought. And then another two, emptying both bowls of nuts and raisins at the bar to keep me going. I said that life in the services was the last thing that I'd want.

'Oh, of course, not for a family man. And you're too young to have done National Service. That was a game. How many bloody angry young writers have pissed out their memoirs of those glorious chapters of British history —Cyprus, Singapore, Eden, Berlin and Brecon.'

I asked him what his war experiences had been. He finished his pint in a long swallow before explaining that they'd found one of his legs shorter than the other and that he'd been restricted to working as a journalist in Fleet Street for the duration. I later heard a story about Griffiths's pal sorting him out a friendly doctor who'd signed him out of the war. That might have been true for all I know. I couldn't imagine that Griffiths's body, even then, would have made a significant contribution to our fight against fascism, and that way, at least, he'd not been wasted like poor Alun Lewis. He went on about Dylan making good out of the war, with scripts and talks and screenplays. He'd seen him from time to time in London. 'Drinking with the smart thinkers—directors, BBC wallahs and the publishing boys. Propaganda was his line, as far as I could see. No bugger's made his fortune out of poetry—except Browning, Eliot and some of the circus-ring Yanks.'

I'd had three or four Camparis by this time and the medicine taste had softened and mellowed. The salted nuts had run out and I was taking less and less soda in the drink. I think at this point I went into a long monologue about the vivacity of the Americans. How I'd rather write like Lowell or Plath than Dylan and Watkins. Brought up as a television kid, it was the pop music and films of Hollywood that nourished my imagination: rites of passage that went from Buddy Holly through to Del Shannon and the Beach Boys.

'Different times—different games,' he said, and bewailed the passing of the cinema at its prime. ' *Gone with the Wind,* Edward G., Garbo, Lana Turner, *The Cruel Sea.*'

It was past nine and Jeremy had promised a launch by 9.15. We left the hotel bar and at the front door I nearly keeled over. The salt air of the Irish Sea scoured the inside of my skull. It was a slow walk down to the quay side. From there we had a good view of the ship—metallic grey, the ensign waving at her stern and the glint of brass in the last of the evening sun. The horizon was far and clear, so you felt as if you could have stood on a ladder and seen Ireland. The *Cassandra* looked a fine ship—so fine it made me want to cry. Whether it was the drink, or all those stiff-upper-lip war films dredged up in the mind, I don't know. Most likely it was the drink. But there was strange feeling of potency and significance that she gave off.

'That ship could ride the whole world,' I said.

By ten o'clock the sun had fallen, we had paced the whole quay, and the mystery had all but evaporated. It was getting chilly and there was still no sign of the launch. Griffiths was for giving it up. But a patrolling docks copper came past and proved sympathetic. We got him to radio through to the *Cassandra.* They were awfully sorry. Of course. They'd picked up the singer earlier, but the launch was coming back over in a short while to collect us.

'The bastards don't want us,' grumbled Griffiths. I resisted the temptation to say I told you so; I wanted to reach that ship. I was still high on the Campari and getting a dry, sandy mouth. I wanted to finish the trip.

The launch duly arrived and we were ferried out. An officer saluted us and we were piped aboard as we climbed up the steps at the ship's towering side. This mark of respect obviously tickled Griffiths and he was in high spirits again as we were shown to the Petty Officers' quarters. The singer was finishing of his stint, apparently, and we were to join him in a while at the captain's party. There was no mention of our reading poems.

The P.O.'s were drinking in a room which seemed incredibly small. Four of them slept there and in one corner they had arranged an improvised bar with a fridge, several cases of beer and an assortment of bottles of spirits. They were as bemused as we were at our arrival and the captain's request that they entertain a couple of poets. They'd had worse jobs though, and were a sociable bunch. There was a cockney and a couple of northerners. They'd seen the world and it had seen them often enough. 'It doesn't matter a toss where you are after a while—hot or cold, yellow or pink,' one of them said. I wanted to hear about it all—the Far East and the women and the fights, but Griffiths started on about the beer, which was clearly to his liking. They explained that it was an export brew and their staple diet while at sea. The two cans I got through almost demolished me. I remember being shown down a corridor and a flight of steps to a lavatory. Standing there at the shiny, metal urinal I felt as if all the acid in my life was draining away. The whole ship was metal: metal handles, metal doors, metal walls and ceilings. Warm, grey metal most of it. When I leaned against the bulkhead it felt like it would melt. Somehow I got back up to the mess.

'What do you lads do? I mean, what's all this for?' asked Griffiths.

'The defence of our glorious country,' the cockney said, 'We are yer floating weapons system. Missiles. We could take out a ship or a town, makes no difference, at several miles. Just blow the whole fuckin' thing apart. Do you boys want to see the stuff? Think we can trust 'em, lads? Come on then.'

We followed him through a maze of those metal tunnels, clanking down past a small-arms and rifle rack to a locked door. 'Have a butchers,' he said, sliding back a spy-hole.

Griffiths pushed forward and thrust himself against the door. 'Take a look in there, boy. There's more heads in there than our audiences.' I pressed my eye to the hole and its

222

glass lens. The room beyond mushroomed out, lit by a low, yellow glow. Ranks of missiles stood in there. They were single, discreet blind shapes in rows stretching for yards. I thought they were a true obscenity. Lines of polished, sharpened weapons, a sprouting of evil, neat as asparagus in a bundle.

On our way back, at the top of some stairs, we were met by a seaman who said we'd been summoned to the captain. We clanged our way after him as he led us up more flights of steps. For me the thing was turning sour, but there was a real shock when we reached the reception room, which was brightly-lit and perfectly circular. I felt dizzy and confused, the noise of talk and laughter and the smoke made me want to return to the clean, stark purpose of the ordnance bay.

'Here's our Welsh poets,' said Jeremy, who was wearing a starched shirt, dress trousers and cummerbund. Welcome aboard, chaps. Perkins, get them a drink, would you?'

I was about to say that we'd been kept waiting on the dock and then on board his bloody ship for an hour or more, and had only been picked up as a sort of afterthought, but Griffiths stepped in front of me, shook the captain's hand and ordered drinks. Then I realised that Jeremy was pretty glazed himself and that it was he, not the ship, which was swaying. There was a gauze of socialising noises punctuated by loud bursts of male laughter: it looked like all the other officers were pissed too. Jeremy explained that the *Cassandra*'s forward gun turret had been rendered redundant by the advent of her guided missiles. It had been his idea to carpet and decorate the place, making it a circular reception room. 'Damn hard when it comes to hanging pictures,' he said, and emptied his glass. Scotch and water was the drink to have, but I stuck to orange juice from there on. It was a case of surviving, for the only food left was on a central table, the leavings of a finger buffet which I picked at whenever I had the opportunity. There was a tableau of white-shirted young officers in various states of animation; they lined the walls like a frieze. The only dash of real colour was a woman in a long evening dress.

'There's Dawkins's piece,' said Griffiths, 'What's she doing here? Isn't it supposed to be bad luck or something?'

I turned and focussed on her. Bad luck—who would care? In those surroundings she was a vision of coolness and depth. I half closed my eyes and she was a kingfisher glimpsed through river mist. I breathed deeply and cleared my head. We were side-tracked then by a group of young officers who knotted themselves to us and practised their socialising skills. Luckily, Griffiths had drifted into a mellow phase and responded to them warmly. Why not—drink was flowing and the evening had risen a few notches socially. All was compliments and friendly banter until the door opened and the sozzled singer was half carried in between two sailors.

'Sunk without bloody trace my little songbird,' he called across the room, 'What sort of a bloody poof name is Jason, anyway?'

One of the older officers intervened and the strummer and his guitar case were ushered out of the room. Griffiths launched into a ramble about men and ships: real men and real ships. Then he was striding through a discussion about N.A.T.O. and the Russians with a bevy of listeners, openly filling his hip-flask from a bottle of scotch too. 'Keeping the Great Bear in chains ... That bastard Stalin was worse than the bloody fascists... ruling the waves for freedom of the artist's voice... I've been with the enemy in the East, you know.' He was spouting at speed, on automatic pilot. That's how he managed those famous radio talks, I'm sure: as long as he had an audience, it just flowed.

I think I'd slipped down onto the carpet and was propped up against the hessian of the wall shortly after that. At any rate I was becoming completely absorbed in the scene unfolding directly across the diameter of the room. Audrey Dawkins had her back to the wall and Jeremy was pressing closer to her. Of course, I could hear nothing above Griffiths's performance and the general chatter, but I could make out her lips saying yes and no. She was saying little else, but her face was doing a lot in response to the stream of talking that came from the captain. As the drinks tray came around she put her hand firmly over her glass and he waved the man away. Soon afterwards he put his hand to the curve of her neck. Her free hand came up to cover his, but she didn't brush it away. He held her fingers and she closed her eyes, swaying a little. It was as if I could hear her moaning softly, on a separate sound track. I wanted to be where Jeremy was, but I was miles downstream. I struggled to my feet in order to work my way closer too them, but at that moment Griffiths brought the whole room to a standstill with a bellowing declaration : 'This has been a fine night, a marvellous night! We owe it all to the Senior Service —The British Navy!'

The group around him shouted, 'Bravo!' Then he announced that he would read a poem.

'A poem written this evening. A poem about a war experience that has stayed with me. The story of a seaman who died in the Atlantic.' He took out of his jacket's inside pocket some scraps of paper, unwrinkled them and then read a piece about the death of Jack Cornwall, his eyes closed for much of the performance. It was raw, but fine and stirring. Jesus, I thought, he's magnificent. I never saw him publish the poem, and when I mentioned it the next day, he said it needed much more work. But a few years after he died I came across it again, or most of it, at least. It was in an anthology—Charles Causley's ' Ballad of Jack Cornwall ',—which Griffiths had half memorised and half improvised that night. Still, it was a brilliant move and they all loved it. I got to my feet and clapped.

As more people were drawn into the lionising of Griffiths I felt someone nudge against me; it was Jeremy at my shoulder. He seemed supremely stiff-upper-lipped in an abstract way, and a little drunk. I looked beyond him, scanning the room, but there was no kingfisher blue dress.

'God, I loved her so much,' he said, as if to himself. I thought he was on the edge of something—the prow of a ship clearing ice.' I can talk to you. Poets. Word-spinners. We met at a ball in Portsmouth. Years since. But she married Ralph. I was in the middle of a long duty, based in Hong Kong. Could have jumped the bloody ship when I got the news. It's a mistake, of course. She knows that now. Did you chaps sense that at the house? I want her to leave him. I would resign the service, of course. Ralph's a cold fish. half-brother. Our father. Audrey should...'

'I could see how you felt earlier tonight, when you were with her over there,' I said.

'She's in my cabin. She's there now,' he said.

'Then why...'

'But I want the whole thing. I want all of her to myself. Nights and weekends only make it worse. Damn it—she simply must leave Ralph!' He swallowed the last of his scotch and blinked to clear his eyes. 'Thank you for coming,' he said, quite formally. He was standing upright, 'and thank Mr Griffiths.' Then, pausing to say something into the ear of the steward, he walked out of the carpeted gun-turret.

The party dribbled away shortly afterwards, as if the captain's departure had signalled its close. They took Griffiths and myself back up on deck. He was still holding forth as we tottered down the boarding steps to the launch.

'Home, my young man. Terra firma. The good soil of Wales under our feet!'

The able seaman at the wheel smiled mechanically, and muttered under his breath. Griffiths and I clung to the side of the launch and looked back at *Cassandra*. She was being drawn into the darker grey of the night, her lights the only indication of her shape and bulk. I thought of the fire-power nesting in her belly and the pressed white shirts of the party. Then, in her stern, I caught sight of a movement. It was a blur of blue, like a loosed blue feather. Audrey's blue dress. She was on deck, looking out towards our launch, or the town, or just the sea, perhaps. I thought of that high, sheltered English accent, the world they'd inherited, she and her sailor boys. I imagined, close-up, the line of her back and her lips forming the words yes and no.

'God bless her, and all who sail in her,' declared Griffiths. He unzipped and pissed into the sea. I joined him and we streamed the night's waste away. I think there was no rancour or stupidity or insult intended by either of us then. I looked up and pointed to the smiling moon.

'Yes, a fine night. Life's not all shit. A memorable night,' he said, stretching his arms upwards and belching.

The last words I heard him say on that occasion.

Memory Sticks

I have loyalty cards for all the coffee places on the Gloucester Road, I mean every one of them. And some in the shopping mall. It's almost as if you need another purse to hold them all. But Coffee Casual is my default haunt and so I've chosen to meet her here. The cappuccinos are well up to par, you wouldn't last long around here with anything that wasn't; terrific almond croissants, *pasteis de nata*, and I like the choice of alcoves beyond the counter and front-of-house—one with shelves for the day's papers and one with a selection of books and magazines. The young mothers and professional women après lunch are in the front while the alcoves usually have a sprinkling of the beards, the thirties-forties men with hair and CK tees who settle in with their lap-tops and do their stuff—scripts, ideas for scripts, marketing narratives, new angles on bespoke lighting—whatever. I can only imagine where the furrowed brows and slick digits are taking them, though I wouldn't dream of asking or casting more than a glance at their screens as I pass. Café society protocol.

Is she the one with auburn hair, Apple i-phone intent, cashmere sweater, ears finished with small ovoids of gold, North Face gilet shouldering the back of the chair, settled in? Is that holly454@virgin.com?

I was so much more anxious when meeting sandrij3@btinternet.com who I assumed would be Asian, an Asian Babe, but who turned out to be Sandra Jones from the Cosham leisure centre, who patrols the pool when she isn't running Zumba Inzane three afternoons a week; she of the loose Nordic Noir sweater and the tail or foot of some creature disappearing down her neck towards her right shoulder—a lizard? A snake? That was in the Costa Coffee in the Brunel Mall; I was early, half way through my first latte in fact, and playing the game of Guess Which Woman until this one arrived, undistinguished from the boho others until she faffed about without ordering and scanned the room with that sort of wide-eyed face that is pleading to be spoken to.

Sandra Imelda Jones, both fit—swimming, Zumba—and, I suppose, 'fit': young enough and curvy enough to be what men want, or are told that they want. Evidently, Richard, my Richard, our Richard, wanted something more, something that Sandra the swimmer could offer. Was it the tattoo? Did he want to see where the snake or whatever ended up?

But what did she see in him? Older by fifteen years or so, rather studious in appearance, sort of slimmer Martin Freeman cast as a provincial college lecturer, which he was, until past half-way in the film when this ordinary bloke takes off his shirt and his glasses. But you'd have to have a vivid imagination, or a deep need, to be able to see that possibility—he never dressed well, and Joanna and I told him that, constantly—

'Time to freshen your image, Dad.'

'I'm not George Clooney,' he'd say.

'More Martin Freeman in *Fargo*,' I added.

'Oh, come off it!'

In my coffee meeting with sandrij3 I can't recall that men-of-a-certain-age attraction being so clear in what had gone on, or her attempt to explain her position. Two needy people, my arse.

We all want our end to be arranged, organised, filmable: our own bed, family and friends in staged visits over the final weeks. Music—Mahler, Wham! Vaughan Williams, Elton John, Elgar, Paul Simon. There must be fifty ways to leave your lover. Requests and bequests. Just drop off the key, Lee. And set yourself free. But not to keel over in the kitchen, your boiled egg top-sliced and the yoke running down the side, going cold and hard by the time the paramedics arrive. And they try to be pro-active, though they know and you are realising that it's only to show willing because Richard has died instantly, before he hit the floor. No need to discuss much…

That evening we had planned an early tea and then the Odeon in town—an NTLive streaming of Bill Nighy and an up-and-coming girl in something new—witty, unmissable. Joanna had been due back from university at the weekend following and our trip to Brittany was on the horizon, just like the old days. One more time together, the three of us, perhaps for the last time. Only when I came back in from the garden with a handful of thyme and rosemary I found Richard unconscious on the floor, half in the kitchen and half in the hall, his right arm awkwardly stretched behind him and the cut on his forehead starting to seep blood. From catching the door frame as he fell, I later realised.

The paramedics arrived in less than their target time, apparently—no complaints on that score—but I hadn't managed to get him to respond and I was desperate for them to appear. I'd not been able to lift him and was just pressing hard in the small of his back, though what good that would have done, I don't know. You just have to do something. And I was too shocked to cry, that came later.

His mother and father had both died, but aunties and cousins were supportive, as were my parents and Richard's friend, Alex. After the funeral it was Alex who helped to sort out Richard's things at the office and who came over to clear and reorganise Richard's study in the back bedroom—his desk and two filing cabinets, as well as various box-files stacked in one corner. We returned his company phone. I had no use for the desk-top computer—my *i-phone* does everything I need and Joanna has her own lap-top at university—so it seemed a reasonable thank-you for his help to offer it to Alex. He reckoned that there was a fellow at work could worm his way into it, as I didn't know what Richard had changed his password to after a recent hacking problem; but none of that proved necessary because when Alex started going through family names 'Joanna1' unlocked it and so he brought it back, having decided he'd not needed another computer, and plugged it back in on Richard's desk.

It was a month or so later that Alex and Sylvia invited me over for a meal. I was so grateful, for after all the legal and practical business that hits you after losing a loved one, you are suddenly less occupied, done with it,the house becomes colder and quieter and the evenings stretch out. The solicitor assured me that between my share of Richard's pension and the life insurance policy my job's salary would be ample to let me stay in the place and see Joanna through her masters, though I know that some people do move on from the sadness and memories of their house and start afresh.

Over an after dinner Calvados Alex placed an envelope on the coffee table in front of me. 'We thought that you should have this,' said Sylvia, 'I mean it's time for us to share this with you.'

Alex said, 'It's a stick with Richard's email account, his correspondence. I didn't think to distinguish those from all the business stuff that day when I put the memory stick in, but later I sorted things and separated the personal emails. I wanted to leave the computer clean for you.'

'That's so kind of you,' I said, 'There's so much to think of, and you two have been such good friends over this.'

'We do need to talk you through a few things,' said Alex. And then, slowly, painfully, they began to explain what the memory stick held and how I would have to go through the contents when I felt able to deal with what I would find, what Alex had found.

It was another three weeks or so before I felt able to read the thing; Richard's computer remained switched off. It sat on his desk like a challenge, and even when I got into it I had a back-log of emails—the banalities and annoyances of solar energy offers, insurance plugs and Nigerian legacies waiting to be claimed. The stick had all the stuff that Alex and Sylvia had warned me about: there were three steady contacts that were women, not known to me, but extremely well-known to Richard, it would seem. And not only that, his email account was still active and stuff was coming in. There is a digital media life after physical death it seems; some kind of immortality, until you close the account, and probably forever after anyway, but how many relatives think to do that? What sort of priority does that have at a time of grief and loss? And grief has become such a private thing, internalised, kept in the family. There are no widow's weeds, no set period of mourning. Kids have badges that come with their birthday cards—'7', 'I am 4', 'Birthday Girl'. 'I am 47'. I have blown out all the candles. 'I am a widow'.

Was it my job to tell these women? None of them knew, at least for the first week. Then jean62elders@google.com ceased. Her messages seemed to have been twice weekly about her cats, the caravan at Brixham, a friend's hen night —and then nothing. Had she read the funeral notice in the paper? Was there an association through work that revealed his passing? I tried several emails then the address was unobtainable. She'd switched providers, moved on.

Sandra the swimmer had shuffled a lot, cried a bit, piled clichés like used pool towels in a heap until the whole thing collapsed into an awkward silence with her constantly stirring and fiddling with a skinny latte. I'd let her off by saying that I'd have to leave—an appointment, without even bothering to elaborate—doctor, estate agent, solicitor, therapist, pedicure, let her take her pick. I'd walked out resolving never to go within a mile of her sodding leisure centre. Later thinking: She must have a constant aura of chlorine about her, is that what turned him on?

There was certainly no hint of chlorine about sam4mc4@gmail.com. We agreed to meet at The Pure Bean on the Gloucester Road, 'England's longest shopping street', though I suppose that's not counting London's Oxford Street. Like most 'shopping streets' Gloucester Road can seem like a succession of coffee places and charity shops, though Sam4 probably wouldn't be seen dead in an Oxfam or a Heart Foundation: Burberry scarf and bag and something trench-coaty posing on the peg behind her in the corner table.

'Thank you for contacting me. I realise how difficult it must be for you.' She is used to leading, getting her retaliation in first. The trophy labels, the power bag. So I let her do the talking, delivering what she calls her 'narrative'. How they met after a management seminar she was running in Swindon, just two months before his 'passing'; her fresh and scarring divorce; the bar tab, her suite. Enough, I thought, but in any case that was pretty much it. A one-nighter, which had obviously had made more of an impression on Richard than on Samantha, who was now happily established in a better place, professionally and personally.

'Richard—and I'm not just saying this because... but he did seem remorseful and his emails never suggested that we, as it were, re-engage. Just a bit of nostalgic flirting and, believe it or not, some business issues.' I was learning so much about the man I thought I knew and to whom I'd been happily, ignorantly married for all those years. He could bed someone who said, 're-engaged' and then 'as it were', which Richard had once joked was so 'Oxford'.

Everything can be dressed up: the staff in this place all wear black t-shirts with on the back in white letters framed in a white square 'We work hard/To be nice'. Irony, honesty, ambiguity? And all the girls have jeans with the knees slashed open. What's the point if everyone does it? Style becomes uniform. Rebel without a cause.

Samantha insisted on paying for the coffees and two croissants and I thought, why not? I had done some engaged listening and had not needed to run through our married lives, Joanna's research, the cancelled trip to Brittany and the return of the company Audi. The other two paramours.

I had resolved to stick to the silent stance with Holly454, but she was so uneasy, fidgeting with the phone next to her tea and constantly pulling down and then back up the sleeves of the sweater, that I thought we'd never get round to whatever there was for me to learn. I went through the practised setting out of ground-rules. No recriminations; I simply wanted to learn more about the man I'd thought I knew. Moving on with our lives, despite the raw and still recent loss: neither Lady Macbeth nor Anne-Marie Duff's Hamlet—no ghosts. No mention of my anger, packed in a safe place, possibly to be used on another occasion; certainly not dissipated, though.

'It finished, I mean I finished it late last year. I'm sorry, but I thought it was special. Then I found out about Rachel and...'

'Rachel?'

'Yes, that was her name, wasn't it? Rachel? Cheltenham?'

'So you were quite happy to put up with me, the woman he lived with, but...'

'Oh, I didn't mean to...of course it became clear to me that he was married, but ...I don't know if I should say this, but Richard said that he was unhappy. With the marriage and that he needed something fresh in his life. I knew it was wrong on one level.'

'On what fucking level could it not be wrong?' was me finally losing it, having had the time to register 'Rachel' and the annoying naivety of Holly. I mean, who calls their kid 'Holly'? And how many more Rachels might there be? In Cheltenham, GCHQ, town of secrets? Wasn't that where they monitored all the web traffic? Russian, Chinese, the UK? Somewhere in the trillions of files there must also be Richard's secret, messy trysts with Sam and Jean and Sandra and Holly. And whatever else I might have gone on to discover.

I stood up without another word and stared down at her: somewhere in her thirties, the cashmere rather pilled at the sleeves, her hair worried out of shape while she'd waited for me, her earrings desperate spots of fool's gold, her lemon slice pushed off the saucer by her nervous spoon, half-drunk Earl Grey souring, acquiring a dusty film as it went cold.

Joanna looked so grown-up, professional as she walked across the stage for her degree. Our little girl. My big girl M.Sc. And a career possible in Psychology. Richard would have been so proud. His daughter with the further degree he felt he should have stayed on for. Birmingham does it well; proper, solid red-brick confidence—'As well as academic dress, female graduands usually wear a dark skirt/ trousers, white blouse and dark shoes. Degree Congregations are formal occasions, so alternative to this may be worn—casual attire however is not deemed appropriate.' But some of the long trail of undergrads I then have to sit through are less compliant and there's a variety of hair, shoes and socks—why do people not realise that below the knees is what you look at first when someone goes on a stage? Still, the hair's shorter and tidier and the suits better cut than in Richard's and my graduation photographs. But we met on a new world concrete-and-glass campus in Surrey, the whole place in revolt against Thatcher and Reagan.

In a cold employment climate she's been lucky in securing an intern year—it is most definitely not a 'gap'—because one of her final year tutors recommended her to an older colleague as an assistant/amanuensis. Professor Helen Dowd is emeritus and quite eminent in her field, but has failing eyesight and needs Joanna as a research helpmate —'My eyes and hands,' as she puts it. 'Cognitive Behavioural Therapy as a Shaman's Tool' is the big paper that will become a book. There's no escaping the shaman's tool, apparently.

Richard's graduation photo, and mine for that matter, has been long tucked away in a drawer. I did not share any of my encounters with the shaman's molls with Joanna, though I did talk a bit with Sylvia. No coffee this time but a G&T at the de Vere. She didn't say much but it was clear that all was not smooth sailing with Alex; no proof, no Rachels, no lipstick on his memory stick, but there was a rough patch that Sylvia was sure they'd get through. It may be par for the course, to be expected with couples;

explaining the stuff and dealing with the fall-out from failing relationships that Joanna will perhaps make a successful career out of. If that's what she chooses. Or bereavement counselling. Because she's parked the bus of her father's death remarkably well, or sublimated it—is that what they say?

It was Tim's death that affected her more and we were surprised after that she'd got the grades for a decent uni. Tim the sixth-form crush from the year above, the boy wonder—five star As, if you count Music, and a place at Balliol. So sharp, he'd cut himself, as my Gran would say. He'd come round sometimes 'to revise'—low and distant moans of music from an earlier age—Radiohead, The Smiths—from Joanna's room. It made me feel quite nostalgic, the circle coming back round, like vinyl on a turntable. She said he knew all the lyrics and could play the bass accompaniment to most things with his fingers on the edge of the bedside cupboard. She shared those details tearfully after the funeral. Most people don't know that boys can be anorexic too. Not sure that I did. There was no blame levelled at the university; they'd counselled him and suggested he go down for a term to get help at home. A punt full of Chinese tourists found him floating in the Isis. Joanna and I talked of Ophelia and flowers, but he was probably face down and snagged on an early morning oarsman's blade.

I suppose that was a harder bus to park. But Joanna's set for the moment and so am I. For the moment. I passed on Richard's computer to a local charity's office, but the desk is mine now and I re-decorated the room, several rooms, actually, as a new beginning. Tautology. Sylvia brought up the subject of on-line dating when we last had a coffee. I'm not sure whether that was for my benefit or whether she was floating a possible escape for herself if things didn't pan out with Alex. Or perhaps even if they did. As revenge. My life is on a sort of plateau, not in an indifferent way, or with a continuing numbness, that has gone. And there are still needs, what Sylvia called 'urges' in my life, just not situated centrally in my life. At the moment. A king bed can seem like Siberia on a Winter's night.

Just after Richard's death the newspapers ran with a strange story for some days. A young man, a brilliant mind, 'a genius geek', the tabloids said, went missing and then was found in a locked cupboard in his flat in London. Handcuffed, legs bound. Sexual urges at the centre of his life, and not the sort you'd find in this neighbourhood. Everything complicated by the fact that he was something in Cheltenham, someone spooky, classified. All a bit shocking—like discovering that John le Carré's George Smiley was a flasher; or that Bond did cooking. One of the reasons for legalising homosexuality back in the day was, apparently, to prevent further Russian blackmailing activities of our brightest and best. The locating news reports on the television kept showing that aerial shot of GCHQ. It's as if a spaceship had landed in the green swathes of Gloucestershire and sightseeing cars had circled to wait for the alien ambassadors. Or as if they had decided to bring back drive-in movies, only in rural Britain. Its user-friendly website seems open and welcoming: they accept the nickname for the place of 'The Doughnut'. Like a franchise full of Rachels serving Freedom Fries. All of them clearly on a spectrum, as Joanna would say. But they are keeping us safe. We all need someone to keep us safe.

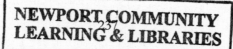